FEAR TO FEARLESS

EVERY PARENTS' FEAR

JOANNA WARRINGTON

Fear to Fearless

Joanna Warrington

Summer 2024

Text Copyright 2024 Joanna Warrington

All Rights Reserved

DISCLAIMER AND BACKGROUND

Fear to Fearless is part of a series, *Every Parent's Fear*. You can read this as a standalone novel, but I hope you will enjoy *Every Mother's Fear, Every Father's Fear, Every Son's Fear* and *Every Daughter's Fear* before reading this 5th in the series. Here is the link to the whole series available in Kindle and in paperback. My Book

All characters in this publication, other than those who are known public figures, are fictitious, and any resemblance to real people, living or dead, is purely coincidental. All opinions are those of the characters and not my personal opinions or the opinions of real people.

This is a fictional story based on the thalidomide disaster, one of the blackest episodes in medical history, which had devastating consequences for thousands of families across the world. Thalidomide was used to treat a range of medical conditions. It was thought to be safe for pregnant women, who took it to alleviate morning sickness. Thalidomide caused thousands of children worldwide to be born with malformed limbs, and the drug was taken off the market late in 1961.

St. Bede's, the school that Toby and Sue attended and where

Bill works as caretaker, is loosely based on Chailey Heritage School in East Sussex, the first purpose-built school for disabled children in the UK. It was founded in 1903 and is where many of the British thalidomide survivors were cared for and educated. There are various schools around the UK called St. Bede's. The name is coincidental and bears no relation to any of these school.

The story reflects the situations and experiences that families and thalidomide survivors might have faced, draws on real events and real experiences, and has been thoroughly researched. I have spoken with many thalidomide survivors at various events.

Lady Hoare, wife of the then Lord Mayor of London established a charitable trust to raise money to provide support for the British families affected by the thalidomide tragedy. She was awarded an OBE in 1972 but sadly died of cancer a year later. The Hoares owned a property called Four Winds in Norman's Bay near Bexhill in Sussex and turned it into a holiday home for thalidomide children and their families where they could relax and play away from the stares of the able-bodied. The provisions were basic by today's standards, but the main purpose was to provide shelter from stigma. The children invented their own games. Fond memories included trips round the bay in an inflatable dinghy. Meeting other families with similar children was a welcome opportunity for parents to discuss their mutual problems. As time passed, the number of visitors to Four Winds fell. The thalidomide children were growing into teenagers, and they wanted to take holidays further afield. In the 1970s, The Thalidomide Trust purchased a property called Haigh More House in La Roque, Jersey and turned it into a guesthouse for thalidomide children and their families. Many friendships were formed here including romantic relationships and new skills were learned from scuba diving to painting.

Bonaparte House is based on Haigh More House. Please

note, Haigh More House did not have any Nazi links. In 2023 I visited Jersey as part of my research for this book. Haigh More House has since been converted into flats. However, the original ramp and swimming pool have been retained. Inspired by a property near Haigh More House overlooking La Roque's harbour with turrets and towers and the intriguing story of the German occupation of Jersey, my imagination was fuelled and so I creatively transformed this story with a touch of author's licence!

The late Queen Elizabeth II visited the island of Jersey six times, more than any other monarch. In 1977 she firmly became the People's Queen, and it is this sentiment I have tried to capture. She had a very busy Silver Jubilee tour taking her to several far-off countries throughout 1977 including Canada and Australia and was therefore unable to visit Jersey until the following year, in 1978. Thousands flocked to see her, and she said she was delighted to be back in the island and talked about the ancient ties that bound together the Crown and the people of Jersey.

The thalidomiders have met many famous people including famous disabled people. I have included the disabled dancer and artist, Elizabeth Twistington Higgins, in this story because her life served as a profound source of inspiration, and disability campaigner, Paul Hunt. I believe that such individuals would have deeply inspired Toby. Please note there is no record of Elizabeth Twistington Higgins having visited Jersey.

Sometimes I use the words 'handicapped' and 'handicap' in this book because this was the terminology used at the time, rather than the more modern terms, 'disabled' and 'disability'.

ACKNOWLEDGEMENT

A book like this would be impossible without the help of the thalidomide community, and the many conversations with survivors about the challenges they've faced over the years, as well as hearing about their many achievements. I hope this book helps to keep them in the public's mind.

Thank you to Stuart Higgins, whose support continues to be invaluable.

Thank you to my cover designer, Jane Dixon-Smith, and to my proofreader, Julia Gibbs.

CHAPTER 1: TOBY

*S*ummer 1977

Toby gazed out of the tiny window with a sense of wonder and awe. The vast expanse of the sky, dotted with fluffy clouds. It made him feel detached from the world and think about how incredible the planet was. The clouds looked like marshmallows and he wondered what it would be like to dive into their embrace, like a bird, high above the land. Maybe this was heaven itself.

He was on his way to Jersey, his first holiday, first time on a plane, first time away with his schoolmates--so many firsts. Excitement fizzed in his stomach like champagne; the anticipation, what was it going to be like, what was going to happen?

Jasper was beside him with his nose in a book, scribbling away like a lunatic, emptying his brain. He wished Sandy and little Angela were here too. Having a little sister was a strange experience for Toby, and he hadn't fully adjusted. She was his sister and yet she wasn't.

As the plane made a graceful turn, the clouds parted to reveal a blue sky and the island came into view. He gasped and jumped in his seat, sending Jasper's notepad crashing to the floor.

'Steady on, fella.'

As he peered through the porthole, mesmerised, his heart soared. The island was breathtakingly beautiful. His eyes scanned the horizon--dramatic rugged cliffs, crashing waves, golden beaches, hidden coves, and picturesque harbours.

Toby's ears were beginning to pop. At that moment a voice came over the tannoy to announce they would soon be landing and for everyone to return to their seats and buckle up. An airhostess moving along the aisle leaned towards Toby and Jasper and reminded them to fasten their belts. Toby glanced up, startled by her beauty. She wasn't much older than him and he fleetingly wondered what it would be like to work for an airline.

'That's an unusual name,' Jasper commented.

Toby read the name badge pinned to her crisp white blouse--Tinika. He wondered how the staff managed to stay so clean and tidy. They were impeccably dressed and with not a hair out of place.

'It's Dutch. Most people call me Tin Tins.'

She smiled and offered Toby a sweet and said, 'Suck this.'

'Only one?'

She grinned and put half a dozen in his lap. 'Cheeky monkey.'

Jasper said, 'Suck hard, lad, it'll stop your ears from hurting'.

Toby looked at him quizzically. 'What you talking about?'

'The change in the atmospheric pressure causes the pain. Keep swallowing, that will help.'

'My God, these air hostesses must suck a lot of sweets.'

A piercing scream rang out from the seat in front of Toby. It was Pete the Parrot. He spoke in threes like a pet cockatoo and was clamping his ears repeating the mantra, 'my ears, my ears, my ears, I didn't want to go on a plane, I didn't want to go on a plane, I didn't want to go on a plane.'

'Yes, you did,' Pete's mother reminded him. 'But it wasn't on my list. I like going to Wales, we always go to Wales.'

'You always moan about Wales, that it rains every day, and the cottage is mouldy,' Pete's dad said with a tut.

'I hate airports, being surrounded by people with a deranged look in their eyes buying up everything from the duty free. You don't go to an airport to go shopping, especially not at three in the bloody morning.'

Toby observed Pete. He only had one limb impacted, a shortened arm. He didn't have to use his feet to perform physical actions. How much easier life must be for him. As he watched Pete bat his ears, he considered how having a single arm might attract less attention from others. There were times when Toby hated people staring at him. Maybe people viewed Pete as more normal compared to his own situation, with hands coming out of his shoulders like flippers. But dwelling on his own misfortune was fruitless, he'd always known that. Far better to concentrate on what he could do and think about the numerous obstacles throughout his life that he'd overcome. The only time his feet were his feet, was when he was walking. The rest of the time they were a multi-purpose tool. And over the past few months, Toby had learned to type using his toes. It was one skill he was immensely proud of. It hadn't been easy, and he'd persevered until perspiration poured down his face and he was exhausted with the effort, but he'd been determined not to give in. The Possum typewriter had been Jasper's brainwave. It was going to be the key to his getting on at college, to be able to type up his essays, it was so much quicker and more efficient than holding a pen between his toes or his teeth. At interview, the head of the academic studies department at the further education college had looked doubtful about his ability to keep up with the demands and pressures of two A level courses. He'd even suggested Toby be fitted with artificial arms. The only thing those unwieldly arms gave was an appearance of normality. He was not incapable and told the man as much. He would manage perfectly well at college without arms and now with the aid of his Possum, he'd prove it. The man had conceded and agreed for one of the students to give Toby a copy of his lesson notes. A copy could be made with carbon paper and that would give Toby the freedom to sit and listen to the lesson as well as asking questions.

As the plane descended, more detail came into view. A castle perched majestically on a rocky outcrop, a fortress, boats bobbing in the harbour, seagulls gliding effortlessly, tiny houses, farms, cows like tiny pinpricks, white blobs of sheep. The scene reminded Toby of a miniature village, Babbacombe Model Village being one of his favourite places.

He didn't want to land, being up in the sky had given him a real sense of freedom and adventure. When the plane touched the runway, Toby felt his heart thump in his chest, the plane was hurtling so fast he thought it might crash. There was a buzz of anticipation that went round the cabin.

Jasper was still frantically writing, trying to beat the world speed record, oblivious to all that was going on around him, locked in his own thoughts. Although he'd come to support Toby and to join in the fun, the primary reason was to document the trip and interview the students for a special feature in the newspaper to be entitled 'Thalidomide Children Holiday on Jersey'. The Thalidomide Trust had purchased a property at La Roque on the southeast corner of the island and adapted it to accommodate visitors with disabilities.

Sally, a girl further along the aisle who'd been chatting to her older sister the entire journey, broke into song, 'We're All Going on A Summer Holiday'. The song resonated around the plane, and everyone joined in. Sue bounced on her seat and shrieked when the plane screeched to a halt, its engines making a thunderous noise. After they'd sung it twice, Nicholas, sitting in the front row, glanced round and started singing, 'She'll Be Coming Round the Mountain When She Comes'. As he sang, he swayed and bumped shoulders with Jerry, sending an array of sweets flying through the cabin.

As they taxied to the terminal, Toby was mesmerised by the propellers. He turned his gaze back into the cabin, looking across at Lucy.

She was paging through a girls' magazine. His heart still ached for her and left him feeling sad. Ever since they'd become friends, a couple of years ago, the sensation overwhelmed him. It generated a feeling of warmth inside him which he didn't understand. She was drop-dead gorgeous, but a girl like her could have anyone and there wasn't a cat in hell's chance, she had so many options. Everything was stacked against him. For a start he was two years younger––and held back by his physical inadequacies. He didn't feel good enough and that would never change. Even if he became rich and successful, she wouldn't be interested. And yet it didn't stop him pining and imagining what it would be like to be with her. And yet, wasn't he worthy of love, just like anybody else?

Her silky blonde hair delicately looped over her ears fell gently down to her shoulders and he wondered what it would feel like swept across his chest. When she glanced over at him, he noticed her thick black mascara and green eyeliner. Lips he longed to kiss, sticky and shiny with gloss. Did she have to tease him by wearing a short tight skirt which accentuated her bottom, flaunting her slender tanned legs, wasn't it hard enough that she'd decided to tag along by offering to run a music session, and play the guitar round a campfire? It irked him, he felt she was just here for a free jolly.

When the plane came to a halt the helpers, who were staff from the school, siblings and parents, stood first and stretched to retrieve bags from the overhead bins. The crowns and outfits the students had made for the Queen's Silver Jubilee celebration in St Helier came flying out. Luckily nothing was damaged in the commotion, but several people had panicked looks on their faces. So much time and effort had been put into making the outfits. The Queen was coming to the island as part of her Silver Jubilee tour and everyone was very excited.

It took an age to get everyone off the plane. There were a few students in wheelchairs who either had no limbs or like Sue, no legs, and they were transferred by passenger service personnel to and from the plane from the air bridge by passenger service personnel into narrow wheelchairs that were able to move along the aisles, where the students then hobbled to and from their seat using a banana board.

Passing through the bustling airport, several students needed the toilet and those who didn't, including Toby, waited outside. The hurried footsteps and animated conversation of passengers and bystanders paused momentarily in their tracks and eyes lingered, their curiosity piqued by the presence of a group of disabled youngsters. A few openly stared and whispered to their fellow passengers with a mix of intrigue and sympathy. Others tried to discreetly steal glimpses, their guilty glances betraying their curiosity.

The Sunshine coach was waiting on the airport concourse and as it trundled down the country lanes towards La Roque, a chorus of delighted squeals filled the air and was contagious. Toby had his nose pressed to the window, captivated by the sea when the driver slowed and turned off the coastal road. His anticipation mounted when he saw a set of tall metal gates leading to a gravel drive. He craned his neck to see a mansion perched on top of a rugged cliff with panoramic views across the sea and harbour. It was just like the house in *The Addams Family*. Large, sprawling, gothic, with pointed arches turrets and a tower to the side, it was every bit as creepy. As the coach swept through the gates in front of the property, every intricate detail came into view from the old sash windows and the climbing ivy to the grand entrance and manicured lawns.

'We've arrived at Fawlty Towers,' Jasper said chuckling.

'That's Victorian. This place is more like the house in *The Addams Family*.'

There was an odd-looking couple standing on the steps at the entrance. 'But see the old boy standing by the door? He could be Manuel,' Toby jested.

He leaned towards Jasper and in a quiet voice said, 'The woman looks scary, reminds me of Diana Dors who played Mrs Wickens in *The Amazing Mr Blunden*.'

Toby hoped the woman didn't have the same vicious temper. She had that same crazed look on her face and one hand was planted on her hip like the handle of a ceramic teapot. She was a large lady in her sixties and dressed in a baggy shift dress and battered cream sandals, her grey hair an untidy mass like a bird's nest. As the coach lurched to a halt at the entrance, Toby noticed a large black wart on her chin, and shuddered. The mark of a witch.

Those in wheelchairs were escorted from the coach first and everyone else followed.

Toby glanced around him and breathed in the clean Jersey air and felt it zing through his body. The house was bigger than he'd imagined, and his excitement mounted. All sorts of adventure awaited. Even a kids' game of hide and seek would be fun in this rambling old place.

'Afternoon, I'm Jasper Cooper.' He shook the proprietor's hand before turning to Toby. 'And this is young Toby.' He put a hand on Toby's head and ruffled his hair before turning to Joy. 'And this here is Joy, year head and the leader of the group.'

Joy shook hands. 'We spoke on the phone. Pleased to meet you both. You've worked so hard to get everything ready for us, thank you.' She glanced up at the house to the small casement windows and then beyond the odd couple to the hallway. A sparkling chandelier hung from the ceiling above a round table which contained a metal stand of tourist information leaflets on the island.

'I'm Miss Trimble and this is the caretaker, my brother, Mr Trimble. Welcome to our magic place. The last of the workmen left late last night. They worked to the eleventh hour getting everything ready. It's been a mammoth project. The house had a new boiler fitted but it was on the blink, all fixed now,' she said in a brisk tone before turning to the other students now gathered.

With a flourish of her hand, she said, 'Come on in, children, welcome.' She beamed at each in turn as they passed her and went into the hall. 'Go into the room on the right, the morning room, door is open. There are trays of squash waiting. I expect you're all very thirsty. Dinner's not till six.'

Toby's stomach was growling, but he'd eaten all his snacks on the plane. The sudden realisation that he had no control over mealtimes created a wave of anxiety. He was in the middle of a growth spurt and the hungry wolf came knocking at his belly at ever more frequent intervals.

As they made their way through to the morning room, Toby couldn't take his eyes off the caretaker and the mangy old dog who trailed faithfully at his side. The dog shared his owner's dour expression. There was something decidedly creepy about the fella and Toby wondered what lay beneath his grizzled exterior. With his hunched back, thinning long grey hair with a shiny bald patch on top of his head, and a permanent scowl etched on his weathered face, Mr Trimble embodied grumpiness in every sense of the word. Now they were gathered in the morning room, his dark beady eyes darted suspiciously across every face in the room like a crow on a lamppost. And then he spoke.

'Boys and girls, ladies and gentlemen. Before you are shown to your rooms, let me make one thing clear to you all. I take my role as caretaker very seriously. A lot of money and time has been spent on restoring this guesthouse and it deserves nothing but the utmost care and attention. I'm here to ensure every aspect of your stay is an enjoyable one but everything must be kept in order.' He scanned the room, his gaze pausing on specific individuals, as if he possessed foreknowledge of mischief or an uncanny instinct to detect trouble. 'I won't stand for any nonsense.

I will tell you this once and only once, the corridor on the left-hand side is out of bounds to everyone who does not wish to suffer a horrible death.' As he paused for effect, Toby glanced round. He could see that the caretaker's words had struck fear into the hearts of a few, while a cluster were revelling in their smug and cocky confidence. This group included Johnny and Mick.

He continued. 'The old punishments work the best.' He glanced at a parent at the front and said, 'Isn't that, right?' before casting his piercing eyes across the room. 'There was a time when detention would find you hanging by your toenails in the cellar. The cellar is a dark and forebidding place, so be warned, children.'

As Trimble rambled on, listing his ridiculous rules, seemingly doing his best to make them feel unwelcome and uncomfortable, Toby, growing bored from standing up at the back, slipped from the room. He was eager for a snoop and just wanted to find out where he and Jasper would be sleeping.

Inquisitive, he meandered down a dimly lit corridor. The air was musty, and his shoulder brushed against a cobweb. He was suddenly aware that he'd wandered off course and was in the out-of-bounds part of the guesthouse. His eyes darted from side to side, as he pondered the mysteries that lay beyond the forbidden doors. Another cobweb was delicately draped across the cracked ceiling, adding an air of mysterious neglect. Toby couldn't help but wonder what secrets were concealed in these rooms, teasing his imagination with a sense of excitement and trepidation.

Startled by the distant sound of voices, he swiftly retraced his steps, rushing back to the reception area. Miss Trimble was handing out room keys and unveiling the practical arrangements: those in wheelchairs would sleep on the ground floor while the more able-bodied were on the first floor.

Jasper bounded over carrying a key. 'There you are, boy, let's get into our room and dump our bags. The caretaker's going to show me round, it's a free-for-all afternoon, don't know what you fancy doing.' He glanced beyond Toby to the window that overlooked the gardens. 'Nice lawn out there and some sun loungers.'

They headed upstairs and Jasper carted the bags in, half unpacking his stuff and throwing his jacket on the bed nearest to the dressing table. Toby looked round. There was a fresh, slightly chemical smell to the room––the scent of paint and new carpet. The swirly pattern carpet was orange and brown and the walls had been papered in woodchip and painted cream. The twin beds were covered in orange candlewick bedspreads.

'You have the bed next to the window.' Jasper nodded to the bed with the best view as he checked his appearance in the mirror, sweeping his fingers through his hair before removing his notebook and pens from his pocket and chucking them onto the bedside unit.

'Right, got to dash, I'll see you in a while.' Toby didn't like the way he casually dismissed him, and a mixture of hurt and confusion washed over him. He plonked himself on the bed and stared out of the window at the garden and beyond it, to the sea. It was unsettling how Jasper kept up this pretence of wanting to share a holiday with him and spend time with him, when it was clear that his true agenda revolved around work. He sighed with irritation. He seemed fixated on reporting about the thalidomide crisis, documenting everything, following the progress of the children as they grew up. Sometimes it seemed that his dedication to work was infuriating. It was the sole purpose of his existence.

Why was he even surprised by this? How Sandy put up with it, he didn't know. No wonder she'd buggered off to her parents' last year for company.

As he glanced round, Jasper's notebook caught his eye. What had he been scribbling on the flight over? He was intrigued to know. He was probably working on an article about the Silver Jubilee, but he opened the book anyway. Using his toes, he flicked through the pages, stopping when he caught the names of his friends, his heart started pounding in his chest. He wasn't happy with what he was reading.

Just wait till I get the chance to speak to him.

CHAPTER 2: JASPER

*J*asper stood at the window of the conservatory overlooking the lawns and the English Channel. Mr Trimble was standing beside him, accompanying him on a detailed walkthrough of the guesthouse while the students were chatting on the lawn and enjoying the sun. He was explaining the difficulties of making changes to the property and how the house had been modified for handicapped guests.

'The furniture in all the communal areas has been arranged so that it's easy for wheelchairs to manoeuvre and to ensure unobstructed pathways.'

They strolled through to the reception area where he pointed out the ramp, slope and handrails that enabled wheelchair-bound individuals to access the building. Doorframes on the ground floor had been enlarged to accommodate wheelchair widths.

'The guestrooms have been renovated for handicapped guests with lower countertops and shelving that's accessible,' Mr Trimble explained.

They were in one of the downstairs bedrooms. 'The bathrooms have grab bars near the toilets and in the shower to provide support and stability.'

They stepped out into the corridor and Trimble glanced up the staircase. 'We couldn't make the second floor accessible for wheelchair users because of the lack of space and cost of building a lift, but the ground floor provides the necessary layout for accessible accommodation. Given the historic nature of the house, it wasn't possible or practical to build a lift outside the house.'

They wandered into the garden where people were milling, sprawled out on the grass, laughing, and chatting and gazing across at the sea. He spotted Toby with Sue. They were deep in conversation and sitting at a distance from the others. He didn't know much about Sue, but Toby had mentioned her a few times. They seemed to be getting close. Maybe he'd quiz the lad later––good prep for an interview with her at some point during the week.

He turned and looked up at the house. The yellow stone needed a lick of paint and there were a few cracks in the stucco. From behind him the wind sucked the conservatory door shut, slamming it with a startling bang.

'What sort of condition was the house in when the Trust bought it?'

'Structurally it was in good shape.'

'Do you know much about its history?'

The air went still. Trimble gave a sharp intake of breath, looked away and shoved his hands into his pockets.

'My family have been here for many years as tenants. There's a dark history to the place. Before the Second World War, the occupants were injured servicemen, recuperating after fierce fighting on the Western Front during the First World War. Some have said the place is haunted by their ghosts. And then, during the Second World War…' His words trailed off and silence gathered in the air. 'That's best left in the past.'

'Wow.' Jasper's curiosity was instantly ignited, like a spark catching onto dry kindling. Rumours of a haunted house hung in the air. And then the Second World War. He was aware the Channel Islands were occupied by the Nazis during the war. Excitement surged through his veins as he pondered the potential in this captivating story. What a fantastic scoop he mused, envisioning the sensational headlines and gripping narrative. This was something he needed to explore, the thrill of unravelling secrets that lay within these walls.

'I guess you must have lived through that period, what was it like?'

Jasper studied his sallow skinned face and wondered how old he was––mid-sixties he reckoned. There was something mildly threatening about him, but Jasper wasn't sure why. Maybe it was the sleeve of tattoos along one arm making him look like a Hells Angels biker or the way his greasy hair was slicked back. But then he noticed on his other arm a long scar about two inches long where the skin had never healed, as if he'd had a tattoo removed.

'Their presence cast a shadow over our idyllic little island. The streets became eerily quiet as people retreated indoors. Our movements were restricted, curfews were enforced, our possessions were stripped away, food became scarce.'

'I can't imagine what that must have been like. We were lucky they didn't reach our shores.'

'There are families that fell out in the war and have never spoken to this day. The war may be over, but for some it will never end.'

A frown came over Trimble's face and he just stared straight ahead. Jasper stayed quiet. Something troubled the man; he'd witnessed a chapter in history he'd never forget, maybe he'd lost someone. It wasn't for him to pry though, Jasper found it hard; he was a journalist after all and asking questions and eliciting information came naturally to him.

'What a lovely garden.' He gazed at the colourful beds of flowers flanking the lawn, his heart suddenly plummeting as the bitter reality settled inside him. The mere thought of pitching an article encompassing the intertwining realms of Nazis and ghosts was exciting, but it was unlikely that Sam, his editor, would approve. He could picture Sam rolling his eyes. His restrictive editorial guidelines were well known within the newsroom. Jasper's ambitious aspirations for uncovering the extraordinary had often clashed with Sam's preference for safe, mainstream stories.

I can hardly complain, I'm lucky to be here, what a privilege. Quality time with my son, our first holiday together and the opportunity to interview a great bunch of kids.

The public would lap it up. The progress and challenges of these families. It was sure to be a riveting read. And what better setting than here, on this wonderful island––the first time that many of them had been on a holiday.

It's best I stick to my remit.

Prying into the horrors of these islanders' memories would be distressing for people like Trimble. Even though it was now thirty odd years since the occupation, every man and woman had suffered, and the pain of the past still lingered. Perhaps a conversation for another time.

CHAPTER 3: TOBY

*T*oby was sitting on a bench next to Sue. Bees buzzed around the lavender and the intoxicating fragrance of jasmine and rose filled the air. A towering hedge meticulously manicured shielded them from the breeze wafting from the west of the property. Seagulls cawed overhead in a current of invisible air, seemingly in suspended animation. In the far corner of the garden was a wooden gazebo standing proudly and adorned with cascading flowering vines. Toby sat back against the wooden slats appreciating it all. He didn't want to admit this to his friends because they'd say he was like an old person.

A cluster of lads were sprawled lazily on the grass behind them making jokes and bantering.

'Lucky the flight was only an hour, what if we'd needed the bog?' Johnny asked another lad. 'Those toilet doors are way too narrow and there's no room for a carer.'

'Don't suppose we'll be going on a long-haul flight, imagine the difficulties we'd face.'

Toby felt lucky, he could have managed the plane's loo even though the cubicle was small, but some of his peers on this trip were severely handicapped. Without warning, a sense of sadness washed over him.

'That airhostess had a nice pair of knockers.' Mick laughed.

'How many points for the tall dark one and how many for the short blonde one?' Johnny asked his mates.

'Did you see the blonde one bend over, I had to stop myself from grabbing her arse.' Mick chuckled.

'I'll give her tits seven but her arse nine.'

'Nah,' Fred said, joining in the discussion. 'More than a handful's a waste. I like something to grab hold off, doesn't have to be tits, could be a generous thigh.'

Johnny piped up. 'I'd love to grab her arse. I'd love to have someone who was built for comfort. A nice pillow to rest my head on.'

Sue turned round and glared at the boys. 'Do you mind? I don't want to listen to your smut.'

Toby tutted. 'I bet if a girl approached them, they'd run a mile, they wouldn't know what to do, wouldn't have the first clue, it's all bravado, Sue.'

She raised her eyebrows. 'They wouldn't have the first clue, sounds like you would?'

'Me?' Suddenly put in the spotlight, Toby was embarrassed and felt his face redden. The only girl he'd ever lusted after was Lucy, but she was way out of his league. It didn't stop him though, he still lived in the hope that one day she'd see through his disability and love him for the person he was.

'What's your type then, Toby?'

'I hate that term, it makes me imagine people in boxes sitting on a shelf and you just reach up and take the right one down. Life isn't like that.'

'But at least if it was a box, you could swap it for another. Wonder if you could do a Woolies Pick n Mix.'

'Love a Pick n Mix. Maybe we should go and explore, see if there's a Woolworth's in town.' Toby's stomach was growling.

'I've heard people use some awful sayings. When my cousin got married, my mum thought her new husband wasn't good enough and said she could have done better.'

'I don't have time for girls, most girls are silly and giggly and only interested in make-up and Donny Osmond. Or David Cassidy or David Essex. I think I'd get bored.'

'Cheers, Toby, I'm boring?'

'I can't answer that, I don't really know you.'

She turned to him, and their eyes connected. 'You know me better than any of the girls do. Those conversations we had in the garden, I don't think I've ever opened up to anyone like I have to you. You're different to other boys. You seem to understand, and you listen. Most boys are only interested in getting in a wisecrack or trying to impress in some way. All the bragging and blagging about what they can and cannot do or droning on about trains or motorbikes or some other boring stuff.'

'You've met some creeps then. Hope I'm not like that.'

'No, Toby, you're different. Their conversations are constant innuendo. Pointless, silly stuff. I can't be doing with it.'

They fell silent and Toby gazed off to the sea as he pondered their striking similarities. He felt himself inexplicably drawn to Sue, though he couldn't pinpoint whether it was genuine attraction or something else entirely. He couldn't deny the presence of a connection between them, and whatever it was, it was intensifying. He wasn't sure what it was, but there was something there and it was growing, but it was a completely different feeling from the feelings he had for Lucy.

Despite his growing fondness for Sue, he couldn't shake his lingering desire for Lucy which had persisted for so long. His mind was constantly plagued by thoughts of her.

At that very moment, as if he'd conjured her by magic, she effortlessly shimmied into his line of sight much like the graceful sway of a dancer. She was at the bottom of the garden with a girl called Maureen. Toby's eyes followed Lucy's graceful legs, her ample bottom, her nipples pushing through her top. In the sunshine, her hair gleamed, her skin glowed. He couldn't help feeling overwhelmed by her curve; everything appeared to be in the right places, she was stunning.

A plume of smoke rose from behind the bushes. 'Those two are going for a fag.' Sue tutted.

'Don't know why Maureen still wears prosthetic legs. They must be cumbersome and annoying. Wouldn't she be better off like you, getting around in a wheelchair?' Maureen had arms but her legs were stumps.

Sue laughed. 'Don't you know why she still wears her artificial legs?'

Toby was confused.

'She's always hidden her fags in her legs. And even now she's over sixteen, she keeps her smoking hidden from her mum because she's a bit funny about smoking.'

The boys were still chatting. 'I'm not looking forward to the match tomorrow, we're going to get hammered.'

'We're at home this week, you lot stand no chance.'

'Yeah, but our best striker's back from injury, we'll maul you.'

Toby didn't dare join in the conversation. He was revelling in the flattery and compliments coming from Sue and didn't want to ruin things. Football was on the list of topics of conversations girls hated.

'What do you think of this place? Bit old and rambling, isn't it? What are you looking forward to doing the most?' he asked.

'The learn to paint day.'

'I can't paint or draw.'

'You might surprise yourself, you should come along, you might enjoy it.'

'I doubt it, but we'll see.'

She looked at him. 'And you?'

'The War Tunnels of course, but just spending time with Jasper would be nice.' He huffed. 'I've been looking forward to it for ages. He's always busy working, chasing rainbows or playing with Angela, never has time for me.' Toby glanced round. Talking of Jasper, where was he? He'd disappeared soon after they'd arrived. He thought then about Jasper's notebook--it had made uncomfortable reading. He felt protective of his mates, didn't want Jasper observing their behaviour and scrutinising everything they did as if they were animals at a zoo. It was embarrassing.

The lads had moved on from footie.

'You lot are forgetting,' Johnny reminded his friends, 'we won't get to watch the match, we've got that stupid parade through the town for the Silver Jubilee.'

'The Queen will be there. I hope she shakes my hand.'

'No mate, how's she going to notice us in our wheelchairs?'

'Princess Margaret came to the school once. She wasn't afraid to shake my little hand.'

Toby got up. 'I'm just nipping inside, see if I can find some grub, I'm starving.'

'You lads,' Sue chuckled, 'all you think about are your bellies.'

Toby strolled back into the house through the conservatory doors and through to the reception area. Nobody was around. He peered up at the staircase and left into the dining room, but everywhere was quiet. His curiosity got the better of him and he felt compelled to explore further and learn more about the mysterious corridor that was off limits.

As he prepared to sneak into the restricted part of the hotel again, he heard voices. The Trimbles were talking. He stepped closer to listen, pressing himself against the wall so that he was out of sight.

'Why did you have to invite that journalist fella?' Miss Trimble asked in a snappy voice. 'I don't want him snooping round where he's not wanted.'

'Stop flapping, I didn't know he was a journalist till we got chatting,' Mr Trimble replied. 'Don't you worry, the room's locked.'

'I hope you haven't lost the key.'

'I'm not that stupid. It's still in the Colman's mustard tin at the back of the broom cupboard.'

'Just you mind your tongue, don't let anything slip. The secret's been kept this long, we don't want it coming out now.'

Toby's heart was pounding as he pondered what could possibly be inside the room. What was the big secret? His appetite vanished as a sense of unease rushed over him. He shivered and feeling unsettled crept from the door and retreated into the garden. Lucy and Maureen were just emerging from behind the bushes, and he watched them wander off chatting. Toby admired Lucy, her ability to effortlessly get along with everyone and her natural ability to make friends with everyone astounded him. People were drawn to her infectious charm and warmth.

'Didn't find anything?' Sue asked as he plonked himself back down beside her.

'Nah.' He couldn't wait to tell Jasper about the conversation he'd overheard but didn't want to share it with Sue.

As Toby glanced round the garden, his eyes were drawn to a shaded area. He could just make out the shape of someone peering out. He focussed hard, trying to work out if it was someone in the group or a member of the public who'd wandered into the garden. As he squinted to get a better view, he could have sworn it was a strange old git spying. There was something creepy about him, his shaggy beard, weathered skin. Toby wondered if he was a vagrant or a dog walker, but there was no dog to be seen. He heard a clicking sound and immediately recognised it. Jasper had a top-range camera. Toby would have recognised that sound anywhere. He gasped and the shape was gone.

'What's up?' Sue asked.

'Nothing.' He didn't want to alarm her. 'I was just admiring the trees in the breeze.'

'What breeze? There is no breeze.' She turned to look at him and frowned. 'You can be funny at times, Toby.' He chuckled, still frowning.

Toby couldn't wait to tell Jasper about the events of the afternoon and wondered what he'd make of it all. Jasper and his damn notebook. He hadn't missed a trick, that was the worst of it. He could understand why their lives were being documented and recorded for future generations to understand the thalidomide crisis, but it just didn't feel right. It was an invasion of privacy, intrusive and insensitive, as if their personal experiences and situations were being exploited for someone else's gain. They had consented to be interviewed, but that still didn't make it right and they didn't know how persuasive Jasper could be when trying to extract information. So clever, he could sell sand to the Egyptians. This was supposed to be a holiday, a chance to get away from the incessant media attention that plagued their lives.

CHAPTER 4: JASPER

Jasper plonked himself down at a small table for two in the corner of the breakfast room and waited patiently for Toby. They had barely spoken since arriving yesterday and Jasper had left him to get washed and dressed in peace. Bill had warned him that Toby wasn't the earliest of risers. He didn't mind though, it gave him a chance to scribble some notes, think about the day ahead and down a few coffees. The coffee wasn't up to much though, instant from a jar but it was wet and warm. He much preferred a fresh roasted brew, it woke him and fired his brain.

Last night there had been a quiz event, and the bar area was packed. The atmosphere was filled with laughter, and everyone was clearly enjoying themselves. Jasper managed to sneak in and grabbed himself a whisky. He recalled seeing Toby at one of the tables, his team consisting of Sue, her sister, Wendy, and a couple of boys he didn't know. He didn't want to intrude, quizzes weren't his thing, so he'd left them to their own devices and retreated to his room for an early night.

Not waiting any longer, he wandered up to the serving table where a generous array of juices, cereals, fruit, and breads were spread for guests to help themselves. As he was pouring himself an orange juice, the door creaked open, and a familiar face stepped into the room. It was Ethel, the lady he was scheduled to interview later in the day. She was the aunt of Jackie, a girl born with a facial disfigurement and without arms or legs. In terms of care and support, Jackie needed a lot, and Jasper was aware that as she grew older it would only increase. Jackie had long given up on her cumbersome prosthetic arms and legs, preferring to get around in a manual wheelchair, propelling herself along with the aid of underarm crutches. Jackie was staying in the guesthouse for the entire summer and a weekly rotation of aunts, cousins and other relatives would be assisting her.

'Morning, Jasper.' Ethel helped herself to a glass of grapefruit juice. 'No Toby?'

'He's still in his pit, I've hardly seen him since he arrived. Where's Jackie?'

'She prefers breakfast in bed so I'm going to take a tray up.' Ethel filled a bowl with Kellogg's Cornflakes and milk. Before she headed back to her room, she put a hand on Jasper's wrist. 'I'm looking forward to chatting later. Shall we say three in the garden?'

'Sounds like a plan, I'll look forward to it.'

Ethel left and a couple of kids came in and chatted with Jasper about the quiz he'd missed before sitting down on the opposite side of the room. He gave up waiting and ordered a full English.

Toby appeared looking sullen.

'Morning, Toby, you're late, did you oversleep?' he asked cheerily.

'It's not late, no one's down yet, just because you like getting up at the crack of dawn.' He looked indignant and Jasper glanced at the other guests feeling uncomfortable.

'Anyway,' Toby continued. 'Surprised you even noticed that I was missing. Remind me again why you came, because it doesn't feel like you're here to spend time with me.'

Jasper sucked on his lip. Toby knew the main purpose of him tagging along, for research. Now he realised that perhaps there wouldn't be as much time for Toby as he would have liked, but the lad had his mates, this holiday was going to be good for him, it was important that he developed friendships. He didn't want a needy, clingy son. At home the boy was always cooped up in his room studying. Both Jasper and Bill hoped the holiday would push him out of his comfort bubble and force him to be more sociable.

'What's got into you? I saw you chatting to Sue yesterday, you seemed to be enjoying yourself.'

Toby huffed and slumped in his chair. 'She's just a girl.'

'Well talk to the boys then.' At times Jasper felt despair.

'I don't suppose you remember our War Tunnels visit this afternoon?' Toby eyed him with suspicion.

Oh damn. I've overbooked myself.

He couldn't cancel the interviews. As soon as he had some meat, he could start to flesh out an article. He didn't want to waste the week but equally he did want to spend quality time with his son.

'Tell you what, we can go tomorrow instead. I've got a full day of interviews today.'

'Wow, you sure you can fit me in?'

'Of course, I can fit you in, Toby, don't give me this, I thought you'd be glad of a day with your friends while I get on with some work, then you can have my undivided attention.'

'Tomorrow is the Silver Jubilee celebrations; I'll see if I can fit you in another day.' Toby was frosty. He got up abruptly. 'I'm going for a walk.' Jasper hated this sulky tone.

'Not having breakfast? Wait till you see my full English, that might tempt you.' He beamed at Toby.

'Can't be bothered, think I'll go for a walk along the beach,

I'll catch up with you later if I'm free.' Toby disappeared across the room.

'Hiya, Toby,' Sue said as she came into the room, but he dashed straight past her without saying a word, out of the room and was gone.

Do I change my plans? If I do, then I may not get what I need.

Toby would cool down and Jasper would make it up to him later, maybe with a stroll into town to buy an ice cream.

After breakfast, Jasper stepped out of the guesthouse feeling a gentle breeze brush against his face. He had an hour to kill before his first interview and wanted to nip into town to explore. His heart sank, this was time he could have spent with Toby, but the lad had been so grumpy. If Toby hadn't taken off, Jasper would have suggested it. He felt disheartened, but he wasn't going to feel guilty, the sun was beaming down, casting a warm glow over the day. He looked around him. He was jolly well going to make the best of the week.

As he approached the town, the rugged road led into a cobbled street with quaint shops and bustling cafes either side, each exuding its unique charm and character. The cheerful chatter of locals and tourists filled the air, creating an energetic ambiance that energised him. Potted flowers adorned the windowsills, adding a splash of colour to the already picturesque scene. There was an undeniable joy in simply wandering through the town, but he would have enjoyed it more not in Toby's company but in Sandy's. He stopped momentarily to think about her and wondered how she was. She hadn't minded him spending this time away, but Jasper felt a bit guilty because it wasn't easy looking after a toddler on your own. Angela could be quite a challenge. She had lots of energy and a developing sense of independence that made her a handful at times. She had a knack of throwing unexpected tantrums and expressing her frustrations with loud cries and refusing to cooperate with the simplest of tasks. Everyday routines could be a monumental battle. He'd call Sandy later from a phone box.

He halted as he passed a newsagent and nipped in to buy a paper. He could see the papers ahead of him and sailed down the aisle towards them. Before buying *The Times*, he glanced down at the local paper on the bottom shelf. The headline story was all about the Silver Jubilee celebrations and the Queen's forthcoming visit to Jersey. As he read the front cover, he became aware of a whispered conversation in the next aisle. He couldn't see who was talking because the shelves separating the aisles were so high that even a tall person would struggle to reach items on the top shelf. There was something about the whispered chat that made him stop reading and listen in.

'A holiday home for cripples, who would have thought it, after everything that went on there.'

'Bloody kids. They were talking about sex and smut. Heard it with my own ears and even managed to get a few photos.'

'Be careful you don't get caught.'

'It's our island.'

'I always thought those Trimbles were odd. If they only knew the history of those two, their toenails would curl.'

'I always knew those two were wrong 'uns. They've always been so secretive. We knew nothing about this holiday retreat. Cripples in a crippled house.'

'Something else for them to hide behind.'

'I don't think they've got any friends on the island at all.'

'The secrets that house holds, I'm surprised they can sleep at night.'

Jasper's ears pricked up and a cold chill swept through him. What had the Trimbles done exactly? The man was right, they were an odd couple, but they didn't seem that bad.

'God, the irony of it all. They're helping the very types that Hitler wanted to get rid of.'

Jasper didn't get a glimpse of the pair who were talking

because they left in a hurry. He went to pay for his paper, and as he left the shop he glanced around hoping to see them in the street but there was nobody in sight.

He ambled back to the seafront, forgetting that he intended to walk round the town because his thoughts were elsewhere. He was disturbed by what he'd heard and wished he could have made sense of the conversation. He took a leisurely walk along the sea wall, stopping to lean across the rusty railings as he watched two dogs chasing each other on the vast expanse of sand. The beach was getting busy. The bucket and spade brigade were out. Families were starting to pitch up for the day, children were splashing in the rock pools. Scanning the beach, he noticed a figure perched alone on a solitary rock looking out to sea.

Toby.

He looked so forlorn and isolated, a troubled soul.

Jasper's heart went out to him, and he turned and headed back along the sea wall to be with Toby. He stopped to survey the beach. The tide was right out exposing a huge moonscape of wonderful rock formations. Several boats were hunched on their shoulders. Children were crabbing in the rock pools and splashing in the gullies. He padded over the soft sand, kicking shells in his wake and squinting against the sun. Toby glanced around as he clambered up the rock, then fixed his gaze back to the distant horizon. Jasper gingerly settled himself next to Toby, their shoulders barely touching. The salty breeze tousled their hair, and the cries of the seagulls above created a comforting backdrop. He sensed Toby's heart weighed heavy with unspoken thoughts. Toby maintained his gaze looking out to sea.

They sat in silence gazing out to sea. 'Hey, kiddo, what you looking at?'

'What's that building out there? Is it a castle?'

'No, it's a Napoleonic tower, built to defend the island against the French.'

'Do you think we'd be able to walk out there?'

'Too dangerous.'

'But the tide's out. Goes out for miles.'

'The landmass increases by a third at low tide. Jersey's got one of the largest tidal movements on Earth. But I'm sure plenty have drowned trying to get to that tower, cut off by the rising tide.'

Toby shrugged. 'Looks easy enough.'

'No, lad, trust me, it isn't.' He glanced at Toby, who looked as if he didn't believe him. 'Please, I know you're adventurous, but don't even think about trying.'

'How come you know so much about the island?'

'Don't particularly. I read a few things before we came. Couple of guys in my office have been. You'll see lots of towers and forts, it's a heavily fortified island. There are several castles too. First the islanders had to defend themselves against the French, then during the war, the Germans.'

'Do you have to do your first interview this afternoon?' Toby groaned.

Jasper sighed. He felt conflicted. 'There will be plenty of time for fun, you'll see.'

Toby groaned again.

'Toby, this is a great opportunity for you to get to know some of the people you don't normally see. Make the most of it, I'll be around all your life.'

'As soon as you're back all your time will be spent with Sandy and Angela, so I want to make the most of my time with you.'

A lump came to Jasper's throat. 'I'll leave you to your thoughts, I must get on, and remember, no heroics, I'll ask old Trimble if it's possible to get to the tower safely.'

CHAPTER 5: TOBY

It was Saturday, the morning of the Silver Jubilee celebrations in St Helier, and everyone had gathered in the bar lounge with their homemade crowns and outfits, to go over the arrangements for when the Queen would be passing them on her town walkabout.

Toby's back was to the group as he lingered by the patio doors looking out at the swimming pool, while people flitted around behind him getting themselves a coffee or a drink from the bar before sitting down for the meeting. It was a glorious day and the sun cascaded through the lounge drenching the carpet in its brilliant glow as if seeking to bleach it of all its imperfections. Toby longed to spend the day in the pool rather than wading through large cheering crowds of well-wishers.

Joy, the organiser, clapped her hands to get everyone's attention. 'If you can all sit down, we can go over the arrangements.'

As Toby turned round, his back against the warm window, Joy looked straight at him. 'Now, Toby, if you're happy we'd like you to present the bouquet of flowers to the Queen.'

Jasper's face lit up with a beaming smile as he enthusiastically raised his thumbs in a gesture of support.

'What's so special about him, why's he been chosen, why can't it be me?' Johnny piped up.

Mick swaggered over and nudged Toby. 'You big girl's blouse. And you, Johnny, why would you want to do it? You wouldn't get me holding a bunch of pansies.'

'You're too brash, Johnny,' Joy snapped. 'Toby's polite.'

Johnny grinned and chuckled. 'You're a cretin, Toby.'

'Enough,' Joy barked, and it felt as if they were back in the classroom.

'Well, he is, miss.'

'Any more of this and you won't be going at all.'

Johnny plunged into a chair and removed one of his artificial legs to scratch his stump. 'I don't really care, she's only an old lady with a little black handbag and curlers like my gran.'

'Excuse me,' Joy retorted. 'She's the same age as me, show a little more respect for your elders.'

'Ignore him, miss,' Toby said, bored with the exchange. He was glad to be moving up to sixth-form college in the autumn where the students were bound to be more mature and focussed on their studies. Johnny and Mick were complete morons, and he wouldn't miss them.

Johnny wasn't going to let it drop. 'What's she do anyway, the old Queenie, what's so special about her? Everyone admires her but my mum and dad say the royal family are a pain in the arse and a waste of taxpayers' money.'

'If you feel like that then don't come, we don't want you ruining the day.'

Johnny grunted and slumped in his seat. 'I was looking forward to all that grub.'

'Well tough, you're staying here, and I'll get you doing some jobs,' Mr Trimble said.

'I ain't doing no jobs.' He smirked at the caretaker, a look of defiance on his face. Toby was glad he wasn't going, the event would be much nicer without him there to ruin it.

With a mischievous glint in his eye, the caretaker snatched Johnny by the scruff of his neck and dragged him off. 'Right, lad, come with me.'

After Johnny had left the room, Joy raised her eyebrows and sighed before moving swiftly on, asking Toby how he'd like to present the flowers. He thought for a few moments. He could clutch the bouquet under his chin or armpit, but wouldn't it be much more interesting for the Queen and the cameras to see him present it with his foot? He realised then that this could end up on the news. There had been news coverage all summer about the Queen's visit to different countries as part of her Silver Jubilee tour, but this presentation would be different. How many people had ever passed flowers to the Queen with their foot? he wondered. He noticed a vase of flowers on the bar counter. If he could practise with them, he knew he could do it. It would depend as well on what flowers they were and how they were wrapped. He didn't much like the idea of holding roses with prickles along the stems or bulky cellophane that might be difficult to clutch.

As if reading his thoughts, Joy explained that their group would not be crushed into the crowd of well-wishers but would be set apart and that the Queen was briefed on who would be presenting to her.

In that moment Toby's heart filled with an overwhelming sense of pride. Members of the royal family had visited St Bede's over the years--Princesses Anne and Margaret, Prince Philip, but this time it would be him meeting one of them. The honour and privilege of presenting flowers to the Queen herself, he could barely believe it. Maybe she would ask him a question or two. Would he be overcome with nerves? He hoped not.

Toby found his mind drifting and was vaguely aware of the drone of Joy's voice as she strolled round each table explaining the procedures for the day, inspecting the crowns and costumes, praising, and pointing out small changes that could be made. It was only when he heard his name being called that he was fully alert again.

'The bouquet you will be presenting is a replica of the Coronation flowers and includes lily of the valley. The Queen loves lily of the valley. They're a symbol of good luck and motherhood.' She paused, her face taking on a serious expression, and glanced round at the mothers in the room. 'All of you are strong women. Our mother's love is the fuel that enables us to do the impossible. No one said being a mother was easy, no one warns us of the pain either.'

Toby hadn't a clue what those flowers even looked like. He imagined they were probably white, but he didn't care what colour they were as long as the stems weren't prickly.

'Sweet peas are also one of her favourites and the flower of her birth month, April. And white roses, associated with loyalty.'

Oh hell, roses.

'Miss, how will they be wrapped up, what about the thorns?'

'I've taken them all off, there's nothing to worry about. Right, everyone, remember, I want you all on your best behaviour, no pranks, no silliness, I want total respect, you can let your hair down later and don't forget to smile, it may be the only chance to meet Her Majesty.'

CHAPTER 6: JOHNNY

With a hard shove, the caretaker pushed Johnny out of the front door onto the gravel drive. He knew he'd been rude and surly, but he hadn't been expecting such brutal treatment and it took him completely by surprise as he lost his balance and toppled to the ground, reeling in shock.

'Bastard', he muttered under his breath. Trimble reminded him of his dad; he was an overbearing and loathsome brute. The fall dislodged his artificial legs. They didn't feel right and as he struggled to his feet, a sharp pain shot through his stumps. He often joked that he wished he was a car because cars had shock absorbers. Socks worn over his stumps and foam were supposed to help and protect but he struggled with the heat in the summer. The legs had never been comfortable, but he could walk okay on them, just not very far and they caused blisters and boils and other issues and had a terrible squeak. How he longed for a new style of legs made of the modern polycarbonate material that would cling on like a pair of gloves. His artificial legs were made of wood and leather with leather straps and were referred to as 'Number Eights.'

Trimble sneered down at him. 'That'll teach you, you little

shit, I don't stand for nonsense from anyone, especially not Scousers, you've been warned.'

I'm going to make him pay, nobody gets the better of me, especially not a scrawny old git.

Johnny looked round, unsure how he was going to get up without assistance. Noticing a handrail drilled into the wall he inched towards it on his bottom and grabbed it and with the full force of his upper body managed to haul himself up.

Trimble showed no concern and was already walking off towards his Ford Cortina parked along the side of the drive. He called over his shoulder, 'I've been told you're good with cars. It wants topping up with oil and water. I'll leave the bonnet up and everything you'll need is in the garage. I've got to drop everybody off in town shortly in the minibus. I'll be gone a while. I'll leave the garage door ajar. And when you've finished, you can clean the kitchen floor. Miss Trimble's got enough to do looking after you ungrateful lot. She's nipping to the shops to buy more food. You'll be manning the fort. And don't even think about sticking your fingers into the trifle, otherwise I'll have your bags packed quicker than you can say Jack Robinson.'

'Who was Jack Robinson? I suppose Bob's my uncle too.' He chuckled. He liked to wind adults up. But the one person he wouldn't dream of winding up was his father. For that he'd get a beating and it would hurt.

'Less of the cheek. You're living on borrowed time, son.'

Twenty minutes later, Johnny stood in front of the house and waved as the minibus pulled away. 'Have fun,' he called sarcastically. 'Say hello to the old dear from me.'

He wondered what job to get on with first. Trimble had left a long list of chores, and many of them were ridiculous given his capabilities. How on earth was he expected to stand on a ladder and clean the tops of the kitchen cupboards? Trimble just wanted him to fall over again, but next time not to be able to get up. Setting the list aside on the hall table, he looked around him relishing in the prospect of having free rein of the whole house for the entire afternoon. The first thing he wanted to do was go on a snoop. He wondered what the others had brought with them. There was bound to be sweets and fags, and maybe loose change lying around. He despised the fact that everybody trusted each other. And everyone seemed to have more money than him. They hadn't a clue what it was like out there in the real world. They'd been cocooned from the year dot. That wasn't the case for him. Every time he went home, his dad stole the birthday and Christmas money his nan had given him. He'd learned to have his wits about him.

He glanced along the corridor, wondering which room Sue and her sister were in. Sue's sister was a bit of all right, he wouldn't mind a grope.

He crept into their room. They were sharing a double bed which was very messy. Their nighties were strewn across the sheets and there was a pile of clothes in the corner of the room. They hadn't bothered to put their clothes in the chest of drawers. He rifled through the clothes until he found a large white bra, picked it up and slung the straps over his shoulders. The cups were huge; must be Sue's bra, he thought, because her sister, Wendy, had small pert breasts. More than a handful was a waste. Big ones turned him off, but it was funny to try the bra on. If she could see him now. He came across a few pairs of panties, black, red, and pink and imagined them on the girls. He collapsed on the bed laughing at the audacity of his behaviour before remembering to hunt for sweets. He found a packet of Sherbet Dabs and some Parma Violets and wine gums. They weren't his favourites, but he'd take them anyway.

Afterwards, he headed towards the kitchen to inspect the trifle. He yanked open the fridge door and his mouth watered as he feasted his eyes on an enormous bowl of succulent strawberry jelly and fruit, layered with a generous topping of thick custard and finished off with fluffy cream. About to dig his finger in, he was distracted by the disgusting sight of a pile of kippers wrapped in greaseproof paper, an idea quickly forming in his mind. He carefully unwrapped the paper and took out one of the cold slippery fish. It slithered in his fingers. It smelt horrible. He hated fish––another reason he didn't like going home––his mum always made fish pie for his homecoming even though she knew he loathed it. It was as if she cooked it deliberately, to put him off coming home. He took it out to Trimble's car and opened the driver's door. He lifted the mat and slid the fish under it. That would teach the idiot not to mess with him. The more he thought about it, the more Trimble reminded him of his dad, a complete arsehole, and a bully to his mum. He couldn't bear to watch how he treated his poor mum, but he had no sympathy. She could have left him but chose not to.

Funny how Trimble had entrusted him with his car, Johnny thought. Anything could happen, he could get a wire coat hanger and start the engine and drive off. Or he could fill the oil tank with orange juice or pour sugar into the petrol tank. No, maybe those ideas were too extreme, even by his standards. The kipper was just a bit of harmless fun and wouldn't affect his end-of-school report. He wasn't completely dumb, he'd need a reference to get a job and he had big ambitions.

After topping up the car with oil and water, and washing it, he wandered back into the house to consider what to do next and found himself in Mick's room. He rifled through his case eager to find sweets and laughed out loud when he found a plastic rat with big teeth and a dribble of blood running down its mouth.

'Nice one, Mick.'

What was Mick planning to do with it? He picked it up, thinking it looked very realistic, especially the teeth and ridges along its back. He headed back into the kitchen to look for somewhere to plant it. He considered the fridge but thought it unlikely a rat would find its way in there. Rats were usually found in cellars, did this house even have a cellar? He looked around and noticed a wooden door in the corner of the room. Maybe it was a pantry, a good place to discover a rat among the bags of flour and sugar, or it could open onto a set of stairs down into a cellar. He pulled on the latch and the padlock sprang open. To his delight there were stairs leading down. He found a light switch which was wobbly but worked and illuminated his way, and a handrail to clutch hold of. Brushing away a few cobwebs and spiders, he began to descend. The air was instantly chilly and dank. He gripped the handrail tightly and took careful steps. He didn't want another fall, to lose his legs in the gloom and be trapped down there for hours. It didn't look as if the cellar was used for anything. He might never be discovered if he had an accident.

Reaching the bottom, he found the smell of mould was overpowering, and he sneezed. Apart from the dripping of water, there was haunting silence. He imagined the grimy red bricks underfoot were cold but, on his prosthetics, he wasn't going to know. Ahead, there was a crate of what looked to be wine bottles and a case of whisky. What a shame he didn't like either of those drinks. There was a door to the left of where he was standing, rickety and splintered. He pushed it gently; it wouldn't take much for it to collapse. When he switched on the light, he looked up and saw a bare lightbulb covered in dust and cobwebs hanging from the ceiling, casting eerie shadows across the room.

His eyes were drawn to the bare concrete floor, to a rough area where there were four square markings. Something had been fixed to the floor and he tried to work out what it might have been. It was as if this room contained secrets locked away like ghosts seeking release. His eyes widened. The room stretched before him like a morbid abyss. He could see something in the far corner like a coiled snake, but on closer inspection he saw that it was just a frayed brown leather strap, its surface etched with signs of use. And a coil of old rope. Beside it lay a pair of rusty pliers.

The bulb flickered, casting elongated and distorted shadows. He couldn't wait to return to the kitchen. Being down here creeped him out.

Hearing noise from upstairs, he turned in a rush and knocked over a few boxes. He was scared, he didn't want to be caught, he had to get the hell out of there. He yanked the door, but it wouldn't close.

Back upstairs he stood in the kitchen listening. He'd thought they were all back, but the house was now quiet, and glancing out of the window he saw that the minibus wasn't there.

He headed back to Mick's room hoping to find something else to make him laugh, to take his mind off the cellar. Soon everybody would be back, and the party would begin. At school they'd been asked to make a compilation of music for the Jubilee party and long negotiations had followed. David Soul was an early controversial choice, then Abba, Roxy Music, the Stranglers and Boney M were added, but when someone threw David Essex into the mix, the fragile civility of horse-trading had broken down. Sue had listed all the tracks because she could write fast, and Mick had volunteered to tape them over the course of a weekend. In the end it was a hotchpotch, and worst of all the Sex Pistols were banned.

He spied a bag paper bag printed with a logo of the local record shop they all went to in Guildford. He picked it up and pulled a square royal blue cardboard from the bag. The cardboard had the familiar cameo of the Queen in its centre, the same oval that now decorated the windows of houses and cars, petrol stations, mugs, and soaps. But in the picture the Queen's eyes were blindfolded and her mouth gagged with strips of words seemingly cut from a newspaper, ransom-style, 'God Save The Queen', it said. The Sex Pistols.

'Mick, you old son of a gun, good on you, smuggling in the best record of all time.' This had to be played at full volume. Suddenly he was glad he hadn't gone to the procession, to be given the chance to play this great record, feel its pulse inside him, let the animal rage through his veins. How he liked to be the class rebel.

He went through to the lounge where he found the record player all set up in the corner of the small stage. As the record started, he could feel the hairs on the back of his neck stand up and his skin tingle. It made him feel sort of strong, and an unbeatable power surged through him. He wanted to do something with the power, break ornaments, destroy belongings, anything, he didn't care, he just felt good. He closed his eyes and consumed the beat. He was free, free of his parents for this limited time away. His head filled with the noise of 'God Save The Queen' and he clenched his feet and shuffled and twisted and punched the air. The song ended in a messy drum roll, a final percussion, a flourish, and he yelled at the top of his voice with the noise banging in his head because he could, nobody was there apart from a manky dog and cat.

CHAPTER 7: JASPER

Mr Trimble opened the gates at the end of the driveway and jumped back into the minibus and off they set on the short journey along the coastal road towards St Helier. David Soul was singing about rain and stars and as the song finished, a news commentator came on air and announced the Queen's arrival in St Aubin's Bay on the Royal Yacht *Britannia* where she'd hosted a reception the previous evening for 200 guests including the new Bailiff, Sir Frank Ereaut. There was a palpable sense of anticipation and excitement in the commentator's voice as he went on to explain that the Duke of Edinburgh would be meeting youngsters involved in his scheme who would be presenting him with a prize Jersey cow worth a thousand pounds. They would also meet Channel swimmers to present awards. The Queen was going to be meeting primary school children who would be presenting her with a soft toy, a Jersey cow for her first grandchild, due in November.

'What about us?' Sue asked in a whiny voice. 'He's not mentioned us.'

As if on cue, the commentator added, 'The Queen will also

be meeting a group of thalidomide victims staying on the island this summer.'

'Victims?' Toby looked incredulous and made a fist. 'We're not victims, we're survivors.'

A cheer rang out. Jasper's heart swelled with love and admiration for the indomitable spirit and courage of these kids.

'Quick run-through,' Joy said, turning round from the front passenger seat to look at Toby. 'There will be a white C painted on the tarmac where you'll stand and don't forget to bow. You'll be great, nothing to worry about.' She reached over, smiled, and patted him on the leg.

This was going to be a proud moment for Jasper, and he was sorry that Bill hadn't been able to witness it too, but Bill couldn't get the time off work. He cradled his Nikon on his lap. He'd make sure he took some great shots.

Jasper had been about the same age as Toby the year of the Queen's Coronation. He had vivid memories of that special day. His mother, a staunch supporter of the royal family had wanted to be a part of that momentous occasion and they'd travelled into Central London to watch the procession. Driving now towards St Helier in the minibus, with the sea to their left, the stunning sight of Elizabeth Castle perched on a rock, Jasper cast his mind back to that glorious day in 1953. He remembered the crowds along the Mall, everyone peering through cardboard periscopes to catch a glimpse of the golden carriage and many people having camped all night to ensure they got a good view. Planned to military precision, the colours of the procession were stunning and went from one colour to the next: dark blue for the Royal Navy, then khaki for the army, pale blue for the Royal Air Force. To be a part of history, ushering in a new age, he'd never seen anything like it, and would always be grateful to his mother for that day. Their neighbours had watched it on the Moores' TV, crammed into their poky living room at number five because they were the only family with a television.

'What's for tea later?' Mick asked, leaning towards Mr Trimble as he indicated to pull over. There was a yellow sign in the middle of the road which was blocked for pedestrian use only. 'I hope Miss Trimble isn't making disgusting Coronation Chicken sandwiches.'

'You'll be grateful for whatever you're given,' Mr Trimble said sternly.

'You can't not have coronation chicken today.' Jasper chuckled. 'That would be like not having Brussels sprouts with Christmas dinner.'

Mick pulled a face. 'They're disgusting too.'

'Coronation Chicken was very exotic back in the 1950s. Someone concocted it specially for the occasion, as a tribute from the Empire. It's got food from every country of the Commonwealth.' Jasper liked extra plump raisins in his Coronation Chicken.

'It's too spicy, I'd rather have a hamburger.'

'That's okay if you're celebrating America, but this is a day to be proud to be British.' Jasper smiled at him.

Mick raised his eyebrows and tutted.

As they all piled out of the minibus and made their way towards the centre of the town, Jasper looked around him. People of all ages and backgrounds had come together in joyful celebration to welcome the Queen to the island. The whole year of Jubilee celebrations were a much-needed escape from the difficulties the country had been facing––rampant inflation, industry beset by strikes and the struggle to find a way out of recession. During spring he'd noticed a change of mood in the nation, a renewed sense of unity as everyone eagerly engaged in the planning and organising process, committed to that feeling of togetherness and celebration, a collective determination to make the Jubilee celebrations memorable and uplifting.

The streets were filled with a frenzy of festivity. Bunting in red, white, and blue cascaded from one end of the road to the other, adorning houses and lampposts. Union Jacks fluttered in the breeze, adding to the patriotic spirit. Neighbours of all ages gathered outside their homes, children with their faces painted in red, white, and blue. Street stalls were set up offering a delightful array of treats. Trestle tables in a long line overflowed with cakes, sandwiches and pies, a feast fit for royalty.

Every family was out, every child squealing at each other. All that noise fighting with the music and the music was fighting with itself. It was the usual crappy mashup, Abba mixed with Rod Stewart mixed with Wings and other chart records.

Joy led the way as they snaked through the crowds to get to the allotted location. People turned to look, startled by their presence. Some stepped back to allow the wheelchairs through and with pity plastered across their faces. Jasper knew what Toby would be thinking. He hated pity and didn't want people to feel sorry for him, he wanted recognition of who he was as a person, their sympathy was cringe-worthy, condescending and insulting. But Jasper knew that people couldn't help being this way and that pity was their instinctive gut reaction, the emotion of people who felt helpless and hated their inability to do anything. As they continued to thread through the crowds, he noticed a mixture of reaction, fear, unease, shock, a subtle downturn of lips, heads tilted, looks of sorrow, or raised eyebrows. People covered their mouths to whisper but there was nothing subtle about their behaviour. 'Who are they?' people asked, 'look at them,' 'they're not normal.' But as they stopped, now in position behind the metal barriers, but separated from the rest of the crowd, worse was to come.

'Oh my God,' a tubby bald man said loudly to his wife. He sneered. 'It's turned into a freak show. They're going to spoil it for the kiddies.'

'Stop it,' his wife said. 'Don't be so rude.' She pursed her lips and looked embarrassed as she smiled awkwardly at Joy by way of apology for her husband's behaviour.

The man turned to the crowd behind him as if looking for support from others and to stir up trouble. Some people might not have noticed the disabled party if he'd stayed quiet but now, they were all staring, and small children were hiding behind their mums. The bald man laughed and pulled a face at one small child clutching its mother's legs. 'They're monsters coming to get you.'

The child began to cry. 'I want to go home, Mummy, it's horrible. Are the Daleks here too?'

'My God, are they for real?' a teenage boy called out.

'They're here on holiday,' his dad replied. 'Although what sort of holiday is that? Maybe they have prosthetic leg throwing competitions.' The man let out a laugh and a few others joined in.

Jasper was listening to every word and made no comment as he scribbled notes, not wanting to forget the appalling things being said.

Toby stood beside him looking indignant. 'How can you let them get away with that?'

'I'm writing.' His manner was brusque, he just wanted to get it all down on paper. He was appalled and deeply saddened, but equally fascinated by the public's reaction to the children.

'That's all you're interested in, all you're ever interested in. You don't care what we have to put up with.'

'It's all ammunition, lad. Sometimes you have to let things develop before you can change people's attitudes.'

Toby looked blankly at him. 'Sometimes you talk twaddle.'

'Quiet, I'm still listening.'

As Jasper tried to work out how he could take pictures of faces, capturing the wide eyes, the horror and disdain, a boy stepped towards Toby and as bold as brass asked, 'Er, mate, where's your arms gone? Are they telescopic?'

Jasper waited for Toby's answer and knew it would be clever. He'd had years of this stupidity, he was bound to come out with a quip or two. Jasper knew that he wasn't going to let it upset him.

Before Toby had the chance to reply, a girl who looked as if she might be the boy's sister joined in the jeering. 'Is it contagious?' she asked Toby before looking at her mum and asking, 'Am I going to catch what they've got?'

'My parents took me on holiday and while I was there, I was eaten by a tiger and all they could do was stitches my hands back on.' He looked over at Sue and smiled. 'I'm a twin. She had the arms, and I had the legs.'

The girl stood back in horror, and Sue was doubled up laughing so much that tears rolled down her cheeks. 'I'm your twin sister, am I now?'

Toby laughed.

'I just love how quick-witted you are.'

Jasper was looking around. He overheard a lady as she commented to her friend. 'Oh my gosh, their mothers took that drug, thalidomide, those poor souls. I was offered that, thank God I didn't take it.' She patted the arm of a girl who was standing next to her. 'You could have been like them.' She opened her handbag, took out her purse and fumbled for some money before handing her daughter a pound note and nodding in Toby's direction. 'Give it to the poor boy, tell him to treat himself.'

'You treat yourself,' Toby said to the girl. 'I don't need your money or pity thank you.'

Jasper smiled to himself. He admired the lad, so quick with his answers. He wasn't going to accept charity however much was offered.

After Toby turned the money away, the girl looked stunned. She stared at the note in her hand, momentarily unsure what to do with it before stepping back and losing her footing. She stepped back against the trestle table laden with food. There was a thunderous crash and confectionery chaos as cakes performed acrobatic stunts before plummeting to the ground.

A beast had awakened within the midst of the sugary ruins; the woman who'd been managing the table exploded in a rage. 'Who's responsible for this?' she asked as she saw the girl struggle to her feet.

'It's those kids' fault, they made this happen. He pushed her into the table,' a woman shouted as she pointed a finger at Toby.

Jasper could see the headlines.

Fate, flying cakes and furious lady. He intervened. 'That's interesting considering he doesn't have any arms.'

The woman looked all haughty and flushed, and turned on her heels as one of the stewards, dressed in a high-vis jacket, came over to assist. Several people helped to clear the mess; the Queen was within view at the other end of the road, and it wouldn't be long before she reached them.

Jasper caught his first glimpse of the iconic figure in the distance. The Queen was gracefully weaving her way along the crowd; she had an incredible composure about her as she extended her hand to greet the enthusiastic well-wishers, and always with a relaxed warm smile. Dressed in a cornflower blue suit she exuded a timeless elegance, and the tailoring was impeccable. A string of pearls adorned her neck, and she clutched the usual little black handbag on her wrist. Jasper felt a sense of awe wash over him. She was just a middle-aged lady and yet she was so much more. Catapulted to the throne at such a young age and in sad and unexpected circumstances, her loyalty and devotion to the country was steadfast and unyielding. And boy, the energy she had. He was staggered by the miles she'd covered during this Jubilee year. She had captivated the nation. Her presence as monarch transcended time, and he couldn't help but admire her ability to connect with individuals from all walks of life. Jasper had never been a great royalist, unlike his mother, and in recent years had questioned the expense of a royal family. Maybe too it was outdated, an institution of bygone days. But now, caught up in the moment, he tried to forget the public's nasty remarks about the thalidomide kids. They weren't worth the energy. They were just plain ignorant. Instead, he focussed on all that was good about the occasion, and as the swell of reverence built inside him, he allowed himself to be swept away by the magic of the moment.

As the Queen made her way along the throng getting closer, he glanced at Toby and could see the lad was getting nervous. Despite the heat, his teeth were chattering and he was pacing.

'You'll be fine, step forward now, here she comes.'

Joy curtsied and shook the Queen's hand. 'Your Majesty, Toby here is our representative and has some flowers to present to you.'

Toby stepped forward. He bowed, then slipped his right foot out of his flipflop before curling his foot around the stems, firmly clutching the bouquet as he carefully but deftly lifted his leg and handed them to the Queen with perfect composure. Jasper had been holding his breath, worried he'd drop the bouquet, but he let out a big sigh now, relieved the flowers were safely in the Queen's hand.

The crowd gasped and cheered. 'Wow, how did he do that?' Cameras flashed, reporters swooped in, and Jasper's heart swelled with pride. How lucky he was to be his father and in the coming years there would be many moments like this, and Jasper would witness it all. His graduation, his wedding. Would a member of the royal family present his degree? And how would Toby slip a ring on his bride's finger? The lad would overcome any challenge he faced, Jasper was sure of that.

Later on, they all piled onto the minibus and headed back to the guesthouse. Everyone was in good spirits until they turned into the drive and saw a van parked next to the front door.

'Pest control?' Mr Trimble muttered. 'What the hell are they doing here?'

CHAPTER 8: JOHNNY

*J*ohnny lay on his bed in hysterics. The daft old bat had come back, gone straight into the kitchen with her shopping and screamed her head off. She'd only gone and called the pest control. That plastic rat with huge out-of-proportion teeth didn't even look realistic. Johnny's belly ached, he'd laughed so much. Planting the rat in the cupboard was supposed to be a joke. From its beady eyes to its unconvincing fur-like coating, everything about it screamed fake. What sort of fool would be taken in by such a cheap trick?

He heard Miss Trimble coming back into the hallway with the pest control man. He got up and crept to his door to listen to their conversation. He clamped his hand over his mouth to stop a splutter of laughter from escaping. He would have liked to share this prank with Mick; a prank shared was much funnier.

'I'm so sorry for wasting your time.'

'I will have to charge you a call-out fee, I'm afraid.'

Louder this time, Miss Trimble said, 'I've got a feeling I know who the culprit is, and he won't have gone very far on his artificial pins,' raising her voice clearly for his benefit.

After she'd said goodbye to the pest controller, loud footsteps marched across the hall and a hard knock on his door nudged it open and nearly knocked him over.

'There you are. Are you responsible for this childish prank? You've caused a lot of trouble and Mr Trimble will not be at all happy.'

Johnny shrugged. He didn't intend to answer the old bat.

She stood there, her face turning a shade of purple, her hands firmly planted on her hips to give her a modicum of authority. They were all the signs of one frustrated woman. She was just like his mother. 'Anything to say for yourself, young man?'

As if she'd known what he was thinking, she said, 'My God if I was your mother, I'd give you a hard whack round the legs.'

'Wouldn't do much as my legs aren't real.' He smirked; he was enjoying this.

She leaned towards him, virtually spitting in his face as she spoke. 'You think you're clever, don't you? You wait till Joy gets back. You'll be shipped back to London faster than your feet can touch the ground.'

This got better and better. 'I don't have a pair of feet.'

Just then a noise came from the hall, the front door flew open and there was a clatter of prosthetics and screech of wheelchairs on the wooden floor as everybody arrived back. Mrs Trimble turned on her heel as Mr Trimble called out, 'What's going on? I've just met a pest control van leaving the premises.'

She shouted back, 'Now you're in big trouble. Don't think you'll get away with this. That good-for-nothing played a prank on us. He planted a plastic rat in one of the kitchen cupboards. What the hell made you leave that idiot on his own in the house? What else will we find?'

Trimble waved at her dismissively with an irritated look on his face. 'Thank God it wasn't a real one. Could have got us closed. You shouldn't have been so hasty calling that lot and waited till I got back, woman. It'll be all over the neighbourhood tomorrow.'

'Doubt it, folk are only interested in our royal visitors and they'll soon find out it was just a childish prank.'

Johnny heard everyone move into the lounge for the party and considered joining them, but what was the point, apart from Mick he knew they all hated him. Maybe it would be a good thing to be sent home.

He was still considering whether to join the party when Joy peered round his door. 'Mind if I come in a mo?'

He shrugged. She was heading in anyway.

'This holiday isn't working out for you, is it?' she asked him in a calm voice as she leaned against the door frame, her arms folded. 'You were warned this morning and you've not done anything to improve your behaviour, I'm afraid I'm going to have to send you home early.'

She looked at him and he knew she was waiting for a sign of remorse or for him to plead with her. He wasn't going to give her that satisfaction. He didn't care, he wasn't bothered whether he left today or next week, the outcome was the same, he'd still be going home.

'Jasper's going to take you to the airport in the morning.'

'Looks like you've all been talking behind my back and decided what to do with me. Nice.'

'Mr Trimble wants a word. He'll be here in a bit.'

Johnny tutted. 'That old fool.'

'Have some respect. The Trimbles have worked hard to make this a pleasurable experience for us.'

After she'd left, he slumped back onto the bed and looked around. It was a pleasant room, apart from the flowery wallpaper and pink carpet. He was going to miss the double-aspect view over the sea, watching it in all its moods. This room had become a sanctuary, his own safe space. For some reason that he hadn't discovered, he was the only one to have been given his own room. As he prepared to leave, a pang of wistfulness tugged at his heart. It wasn't just the comfortable bed or the cosy armchair by the window that he would miss, or the shimmering sea, it was a sense of longing that welled inside him, to be alone.

A while later, just as he was having a quick kip, Trimble came in and without knocking.

His hair looked particularly greasy today, as greasy as an old frying pan and Johnny found himself staring at the craters on his face, acne marks from long ago. His face reminded him of the rough cellar floor.

'How many of those jobs did you complete, young man?'

'I didn't get them all done.' He could feel the heat rise up his neck.

'And what were you doing down in the cellar?'

Johnny's heart jolted; he must have left the light on.

As Trimble stepped closer, there was a nasty cloud of body odour, and he resisted the urge to flap his hand through the air.

'Wasn't me,' he said rather too quickly.

'You were the only one in the house, you left the door open and the light on and you knocked a few boxes over.'

'Sorry, I got bored, I fancied a nose around.'

'I told you quite clearly, the cellar is out of bounds to all of you,' he said with a stern wag of his finger.

'But, mister, what are the markings on the floor?'

He peered at him through narrowed eyes. Johnny felt intimidated. 'You shouldn't poke your nose where it's not wanted. It's best you don't pry; you wouldn't want to know the truth.'

'There's a lot of angst inside you, lad. What goes on in that head of yours?'

Johnny wasn't going to answer his questions. A part of him would have liked to stay longer, but not with a bunch of adults giving him gip. There was so much to explore on this little island and the weather was good. He felt down, he wouldn't get the chance to find out now.

THE NEXT MORNING, Jasper loaded him into the car and drove him to the airport. Johnny glanced at Elizabeth Castle and the ominous coastal defences peppered along the shore before turning his gaze inland, to the massive houses lining the road and dotted across the hills overlooking the bay. He wondered who lived in those mansions, and if they knew what lucky people they were.

Jasper was on a mission, prodding him for answers. 'Didn't you like it at Bonaparte House? I don't understand why you'd ruin your holiday, it's not as if a free holiday comes along every day. Do you *really* want to go home? Most of us don't want to go home after a holiday, let alone leave in the middle of one, but you don't seem at all bothered.'

He kept on firing questions, and they felt like gun shots ringing through his ears. It was none of his business, what did he know? Jumped-up twat, he'd seen his big, detached posh house with its gravelled driveway, what did he know about how others lived?

'Still, at least your mum will be pleased to see you, mums always miss their sons. It will be a nice surprise for her. When I moved to London, my mum missed me. I was her little boy even when I was an adult. In her eyes, I never grew up. Mums never give up caring, but at some point, we must cut the apron strings and step out into the big wide world, make a life for ourselves.'

Jeez, Johnny thought, *this guy barely comes up for breath.* When was he going to shut up? Typical adult, talking at you rather than with you.

'I guess you're halfway there, lad.' What was he on about now? 'You've lived at St Bede's for most of your life, I take it?

This is the last time you'll be with your mates, you'll miss them more than you imagine, they're your thalidomide family.'

Johnny looked in the car's wing mirror and saw the reflection of his bleak, sad eyes. Jasper was a seasoned observer of human stories; did he sense the weight of unspoken pain? Was that why his prying was so persistent?

He hadn't planned his words, but they burst from his mouth like a torrential downpour, unleashing a flood of raw and painful emotions he'd tried to restrain. 'You've no idea about my home, so don't you dare go making your wild assumptions, you Fleet Street toff. Sniffing round like a vulture, using Toby as your prop, and don't go making out you care about us kids or what our parents went through, you just want to make money out of our story.' As Johnny continued to rant, he thumped the dashboard and even though it hurt his hand it felt good. It was like releasing a beast. A force rose inside him, he was on a roll now. Normally he kept a lid on his feelings, but now the dam had burst, and he couldn't stop because he felt so worked up and annoyed and upset. Hot tears spilled and splattered down his red cheeks.

'You think my mother's going to welcome me with open arms, that what you think? Before you go making assumptions you couldn't be more wrong. She's unlikely to get out of bed because for as long as I can remember, she's always in bed, either that or she's up and in one of her rages. And he's as cruel as she is barmy. In public they're polite to each other, they put up a devoted, united front like actors in a play. But at home they either ignore one another, or snipe. My older sister says it was different before I was born, that things were okay. So, Mr Journalist, that should tell you all you need to know about our family. You can piece it all together for yourself. I've long given up trying. I don't care anymore. Nobody wants me, I don't fit in anywhere.'

'Normal families.' Jasper sighed. 'What is normal for the spider is chaos for the fly.'

'Do you always talk in riddles?'

'Sounds as if you've had a hard life, lad.'

'My sister said when I was born, Dad took off down the pub. He didn't want to think about the deformed baby that had been born, just as he didn't want to remember there was rent to be paid and that he was lucky to be in work. And he blamed my mum for what had happened. According to my sister he blamed my mum for taking the tablets. There you are, satisfied now?'

'I'm sorry, lad.'

'My parents have never had time for me, I'm just the spare part, I don't fit in, not at home, not at school. Nobody has time for me. Alright for you Mr nice guy, nice house, nice job, nice life, just think how crap it would be if you lived in my shoes.' He gave a dark laugh. 'Excuse the pun, I'm full of them.'

'Did you ever get the chance to talk to any of the teachers at the school about how you felt?'

Johnny snorted in contempt. 'That lot just pretend to care, it's what they're paid to do. We're all on our own now, that part of our lives has come to an end, spat out into the wide world to make a life for ourselves. No doubt some will succeed, Toby for sure, but most of us will flounder. What chance do any of us have? Nobody's rushing to support us.'

'Life is what you make of it, some can fake it, you make your own fortune in this world, you can't let your circumstances drag you down. All sorts of circumstances affect our fortunes: race, social background, being in the right place at the right time, and of course disability. I came from a poor background, I didn't have the opportunities open to kids these days, but I guess I was just determined to make something of myself. You only have one life kiddo. You've had a lot of pain, you're still young, but you don't make it easy for yourself, do you? Perhaps you need to try a different approach, there are many ways to win folk over and maybe things will change for you, only you can change your fortune, but you need to change your attitude especially now that you're practically an adult.'

As they reached the airport, the atmosphere shifted and stepped up a gear. The air resonated with a flurry of activity, the hustle and bustle of people lugging cases across the road and into the terminal, taxis pulling up and passengers spilling onto the pavement. Now that he was here, he didn't want to leave, the idea of going home felt as daunting as hell. It would be easy to suggest a coffee, stall for time, pick Jasper's brains for ideas, but he wasn't in the mood. It wasn't his nature to be positive, he'd had so many knocks, he could lift himself. Jasper's words made some sense, but he couldn't help feeling sorry for himself and always had.

JASPER PARKED the car and took him through and handed him over to airport special assistance. Watching him disappear through departures, he observed how tall and lanky he was, but it was sad to watch how he walked, with an uneven gait. He sighed. It was anyone's guess what the future held for prosthetic technology. Hopefully there would be significant advancements so that people like Johnny could walk with a more natural stride. But really, did it matter how he walked, how any of them got about, how they held their cutlery or biros or bags?

Johnny had enough challenges without the big chip on his shoulder. He needed to overcome the challenges he faced. Jasper's heart went out to him, he'd clearly suffered, but he needed to find the strength and courage inside himself to propel his life forward. Otherwise, what would happen? It was just too awful to contemplate.

As Jasper drove back to La Rogue, he pondered what to do. He thumped the steering wheel; he hated feeling useless, all of this was out of his control, the destiny of these kids. He couldn't emancipate them, liberate them from the shackles of their impairments, or reverse the effects of the drug. For once he wasn't mulling over words and sentences, writing in his head, thinking about headline-grabbing stories, he had a different hat on, one of compassion.

As he indicated to turn onto the drive of Bonaparte House, in that moment he knew one thing––their cause was to be his lifelong quest. And that meant using his position to fight the pharmaceutical companies, Grunenthal and Distaval, and the government. Making their lives more comfortable, helping them access opportunities, it was all on his agenda. In the meantime he'd have a chat with Joy, see what she knew about Johnny's life and if there was anything that could be done to help.

CHAPTER 9: JASPER

It was the evening and in the bar lounge families gathered around pine tables to take part in a pub quiz. They were eagerly discussing their answers. The sound of clinking glasses and lively conversation filled the air giving the place a cheerful feel. Jasper sat to the side on a vinyl covered seat away from everyone else, having a drink on his own, doodling notes, putting together a brief description of everyone in the group so that he could identify each family and the disabilities suffered by each child. He glanced across at the barman diligently polishing a glass and thought how unwelcoming the fluorescent strip lighting was. It cast a sterile glare across the bar and an unflattering glow across every face.

His attention was drawn to two ladies. They couldn't have been more different. One was short and plump, and the other tall and slender. There was a significant age gap between them, maybe more than a decade. Surprisingly, the older one exuded a youthful and carefree vibe, flaunting her long blonde locks in a seductive way, clearly knowing that her hair was her best feature and twiddled with her ethnic style necklace made of wood and feathers. She was dressed in red bell bottoms and a

Mexican peasant blouse and embodied the free-spirited essence of a true hippy. The younger one with her bold and severe haircut, blunt fringe and beige dress sought invisibility. She had to be the sensible one. Dull, unadventurous, and practical. Miss Plain Jane. These two women were worlds apart in both appearance and style, yet despite their stark differences, they were relaxed in each other's company and seemed to have found an unexpected camaraderie, as if they were kindred spirits from different realms. He wondered which was the mother of the handicapped girl sitting between them, however he anticipated the older one was despite her bohemian looks and the younger one was maybe the helper or carer given their age gap. As he continued to study them, the younger one glanced over and smiled at him. He looked away, embarrassed. Had he been staring? He looked down at his pad and several moments later, lost in scribbling notes he was oblivious to the fact that someone had approached his table and was now towering over him.

It was the younger woman. 'Are you writing more quiz questions? Why aren't you joining in?'

'Quizzes aren't my thing. I'm just jotting down some background info on the group,' he said, then quickly closed the notepad.

She threw him a puzzled look. 'Why are you writing notes on the group? I thought you were with that young lad.'

'Yes, I'm here with Toby, but I've also got work to do while I'm here. Are you a carer?'

'No, I'm just here to support my sister,' she said and all at once his initial impression of her as stern and cold changed completely when he discovered how warm she was.

Jasper glanced across the room. The second round had just started. 'Shouldn't you get back to the quiz?'

'I'm bored with the quiz, the questions are too easy. I'm glad of a break.' She tilted her head back and gave a tinkly laugh.

'Is that your sister's child? What's her name, how old is she?' He nodded towards the girl sitting next to the other woman.

'Yeah, Jackie, she's sixteen, sadly she suffered like the others.'

'Bet she's had a tough time over the years.' Her took a swig of his beer and wiped the froth from his lip.

'You could say. Poor lamb, she gets a lot of pain in her back.'

'How unpleasant and at that age. Is there anything to alleviate the pain?'

'She has regular spinal injections. She had a Harrington rod fitted.'

When Jasper looked confused, she added, 'They're used to treat deformity of the spine, usually to reduce curvature. I think they attach them using two hooks.'

'Poor kid.'

He gave a sympathetic shake of his head, a frown etching onto his forehead. *My God*, he thought, these kids had so much to contend with.

'She's one of the worst affected. Most children have just upper limb damage, like your Toby. Abnormalities of the lower limbs are less common. And lower limb deformities on their own, as with children like Sue, are very rare.'

'The whole thing makes me very sad, and angry of course but I can see an independent streak in each of them, can you? They're so determined to get round any challenge. How's Jackie faced her challenges?'

'She's amazing, I'm so proud of her. She's strong, takes it all in her stride, but poor lass, she's been through a lot of surgery over the years. When she was young, she wore prosthetic legs, but she kept falling and broke most of her teeth, so she now has dentures. She was also born with an extra toe. That was removed but she suffers a lot of pain in that foot. It was hurting on the plane, squeezed into those narrow chairs. The wheelchair they transferred her into from the terminal to the plane was narrow and crushed her foot. She ended up with a nasty bruise. Her foot is still very tender because of the operation she had all those years ago.'

Jasper winced. He put his pen down and gave her his full attention. He noticed her soft skin and wispy mousey hair. 'Have you got children too?'

'Sadly, it hasn't happened for me and my husband. We've had challenges of our own preventing us from having children.'

'Does Jackie have the classic flipper-like arms and legs?' He couldn't tell as the girl was wearing a long dress and it had puffy sleeves.

'Yes, her limbs are severely shortened.' She sat down opposite Jasper and gave a heavy sigh.

'You must have helped your sister a lot over the years.'

Her eyes repeatedly darted over to her sister. 'I can't say too much, my sister's reticent to talk, especially to strangers, but I'm hoping this trip will help her to be more forthcoming to share her experiences with the other parents. I was only a teenager at the time and still living at home.'

As Jasper continued to chat with the younger sister, who'd introduced herself as Bridie, he noticed the older one crane her head and look over at them with a suspicious and quizzical expression on her face. It made him feel uncomfortable. She clearly didn't like Bridie talking to him. Better to steer the conversation to lighter subjects he thought as he told her a funny story related to the quiz question that had just been asked causing Bridie to give a raucous laugh.

Everybody was concentrating hard on the next question. The sister glared at him again. He flapped his hands. 'Sorry,' he called over, 'didn't mean to be noisy.'

'I think we're disturbing the quiz.' He stood up. 'I might take a stroll along the beach, get a bit of fresh air.'

'Mind if I join you?' she asked. 'By the way, what's your name?'

'Not at all, and I'm Jasper,' he said shaking her hand. As they left the room, Jasper noticed Toby glance across and frown. He was in a team with Sue and a couple of their mates.

The path that led down to the harbour wall was uneven, and in the absence of street lighting, the moon in her dappled glory cast a milky glow over the tapestry of pebbles. The tide was in, and the only sound was the hypnotic swooshing drag of waves. Above, the stars were out, spilt sugar across the sky. The night air was weightless against his bare arms. Jasper cast his eyes across the shoreline and the inky blanket of sea, and out to the shadow of the fort, a menacing reminder of the past. They carefully picked their way across the shingle, their feet reaching the soft sand. If Sandy had been here, it would have been a romantic setting.

'Are you enjoying the holiday?' Jasper asked. 'Where's home?'

'Southampton, and my sister, Jean, lives in Reading. We don't see much of each other. In fact, this is the first time I've been away with her.' She glanced at him and must have noticed his surprise. 'As I said, there's a big age gap between us. She left home when I was still young, got married, moved away.'

'Must be really nice then, to spend time together.'

'Yes, it really is,' she said cheerfully. She stopped walking and a big smile came over her face as if she was acknowledging this for the first time. 'There's so much about her life I knew nothing about. This time away has been about finding each other. It's been lovely.'

'Have you had much time though to talk away from Jackie?' Jasper kicked a pebble in his wake.

'Heavens yes. Jackie is so independent, she just wants to do her own thing, mostly sit by the pool with her friends, but she has been down to the shops on her own.'

'Wow, how did she manage that?'

'She's a capable lass, won't be told what she can and can't do. Her motto is, no limbs, no limits.'

'That's really good.'

'I'm embarrassed to say I've only met Jackie a few times. I don't know her very well at all. My parents never took me over to Reading to see her. They didn't talk about my sister much or Jackie. Jean's always been reluctant to talk about what she went through, she shut herself away for a long time and she became a bit of a recluse. On this holiday, she's opened up and told me how she felt, that for a long time she blamed herself and it's only now that she's been brave enough to come away with fellow parents, but she's still very wary about speaking about the past sixteen years of her life.'

This was an interesting family and there was so much that Jasper wanted to explore, but he had to tread carefully, choose the right words, show sensitivity. He didn't want to be intrusive, invade their privacy and come across as overly curious. As he pondered his next question, she unexpectedly volunteered the information and all he needed to do was gently guide the conversation.

'Jean was a difficult teenager, a bit of a wild child and very headstrong, disobeyed rules, caused our parents no end of heartache, staying out late, partying when Mum thought she was in bed and the more they tried to control her, the more she rebelled. When I reached my teens, they were extra tough with me, didn't want history to repeat itself, another daughter in the family way, God forbid, but I was very different, I wasn't a party animal. I preferred libraries to dance halls. I thought boys were silly at that age.'

There was a nip in the air, and when Jasper saw her shivering, he suggested they turn back. He wished he had a jacket to offer her.

'When Jean got pregnant, it caused a scandal. She hadn't known Tom long. Mum was disgusted. Back then guys were encouraged to do the honourable thing.'

He nodded in sympathy.

The moon was shining on her face, and he smiled warmly at

her. He reflected on his own situation. Sandy had fallen pregnant the first time they'd made love. They hadn't been courting for long. If he'd known she was pregnant, he would have done the decent thing. Now, he loathed the damaging effects of those outdated values which cast stigma and shame on young people, forcing them into marriage before they were ready or against their wishes.

'Jean was just eighteen when she had Jackie, it forced her to grow up fast.'

'That must have been overwhelming.' Jasper shook his head.

'Jean and I now spend hours talking. I thought my own situation was bad enough--three miscarriages--but what she went through was incredibly sad. If I'd been older, I would have supported her at the time and been there for her.'

'You mustn't blame yourself, as you say, you were very young and you were kept in the dark.' Jasper thought for a moment. 'How do your parents feel about Jackie now? Are they doting grandparents?'

Bridie stopped walking and stared at him with raised eyebrows.

'Doting grandparents, you must be joking. They have given no support whatsoever since she was born. They never made time to see Jackie, it's as if she doesn't exist.'

She stared off towards the sea with tears in her eyes. 'Can you believe it? There was always an excuse as to why we couldn't visit. I wondered why they were never included at Christmas and then finally the truth came out. It was the day I shared my frustrations with my mum about not being able to have children that everything unravelled.'

Jasper was silent, overcome by a massive sense of sorrow. The poor lass, to have missed out on such a special relationship. It was downright cruel. When he thought of his own grandparents, now long gone, it was with such deep love and affection. The memories were interwoven with special smells, taste, senses. All at once he saw Grandma Cooper's crispy toad-in-the-hole, her apple crumble that was always served in an old cracked dish and he remembered stories by the coal fire, endless card games, hide-and-seek. Above all though, laughter was served in generous measures like her custard.

Back on the harbour wall, she plonked herself down on a bench. 'She gave me absolutely no sympathy. My own mum. I'd been through three miscarriages and had come to the reluctant decision to stop trying for a family. I couldn't go on, all that living in hope each month, it was just too painful. I wanted Mum to wrap her arms around me like she used to when I was a little girl, but her concern was about her own missed opportunity of becoming a grandma "of a normal child," her exact words.'

Jasper's mind jumped back to how Rona and Bill must have felt all those years ago, the trying and trying and the sheer desperation and heartache.

She crossed her legs and clutched her handbag on her lap as if it were a comforter.

Jasper felt incredulous. He thought of all the joy that Toby brought into his life, and he realised then that he wouldn't change a thing. He couldn't imagine forfeiting the joys of grandparenthood, rejecting your own flesh and blood because of disability. It was appalling and narrow-minded.

'We had a massive barney. I shouted at her, "but you are a grandmother and you have been for the past sixteen years." I could see the shame on Mum's face and then I saw it, as clear as glass, she'd never been able to cope with Jackie. And the more I pressed her, it all came tumbling out. The utter despair of everyone gawping and asking questions, what's wrong with her? And now she is disappointed in me because I couldn't give her a grandchild.'

'My God, so she's pushed you both away?'

'I think she must have felt overwhelmed. She desperately

wanted a grandchild, a perfect one to show off to her friends. Jean and I are made to feel like failures. She longed to take a grandchild to play parks, the seaside and maybe it was the not knowing what Jackie could and couldn't do, how to pick her up, how to look after her, maybe it was just too overwhelming. It seemed as if there were constant obstacles obstructing her path so instead, she chose the easy way out and just pulled away. I was so angry, such pathetic behaviour and poor Jean, she felt so rejected. And even now there's no remorse for how she treated us.'

Jasper's heart went out to her and for a couple of minutes while they were silent, he pondered the missing years of Toby's life when he hadn't been around.

When the breeze picked up, they rose to their feet. Jasper looked across the bay. In the distance St Helier's skyline was a tiara of lights. Below the harbour wall, he watched the waves slap on the boat hulls and was going to comment about the view but knew that would bring their current conversation to a close. Eager to understand more about the family's journey, he asked about Jackie's birth and listened intently as Bridie explained how Jean had gone to the doctor a week into her pregnancy feeling very sick.

'The doctor said to her, "I've got something for you" and then he walked over to a rickety old cabinet in the corner of the room and took out a bottle of white tablets. "Try these and let me know how you get on," he said. The label on the bottle was Distaval and she took one before bedtime and it stopped her being sick until lunchtime. He eventually gave her a prescription and she took it until she was about three months pregnant.'

'And how was the pregnancy after that?'

'She felt well throughout, but alarm bells were raised at around four or five months when the baby hadn't started moving. They sent her for an X-ray. They don't carry out pre-natal X-rays nowadays because of the risks but back then, it was common practice. After she'd been X-rayed, the doctor called her in to explain the results. He was very matter-of-fact, he had a poor bedside manner, shall we say, and told her the baby had some kind of deformity and it was best she had a home birth as there was little hope of it living and it would spare her the agony of seeing the other mums and their babies. Then he offered her a brandy. Poor sis, she blamed herself. Mum said it was punishment for being a difficult teenager and getting knocked up.'

'And you've only found out all this just recently?'

'Yes, only this week. She invited me here when I rang to tell her about my latest miscarriage. She thought a week by the sea would help.'

'I bet it helped you both to finally tell each other to talk about what you've both gone through.'

'I think so.' She went quiet as if reflecting. 'She said she didn't really believe the baby was deformed because how could a grainy X-ray show much? They called her back for a further X-ray and held her down on a hard bed with two straps which they tightened with a lever till her stomach was as flat as it could be. She was treated like a disease not a human. When Jackie was born, and it was in hospital, they put a green curtain up across her belly and doctors in white coats flitted in and out, all staring beyond the green curtain as if her privates were a piece of meat or object of fascination and talking in medical speak, probably Latin. All she wanted to know was whether it was a boy or girl, but nobody would answer her, and she asked if the baby was alright and again, she got no answer. "Doctor will tell you", "sister will tell you." Then the following day Jackie was whisked off to Stoke Mandeville where she stayed for the next six weeks.'

They sauntered back towards the house, picking their way along the narrow pavement.

As they pushed open the iron gate that led onto the driveway she glanced at him, a wicked grin lighting up her face. 'I feel very naughty escaping that quiz. I wonder which team won.'

He smiled. 'Do you even care?' And then they looked across to the house. A woman was standing on the doorstep looking very stern and disapproving. Her arms were folded and she had a scowl on her face.

Jean.

'Oh shit,' Bridie whispered looking sheepishly at Jasper. 'My sister doesn't look at all happy.'

As they approached Jean, she didn't speak but merely grunted and turned on her heel, disappearing into the house. Jasper felt decidedly uncomfortable; it hadn't occurred to him when he'd agreed to step outside with Bridie, that talking in private with her about her sister maybe hadn't been such a great idea. He hoped the conversation on the beach wasn't going to cause a problem for Bridie. He would hate for that to happen.

CHAPTER 10: JASPER

*J*asper loved the early morning. He'd just been for a run along the harbour wall, showered and was now at his usual table by the window, the sun pleasantly streaming through. As he savoured the tangy sweetness of fresh orange juice, he gazed wistfully at the view across the turquoise sea, an exquisite masterpiece painted by the hand of nature. The rhythmic dance of the waves crashing on the sand was hypnotic. He cherished these moments of solitude in the breakfast room, allowing his thoughts to flow undisturbed, the seeds of creativity germinating and firing, a welcome respite from the imminent chaos that would follow when the teenagers burst in.

Bridie wandered in followed by a few others. She smiled and gave him a small wave as she headed over to the table where the coffee and cereals were served. He thought it strange that she didn't come over, he wanted to find out what Jean had said to her. He watched her fill a bowl with cornflakes and take it to a table on the far side of the room. After their previous evening's stroll together along the beach, he was surprised she was choosing to sit alone rather than join him.

He sat for a while watching people come in and spoke to a

few before getting up and heading back to the room to find out if Toby was up. While making his way along the corridor, a familiar voice called his name. He turned to see Bridie, who'd followed him out of the breakfast room.

'I'll have to be quick before my sister comes down.' She hesitated, glanced over her shoulder with panic in her eyes as if expecting Jean to emerge at any moment. 'My sister wasn't happy that we went off together last night. She gave me a really hard time.'

'Why?'

'I can't say too much. We can catch up another time,' she said curtly. 'I didn't realise you were a journalist, had you explained your motives, I wouldn't have told you half of what I did.' Her words pierced like tiny knives; upsetting one of these families, how could he ever forgive himself? His reputation, professionalism and sensitivity meant everything to him, but now the air between them had turned chilly.

'I would never do anything to harm any of these families here. I'm keen for the public to understand the truth so that they get the recognition and justice they deserve. You'll have to trust me.'

She scoffed and peered at him through daggered eyes. 'How, when I don't even know you? My sister says you can't trust any journalist no matter what they say. Over the years she's had endless phone calls, prying reporters trying to find out more, tricking her into giving information to sell her story.'

'Let's step outside a minute.' He put his hand gently on her shoulder and pulled open the door open that led onto the drive. She followed. He could see reluctance in her eyes and demeanour in her body language.

Her tone was blunt but civil. 'You come across as a perfectly nice man, but I've told you too much and I don't want any of it to be used in your story Do the others know what you're really here for or have you kept it a secret from them too?'

'Look, I may be a journalist, but you must also understand I have Toby's interests at heart too and would never do anything to hurt him or any of you. My motivation is to get the pharmaceutical companies to accept their liability and rest assured I'd never betray you.'

Just then, Jean appeared at the doorway and glared at her sister. 'Couldn't help yourself could you, taken in by his charms again?' Her hands were on her hips, and she looked cross.

She stepped outside and confronted Jasper. 'I don't think much of you, the sneaky way you got information out of my sister last night.' Her lips were curled. 'I know exactly what people like you are, I've had years of dealing with you lot. You need to be careful. You press are the scum of the earth.'

'Please don't put me in the same box as others. You shouldn't judge me before you understand where I'm coming from.'

She pointed a finger at him. 'I want you to stay away. I wonder if all the others know you're sneaking round trying to get a story.' There was genuine venom in her voice, and he felt extremely uncomfortable.

'Have you read any of my articles? I can drop a few to your room later? If only you knew what I'm really trying to achieve. I want to help you get better compensation. I'm willing to spend all my time and energy on the families, getting them help, and publicity is the only way. Your stories need to be told. Of course, I won't mention names and places. You will be anonymous. My attitude is that you don't just write about it once, you don't just write it twice, you go on writing until people are almost bored. I hope to God that eventually we'll get you the compensation and recognition you all deserve.'

'You think you're some kind of hero riding to our defence? We can fight our own cause.'

'I want readers to feel anger for what happened to you. Society has conspired to contain the information, isn't it time the public knew about the challenges you face?' Jasper felt passion flood his veins, he'd carry on fighting because this was a cause he believed in so strongly.

Jean was so worked up that she started shouting at him. 'You're completely deluded if you think readers and society will be on our side. Surely, you've seen how crowds disappear when we walk onto the beach. We're shunned, and we mothers are blamed for taking the bloody pill, accused of being neurotic hypochondriacs.'

Out of the corner of his eye, he saw Bridie quietly shrinking away. He'd dealt with challenging characters over his career, but this really intimidated him. Was this how they saw him? *Am I one of those vultures that would do anything for a story?*

CHAPTER 11: JASPER AND TOBY

The following morning Jasper came down for breakfast armed with his newspaper articles, and when Jean and Bridie entered the room and sat down at their usual table by the window, he sauntered over and gently put the articles onto their table.

'Look, I'm sorry we got off on the wrong footing, and I'm sorry you've been let down by everyone else, but keeping the stories out of the press prevents the truth being told. Just have a read,' he said, nodding to the articles. 'Then maybe you'll understand where I'm coming from and why I'm so keen to help you.'

Jean glanced at the papers with a sneer on her face. 'I'm not reading that tripe.'

Bridie was struggling to look at Jasper, her face flushed, and she was clearly embarrassed by her sister's attitude. 'I'm intrigued. Maybe we should at least read them.'

Jasper looked at Jean and in a soft voice said, 'I think you'll see I'm not the beast you think I am.'

Bridie put her hand on her sister's arm. 'Maybe we should give him a chance,' she said softly.

Jean brushed her off and her face hardened. 'Everybody

thinks they know best. None of you have a clue of the difficulties we face.' She rose to her feet and pushed her chair back.

'I'm beginning to understand but I'll never truly know unless you are prepared to share your stories with me,' Jasper said, trying to pacify her. 'All I want is to pursue truth and justice. It's not an easy task. The government wants to bury the story and write the children's eulogies, ministers like Enoch Powell didn't give a fiddler's monkey, like they are trying to do with the coal miners.'

'We aren't interested in justice. Grunenthal is a machine, it tried to suppress the truth, its eyes are only open to money, they don't give a flying fig what they did, so what's the point in you writing about it? We are all too preoccupied trying to raise our families.' And with that she stormed out of the room and all Bridie could do was look at Jasper, shrug her shoulders and sigh.

'Jasper, I'll read your articles and encourage my sister to do so too. If you are true to your word and want to get anywhere with Jean though, just a word of caution, she has a lot of ill feeling towards the press, she's faced constant intrusion by journalists, it'll take a lot to persuade her.'

Jasper felt a sense of shame. He had no intention of causing distress, but he was also determined.

He sighed and when Bridie picked up her piece of toast, he knew it was his cue to leave her in peace. He glanced at his watch. 'Goodness, is that the time? Trimble's kindly offered to take us to the War Tunnels.'

'Maybe that's what you should be writing about instead, the German occupation of the islands.'

Jasper smiled. 'I'm sure plenty already have. I'll catch up with you later, have a good day.'

. . .

TOBY PEERED through the car window at the imposing entrance to the Jersey War Tunnels. His mind swirled with a multitude of questions.

'Oh my God, what is this place? Who built it, why was it built?'

He couldn't help himself, when something captured his imagination and intrigued him, he had an insatiable thirst to know more. That was how he felt right now. He wanted to know everything there was to know about these war tunnels.

'Why is there a red cross?'

'That's the emblem for the Red Cross,' Jasper explained. 'A red cross on a white background, it symbolises protection and medical services. The tunnels were built as a bombproof munitions barracks but some of it was converted to receive casualties after they feared an assault on the island.'

Toby screwed up his face. 'An underground hospital in a hillside, how weird. Dripping water, dark with rats scurrying around. And it's not exactly an easy place to get to, look at the journey we've had. You could bleed to death before you get here.' He shuddered. 'Must have been smelly and damp. And how did they heat the place?'

'Steady on, lad, your mind's running riot, where's all this come from?' Jasper chuckled.

'Here, Jasper, do you think there are any gory relics left over? Maybe we'll see skeletons. I wondered how many people died here. Perhaps there are some ghosts.'

Trimble reversed into a parking space. 'This formed part of a huge defence fortification, a series of coastal defences built by the Nazis to protect them from an Allied invasion, they called it the Atlantic Wall. It was dug out by slave workers, mainly from Russia and Poland. The working conditions were horrendous, many died. The Germans knew it wouldn't be bombed by the Allies because the Geneva Convention protects medical facilities.' Trimble's voice was flat and unengaging but there seemed a slight reluctance to talk about the past. His face looked grey and ashen.

'I bet you have a lot of stories to tell of that time.'

'That's in the past, boy. Things you wouldn't want to hear. Nothing to be gained by revisiting memories. Best forgotten. Ain't that right, Jasper?'

'I don't know about that. Sometimes it helps to revisit the past and it helps us appreciate what we have and what people went through so that we can have a better life.'

Toby didn't want to let it drop, he was fascinated and wanted to know more.

'I've never visited the tunnels, I have enough of my own memories, can't understand why people would pay good money to see such cruelty.'

Jasper smiled at Trimble and said, 'That's a shame.' He opened the passenger door to get out. 'Thought you might have given us a guided tour.'

The engine was idling. 'No thanks, I've no desire to go in there. I'm going to pop in and see my old miller friend over the road. Come and find me when you're done.'

They got out of the car and after paying their entrance fee headed into the gloomy interior. It smelt damp and musky. They peered into every room, their eyes slowly adjusting to the gloomy light. The air was dank, and a strong smell of mould filled Toby's nostrils. It was chilly and as he shivered, wishing he'd worn a jumper over his t-shirt, he glanced round finding it hard to believe the Germans planned to use these gloomy, damp tunnels as a makeshift hospital. Hospitals were warm, bright, and pristine, sheets were crisp and smelled of fresh spring flowers. But as Trimble had pointed out, the large red cross at the entrance to the tunnels was a façade to divert the enemy from its main purpose, the storage of munitions. How sneaky, Toby thought.

He wandered over to a few exhibits, old remnants and newspaper articles that weren't part of the main display. Looking at a range of old photos, he was about to move on when his eye was caught by one in particular. It was an old sepia photo of a house. He immediately recognised the turrets and chimneys that looked like fingers pointing to the sky and the observation tower to the east of the house. It was such an unusual property, he'd recognise it anywhere and was just as creepy in real life as it was in the picture. He stopped abruptly and took a few steps back to peer at it more closely.

'Jasper, quick, quick, come and look at this,' he called as if the picture was about to disappear.

Jasper came rushing into the room. 'What's up?'

'Look what I've found.' He couldn't contain his excitement. 'It's Trimble, it's Trimble.'

Jasper looked over his shoulder. 'Bloody hell.'

Toby read the writing under the photo. 'Bonaparte House was used in the war by the Nazis as a command and interrogation centre. Many islanders thought to be guilty of offences were brought here for interrogation, which was often accompanied by physical abuse. Prior to the Second World War, the occupants were injured servicemen, recuperating after fierce fighting on the Western Front during the Great War.'

A couple of German officers were posing next to a car, the occasion being a visit by the chief of the Gestapo. Their uniforms were spotless and adorned with medals, and their polished boots gleamed.

'You never see them in any other footwear other than jackboots. They probably kick their way out of the womb.' Jasper chuckled.

Toby took a closer look. A man and woman stood close to the entrance of the house and the woman was shaking the hand of one of the officers, a big smile on her face. There was something strangely familiar about them. And then it struck him.

'That's Trimble's sister.' He turned round excitedly and looked at Jasper.

Leaning closer, Jasper squinted at the picture. 'I think you're right, lad,' he said with surprise in his voice. He read the information under the photo. 'The Trimbles were market gardeners and owned a flower shop in St Helier which Mable Trimble continued to run throughout the war. John and Clare Trimble are seen here. John worked as a gardener at the house and Clare was a record keeper.'

Jasper frowned. 'There are three of them, I'm confused.'

'The other must be his wife. I imagined he'd never been married. How odd. He's never mentioned a wife.'

'Why would he tell us his life story?' Jasper shrugged.

'Whole thing is really creepy. Imagine the house being used as a Nazi headquarters.' Toby was intrigued. 'Could this all link in with the area of the house that's out of bounds? They're hiding something.' His mind was racing. He couldn't go off exploring on his own, he needed an accomplice, but Jasper would never agree to snooping round the house.

'I'm not sure, lad, it's all very curious.'

'We could have a look.'

Toby wasn't expecting Jasper to agree, but to his surprise he did. He rubbed his chin. 'How the hell would we get in? It's bound to be all locked.' He looked at Toby. 'I wonder if this is linked to a conversation I overheard in the shop.' He seemed reluctant to continue.

'What conversation? You didn't say.'

'It was the first morning, you were in one of your moods.'

'I was not in a mood, I was just annoyed with you, sometimes you're only interested in your interviews and writing your articles.'

'Yes, but never mind that for the moment, we need to think. I was in the shop, and I overheard a couple of locals talking about the Trimbles. The locals don't seem to like them, I'm not sure what they did but something happened during the war. If only we could find out what.'

'We need to ask Mr Trimble.'

'We can't just ask him, we've got to be clever. Here, lad and we don't want to be caught snooping otherwise we'll be on the plane back too.'

'Can we be detectives, like Starsky and Hutch?'

'I'll be Starsky, he was better looking.'

'Okay, be serious, let's have a think, we can get our heads together later and come up with a plan.'

As they sauntered back into the bright daylight, they saw Trimble parked up and waiting for them. He waved across, and from the relaxed look on his face it seemed as if he'd enjoyed his coffee with the miller. They got in the car and the atmosphere was cheerful as they trundled down the hill. Trimble commented on what a lovely day it was and that the mill was busy with visitors. As they turned onto the main road, Toby couldn't contain himself, he was so excited and blurted out that they'd seen the photo of the house. He caught a glimpse of Trimble's face in the mirror and immediately regretted speaking as he watched the man's jovial demeanour darken at the mention of it.

'Wow, you didn't tell us the house was a Nazi command centre during the war,' Toby gushed.

Jasper turned in his seat and glared at Toby. They'd promised not to tell Trimble.

'I don't know anything about a photo.'

'But you must know about the history of the house, what can you tell us?'

'Drop it.' Jasper glared at him.

'Some things are best left in the past, lad.' Trimble put his foot down and speeded round a bend. Jasper gasped and grabbed the door handle. It felt as if Trimble was escaping the past and their conversation.

'But who were the women we saw in the picture? I recognised Miss Trimble but who was the other lady? Was it your wife?'

'I've never been married. Maybe my other sister.'

'You have two sisters? That must have been horrible. One is bad enough.'

'Where is she now?' Jasper asked.

'I don't know, she disappeared during the occupation and I've never seen her since. I don't want to talk about it, boy.'

'Disappeared?' Toby piped up. 'Wow that is amazing. Was she a magician?' He laughed.

Jasper looked sternly at Toby.

'No boy,' Trimble said. 'She just disappeared, and nobody ever saw her again.'

Toby's interest had piqued to a new level now. He wasn't going to let it drop. 'Did you send out a search party, everyone must have been so worried, you cannot just disappear.'

'All sorts of people disappeared during the war, and for all sorts of different reasons. I don't want to talk about this, the subject is closed, as I've said before, it was a time we would all rather forget.'

'But…'

Jasper glared again at Toby. 'No buts, you heard what he said.'

They drove the rest of the way in silence, only broken by Trimble grumbling at the state of the roads and the crazy driving of the holidaymakers and Toby making comments as they passed through the local villages.

When they drove through the gates of the house, Jasper thanked Trimble for taking them and after getting out of the car Trimble shot into the house before anything else could be said. Toby followed Jasper to their room and when they were safely inside, he said, 'He's hiding something, I know it. Did you see his face when I asked the question about the photo? He's creepy, glad we are only here for a holiday.' He paced the room feeling more and more frustrated. 'For God's sake, how can you lose your sister, that is careless, perhaps she was tortured, murdered and fed to the wolves Perhaps her skeleton's in the cellar.'

'That's enough,' Jasper shrieked, throwing his notepad onto the bed. 'Your crazy thoughts will get you into trouble. Off you go and play with the others, I have work to do now.'

'You and your bloody work, you need to get a life, Jasper, there is more to Jersey than note-taking and interviews, so much to see and do. I'll see you at dinner.' And with that he opened the door and left.

LATER, after dinner, Jasper strolled into the garden and gazed at the inky expanse of the sea. Waves pounded on the rocks, and he could hear the distant clinking of halyards against masts. He felt the cool embrace of the evening air. The afternoon had been productive; he'd interviewed another mother, this time of a girl named Josie, and now pondered how best to write her story. Josie had the same impairment as Toby, foreshortened arms, and Jasper found her story fascinating. Although thalidomide families shared similar experiences, each story was distinct, unique, and always shocking, heartbreaking and sometimes both.

Jasper shook out a fag from his jacket pocket, lit it, took a drag and watched the plume of smoke eddy into the air. Filling his lungs, he felt a sense of calm washed over him, all the tension that had been building inside, exhaling all the shame he'd felt earlier on, all those feelings of self-loathing and doubt. But what was he doing? He'd quit years ago; puffing away on a cancer stick wasn't going to help, it had got his mother in the end. Puff, puff, puff like a chimney. That's how he remembered his old ma. And what the hell would Sandy think if she discovered his dirty little secret? He consoled himself, it was only the occasional fag, perfectly harmless, but she wouldn't see it like that and was bound to explode and warn him never to smoke around Angela. Ever since Sandy had returned from her parents', their relationship had been good, very good in fact, and the last thing he wanted was to spoil it.

He allowed the cigarette to burn almost down to the filter; that was a first, an indication of how much he'd craved that hit. He dropped it on the pathway and as he ground it beneath his shoe, someone coughed nearby, and he turned to see Jean in the gloomy light clutching his articles.

She looked awkward, her head dipped, and she couldn't look him in the eye. 'I read one of your articles and I'm sorry I reacted the way I did, I can sense you're different to the rest. You're for us not against, but I still feel I'm not ready to share my story.'

Her words lifted him; he'd started to feel doubt and unease about his work, but this was a minor victory. 'There's no pressure at all. But if at some point in the future you do feel able to, you can remain anonymous. No names, no pictures. Just share what you want to, what you consider to be important. But as I say, there's no pressure. Do what you feel most comfortable with. But I'm sure you feel the same as I do, that it's time the government and Distillers took responsibility for their failings. I can't do this alone and need your help to get your voices heard.'

She turned away and gazed out to sea. 'The press is a double-edged sword, holding the power to shed light on truth and incite positive change, yet also capable of causing harm and misinformation.' She looked at him and he saw the pain in her eyes and all that she'd endured. 'It depends on the hands that wield the sword and the integrity of its blade.'

Her words were profound, she'd clearly thought long and hard. He wanted to be the blade that cut through the confusion and the misinformation and shine his beacon on the truth. His integrity was the sharpening stone, not all journalists were professional, they hounded, they tapped phones, recording people without their permission, and were hot on pursuit with their telephoto lenses. He was different, he respected privacy and boundaries and didn't overstep the mark. He took his responsibilities seriously and it was the way he wanted to remain. He took pride in his work.

CHAPTER 12: TOBY

Toby and Jasper were getting ready for the evening ahead. Jasper was slumped on his bed having showered, dressed, and run a comb through his damp hair, but Toby was taking longer. Why did Jasper always look catalogue handsome no matter what he wore or how long he'd taken to preen himself? It wasn't fair. He had the kind of looks that launched a woman's dreams. His skin glowed and had the warmth of the Mediterranean and it was the way he carried himself, like somebody of importance. There were times when Toby wished he looked more like Jasper, like this evening because he so wanted to make a good impression––a lasting one with one particular person.

Lucy.

He stood in front of the mirror. His beloved black t-shirt hung on his wiry frame, the one that never failed to earn him admiration from Lucy. He'd slung on his signature flares and asked Jasper to weave his CND buckle belt through the loops. He studied his reflection. How he wished he was older, taller, better looking, he might stand a chance with her. He was hardly a babe magnet. She was well out of his league and that would never change. He wasn't likely to get anywhere with Lucy, yet an inner voice urged him to cling onto hope.

'I'm really looking forward to tonight, Lucy's performing.'

Jasper was reading a book. He glanced up and smiled. 'Yes, I know, lad. It's all you've talked about all day.' He chuckled.

'No I have not,' Toby said defensively.

'Ah, lad, you have a soft spot for her. But I should be careful because I've seen the way Sue looks at you.'

Feeling his face flush, Toby turned away. 'Sue and I are just good friends.'

'Ha ha, I've heard that one before.'

It was Toby's turn to wind Jasper up. 'Well, what about you and that Bridie woman? You snuck off for a romantic late-night walk with her, wonder what Sandy would have to say about that.'

Jasper winked, and teasing Toby said, 'I have chicks falling at my feet, lad, falling at my feet.' Laughing, he picked up a comb and flicked his hair, Elvis style. 'Perhaps you'd like to me to give you a few tips.'

Toby headed downstairs and into the bar area where the disco had already started. A kaleidoscope of swirling colours and the pulsating beat of *Earth, Wind and Fire* washed over him. Lucy wasn't on the stage yet and until then, a DJ was playing tracks and engaging with the audience. The tables had been pushed to the side of the room to create a dance floor and the air crackled with excitement and energy. He spotted Sue in the corner by the window chatting to a friend. The mums were sipping their usual tipple, Babycham. He hated the stuff, it was too sickly, but it seemed to be the drink of the moment among women. He wondered what the appeal was, maybe it was the sweet taste or the way the translucent liquid shimmered under the light and created a mesmerising display of tiny bubbles that gracefully ascended to the surface forming a veil of delicate foam, or maybe it was the picture on the bottle of a cute Bambi with a blue ribbon around its neck. He didn't care, he knew what drink satisfied him and he was heading to the bar to grab himself a shandy.

Clutching his glass under his armpit, he glanced around the room suddenly feeling all conspicuous and hoped someone would invite him to join them, but everyone was busy laughing and chattering, huddled in their groups. Sue had noticed him though. She waved him over and patted the chair beside her.

'Oh my God,' he said as he leant close to the table and carefully put his glass down. It was always a challenge holding a pint glass, but he'd developed a good grip and only ever filled it half full. 'I've been looking forward to tonight. Lucy is performing.'

Sue's posture tensed and she tutted irritably. 'What's so special about her?' she snapped. 'She's just a bit of blonde fluff.'

'She's more than special. She's lovely, she's brilliant.' Toby beamed and glanced round to see Lucy make her grand entrance. Several people whistled and whooped, and the DJ welcomed her to the stage.

'Great to know you are so shallow, Toby,' she said frostily. 'You of all people are supposed to look beyond beauty.'

'Well, you know, she's my mate, we go back a long time, she treats me like a normal person. She's the perfect woman, she's got everything going for her. Reminds me of Suzi Quatro. I wish she was my girlfriend.'

Her head shot back, and she looked at him in horror. 'Don't be ridiculous, Toby.'

A pang of hurt swept through him.

'How do you know her anyway?' The way she phrased the question, it was belittling.

'As I said, Lucy and I, we go back years.' That was all he was prepared to tell her. Let her wonder.

'What would you do if you went on a date with her? She'd eat you for breakfast, then spit you out.' She laughed in a mocking way, but it wasn't funny, it was spiteful. 'Would you wear your artificial arms to look normal? One thalidomide guy did that, and a few dates in, she pulled his arm, and it came off and gave her such a fright, he never saw her again.'

'Lucy accepts me the way I am,' he said coldly. 'And actually, I have already been out with her a couple of times but not on a formal date.'

'Why haven't you asked her out yet? You muppet, get on with it.' She laughed, a full belly laugh. 'You don't want to, you know you stand no chance, just as I stand no chance with some of the able-bodied guys I know. Time we accepted we're basically losers.'

He hated the way she casually hurled a grenade into his world, shattering his illusions. He could dream. He wasn't inadequate. He was going to make something of himself, and years from now she'd regret those cynical words. He'd show her. He wasn't going to be defined as Toby with no arms, he wanted to be remembered for something he'd achieved, and he realised then that he had to make a name for himself, make a success of his life, be something other than handicapped Toby. 'It's nothing to do with my handicap,' he said firmly. 'Lucy's older than me. If I want a girlfriend, I'll chase someone my own age, but I won't ever settle for second best because I'm handicapped, and you shouldn't either.'

When Lucy starting singing, the music drowned out their conversation. Sue fixed her gaze on several girls who were dancing. Like Toby, they had legs but no arms. She leaned towards him and in a loud voice said, 'wish I was able to wear clothes like that, such beautiful legs.' Toby saw the sad look on Sue's face and although he felt sorry for her because he knew she probably wished she had legs like those girls, he was soon distracted by Lucy strutting across the stage, giving it her fully welly as she belted out her first song. He watched her perform, awestruck by her presence. Her beauty was captivating, from her slender legs encased in fishnets to the short black leather skirt and stylish stilettos. Her sparkly red top accentuated her magnificent breasts. He was unable to tear his gaze away from her cleavage and the contours of her body. She looked so desirable, and he felt overwhelmed. And he loved the way her hair delicately framed her shoulders, and in that moment, it was as if she had been carved from the finest of heavenly materials.

During her third song, 'Jolene', he glanced round, his eyes scanning the crowd for Jasper. It was odd, he wondered where he'd got to, then realised he'd probably gone for one of his evening walks along the shore. Bridie wasn't in the room either; Jean was sitting on her own.

While it was quiet at the bar, Toby got up to buy more drinks. At the far end of the bar, the barman was busy polishing a glass and talking to Trimble, oblivious to his customers. The look of concern etched across the barman's face caught Toby's attention as he watched the man put the glass down, his furrowed brow indicated that he was contemplating something important. Trimble looked visibly distressed, his features were pinched. Pain was banking in his eyes. Something had happened, but what? He'd seemed okay yesterday.

When Trimble turned and headed back into the hall, Toby decided to follow him. Rounding the corner near the toilets, he stumbled on an intimate moment between the Trimbles. He held back, they hadn't seen him. Trimble's hands were resting consolingly on his sister's shoulders. She looked upset.

At the end of the evening, when Toby headed up, he found Jasper in the bathroom cleaning his teeth and getting ready for bed.

'Where were you? You missed a good evening.' He was disappointed that Jasper hadn't joined the party, especially without telling him, but his absence had given Toby the chance to enjoy his friends' company. Sue had been off with him though, and after his comments about Lucy, she'd practically ignored him for the rest of the evening. Women, he couldn't fathom them.

'Sorry, lad, I went for a walk with Bridie.'

'Another walk?' Toby's eyes nearly popped out of his head. 'People will start talking.'

'She's a nice lady, we have a lot to talk about.'

'Yeah, heard that one before.' He laughed as he slipped his loafers off and plunged onto his bed.

Jasper, with his mouth full of foaming toothpaste, leaned out of the bathroom and said, 'Some development, lad. Trimble asked if he could leave me in charge tomorrow. His sister is going for a medical check-up. He'll be gone all morning.' Toothpaste dribbled down his chin. 'Looks like we have our chance.' His eyes were twinkling with mischief.

'Better put our thinking caps on then,' Toby said excitedly. 'Work out where they keep the key for the cellar. Johnny went down there, did he tell you where it's kept?'

'No. I heard the sound of drilling this afternoon coming from the cellar, something's been going on.'

'How strange. Well, we have all morning to find the key and get down there.'

'Okay, lad, let's sleep on it, we'll devise a plan in the morning.'

CHAPTER 13: TOBY AND JASPER

The following day, shortly after lunch after the Trimbles had left, Jasper and Toby wasted no time. They didn't know how long they had. 'You know what hospitals are like,' Mr Trimble had said. 'Could be all afternoon or could be back in an hour.'

As luck would have it, everybody had gone to the cinema. A volunteer driver had driven them into town in the Sunshine coach. 'You're all off to the cinema this afternoon,' Joy had announced that morning.

With a sense of purpose, Toby strode across the kitchen towards the door tucked away in the corner while Jasper glanced out of the window to check the coast was clear. His foot reached out, firmly grasping the knob and he attempted to twist it open.

'Damn, it's locked.' He surveyed the room, and with a sudden flash of inspiration, remembered the conversation he'd overheard on the first day. 'They mentioned a key in a mustard pot. Wonder if they were talking about the cellar key.'

Jasper scratched his forehead. 'I hate snooping around, doesn't sit right.'

'You love it,' Toby chided. 'You should be used to snooping round, it's what you journalists do.'

A cheeky grin spread across Jasper's face as he began opening and closing cupboard doors pushing Marmite jars, tins of soup and condiments aside. He was like a kid rifling through his Christmas stocking before dawn had broken. 'Nothing wrong with an inquisitive mind, lad. Seek and you shall find.'

'Is there nothing sacred?'

'No, not in my world.'

Toby gingerly opened the broom cupboard. The broom and the mop fell out, whacking him in the face as if guarding against intruders. There on the shelf at the back between the silver polish and the floor polish was the old, battered Colman's mustard tin. 'Think I've found it, Jasper. Can't reach to get it.' Tins crashed to the floor and Jasper dashed over, picked up the broom and put it back in the cupboard before reaching up to the mustard tin to take off the lid.

They both grinned when he produced a large key.

Returning to put the tins in place, Jasper said, 'Damn, this baked bean can is now dented, I hope they don't notice.'

Jasper took the rusty key and opened the door to the cellar.

A waft of mould and damp hit his nostrils. Jasper switched on the light. There was a scurrying noise and Toby gasped.

'It's okay, it's only a rat, you're never far from a rat.'

'I know that, I'm standing next to one.' He nudged Jasper and chuckled.

They inched their way down the brick steps, Toby hugging the wall so that he didn't trip. 'Are there any spiders? You know I hate spiders.' He shuddered, glancing into the gloom, his eyes adjusting.

There was an old door, to the left of where they were standing. He nudged it. When he switched on the light, he looked up and saw a bare lightbulb hanging from the ceiling.

Toby's gaze settled on the rough concrete ground where a

patch bore scratches and signs. He couldn't make out what it was.

Jasper was behind him. 'Looks like something was fixed to the floor, but what?' he mused.

His eyes darted to the corner of the room, and he thought he could make out what looked to be a leather strap. Beside it lay a pair of rusty pliers.

'Looks like they're into bondage, very kinky.' He laughed.

'Toby,' Jasper chided. He looked like a startled rabbit as he turned to stare at him. 'You're not supposed to know about stuff like that.'

'You'd be surprised what us crips know and get up to.' A raucous laugh escaped his lips. 'Besides, you should see the magazines Dad's got stuffed under his bed, the dirty old sod.'

Jasper tutted, then went over to the strap, kneeling to inspect it. He glanced up at the ceiling and was quiet for a few moments before letting out a heavy sigh.

'I think this is a bit more than bondage,' he said in a solemn tone before getting up and brushing his knees.

'What do you mean?'

'I'm not sure, but something was happening in this room, I'm just not sure what.'

They left the room, pushing the rickety door shut.

Ahead of them was another old rickety door with a shiny padlock attached in addition to the existing lock.

'Looks like they've fitted a new padlock. I bet they did that after Johnny came down. Why would they do that unless they've got something to hide?'

They looked around in the dim light to see if they could find the key. Jasper glided his fingers along the upper edge of the door frame and expected to find the cold metal of a key. Instead, all he found was a fine coat of undisturbed dust which rose into the air making them both sneeze.

Toby reflected whereabouts under the house they were. 'You

don't suppose this door leads to that tower, do you? It could be a secret passageway.'

Jasper swung round, the expression on his face, thoughtful. 'Let me think, you could be right.' He raised his left hand pointing in different directions as he spoke. 'The kitchen is in that direction, the garden that way, so yes, maybe.'

They climbed the stairs, locked the door, and put the key back in the tin.

'Come with me, lad, let's check outside.'

Out on the driveway, they stood musing, looking at the house and its grounds and across to the tower which sat about forty feet to the side of the house. 'It would have to be a secret passageway between the two buildings built in the Napoleonic days.'

'My God, if they come back now, we're going to look like a couple of idiots looking round as if we're prospective buyers. You don't suppose there are dead bodies down there?'

'Don't be daft, lad, maybe a pile of bones and clothes. It's probably just blocked off because it's dangerous, that's all.'

'When the Trust bought this place, do you think they checked the cellars out?'

'Good point, lad. I think the Trimbles were facing financial ruin when they sold it to the Trust. It's a strange arrangement though, to buy a house and agree for the current owners to continue living there. It must suit the Trust, live-in caretakers that take care of the day-to-day running of the place and also suit the Trimbles to protect the secrets it holds.'

'And run these holidays.'

'Exactly.'

'There's potentially a direct line between the cellar and tower but you'd never know from looking at the ground.'

They walked over to the tower to take a closer look and couldn't find any clues.

Jasper went back inside to get on with some work, while

Toby tried to peer through the lowest window of the tower. He gazed up and down to see if he could find an entrance. Round the back was a big solid oak door which looked like it hadn't been opened in years. Cobwebs adorned the door, and the lock was rusty.

As he stood there wondering what was inside, he heard the sound of gravel crunching and peeped round the tower to see the Trimbles returning. He quickly shot in through the back door and hastily returned to his room where he found Jasper searching for something.

'What are you looking for?'

'I can't find my glasses. I think I've left them in the cellar.'

'That could be a problem, the Trimbles have just returned.'

'Shit, now what am I going to do? I need them for reading.'

Toby laughed. 'You'll just have to send them back to hospital.' He laughed.

They both returned downstairs to find Mr Trimble struggling with boxes from his car. 'Here, let me help,' Jasper said, 'where do you want them?'

'They're going down in the cellar. Put them by the cellar door.'

This was his chance to get his glasses. 'I can take them down for you.'

'No, I'm fine, just leave them there, I can sort them when I'm ready.'

Trimble brought the remaining boxes in from the car. Toby could see the frustration on Jasper's face as he attempted again to suggest that he could carry them down, but Trimble said the stairs were rickety.

They went out into the garden and when they were out of earshot, Jasper started swearing and cursing. 'What the hell am I going to do now? I just hope when he goes down there, he doesn't spot them. I'll just have to wait till they go out again.'

As Jasper didn't have his glasses, he couldn't do any reading or writing so they decided to go for a stroll along the beach, and later when they returned, they were about to climb the stairs when Trimble appeared. 'Jasper, Toby, thanks for the help. Ah, Jasper, if I'm not mistaken, I think these belong to you.'

'Oh, thank you,' he said, all flustered. 'I've been looking for them everywhere, where did you find them?'

Trimble seemed to grow in height as he looked at Jasper and with a triumphant look said, 'I think you know full well where you left them. Just for future reference, Colonel Mustard is no longer in his normal residence, snoopers beware. Have a good evening, boys.' Then he turned and walked off.

Jasper looked gobsmacked.

'What did he mean by that?'

Tutting, Jasper swiped him playfully across his head and they walked off into the garden.

CHAPTER 14: JASPER

After breakfast the next day, Jasper went up to his room to collect his notepad and pen. Before turning, he paused, his hand on the doorframe as he thought about the lady who was coming to visit. During his career, he'd encountered a great number of people but without doubt Elizabeth Twistington Higgins was one of the most remarkable and he considered it his greatest fortune to have met her. He'd often thought about Elizabeth over the years and because of the desperate nature of her illness, he'd always doubted she'd survived. And then, he was astonished to see her on *This Is Your Life*. He sent her a letter of congratulations for the MBE she'd achieved and as she was visiting St Helier, he invited her to Bonaparte House to give a talk to the group.

As he walked down the corridor, he was struck by the realisation that throughout history, each era bore the weight of its own distinctive medical battles, from the scourge of the plague, the insidious grip of smallpox to the haunting legacy of thalidomide. Each affliction left its mark on humanity and served as a reminder of the resilience of the human spirit.

Now at the top of the staircase about to descend, he caught

sight of her arrival through the landing window, as her carer guided her in a wheelchair towards the front door. He was taken aback by the noticeable frailty of her form, a sight that stirred a mix of concern and empathy and took his mind back to his own childhood, his parents so afraid of the mysterious deadly disease that was striking down tiny children. He remembered being kept away from public swimming pools and parties. Poor Elizabeth. He could still see the headlines from the early fifties, accompanied by pictures of jam-packed hospital wards, children on crutches or their legs in braces, their small bodies contorted and weakened by the effects of the disease. The sense of helplessness on the parents' faces etched with anguish and exhaustion. They called it the nation's most feared disease.

Polio.

He shuddered pushing the memory aside, and skipped down the stairs to open the door before they reached the bell.

'Jasper, it's been so long. How are you?'

'Elizabeth, how wonderful to see you again.' He leant down and kissed her on the forehead then smiled at the carer and welcomed them both in. Elizabeth's brown hair was neatly tied back into a bun and as usual she was fastidiously groomed. She was wearing a cream silky blouse with a bow. Her hands were folded on a little blue velvet lace-edged cushion placed on her lap. She was completely paralysed, her only movement being in her neck and one of her fingers. 'I can't believe how much time has passed since I interviewed you all those years ago and to see you on *This Is Your Life*, what a surprise that was.'

'You're still the same, Jasper, an old charmer.'

He beamed down her. 'Do come in, the kids are all waiting.' In the hall, they were joined by the Trimbles. Jasper noticed they were subdued and seemed out of sorts after their hospital appointment. He wondered if everything was all right but didn't like to ask.

As they entered the bar area where everybody was seated, the room buzzed with chatter and their eyes were alight.

Jasper introduced Elizabeth but didn't want to steal her thunder. He'd allow her to share her life story with the group.

'It's lovely to meet you all,' she said. 'Jersey is a great place for a holiday and I'm sure you'll all have lots of fun.'

She chatted for a few moments before taking on a serious expression as she glanced around the room.

'In the journey of life, the cherished dreams we have may not materialise as we imagine. Dreams are not shattered, they are merely re-routed.' She looked at the mums in the room. 'The dream of motherhood often encompasses the hope for a perfect, healthy child, but sometimes life throws you lemons and you are forced to adapt. A different dream emerges as you take on these new challenges. It had been my dream to be a ballet dancer after my brother took me to see *Les Sylphides* at Sadler's Wells for my fourteenth birthday and I was so determined. I joined a dance school, and I performed in several shows. But then, in 1953 I contracted polio and my whole world changed. My greatest dream was now out of reach, shattered by a cruel twist of fate. It's hard when you set your sights on something and then that is dashed. The dreams you had, the vision of your future mapped out. I was in excruciating pain, and it left me weak and within a few days I'd lost the use of my legs and arms. At night I have to sleep in an iron lung.'

'What's an iron lung?' Mike asked.

'I wasn't sure how much you already knew, so I've brought along a picture of one.' Her carer showed the picture to the group and Elizabeth explained that the metal tube fed air pressure to inflate and deflate the lungs of paralysed patients. 'It's a miserable existence. I consider myself to be lucky because there is always someone who is worse off than yourself. I didn't lose the ability to use my mouth and like many of you, I've learned to use my mouth to do everyday tasks, all the things my hands and feet were used to doing for the first fifteen years of my life. It's amazing what you do to adapt when you have to.'

'But wasn't that hard? This is all we've known. We were born like this,' Toby asked.

'Yes, it was very hard. I was an active energetic child and always on my feet.'

'How did you learn to paint?' Jasper asked. He was eager to find out more.

She described mastering the art of breathing through her neck muscles, using a method known as 'frog breathing', where each breath is consciously commanded. 'It took me six years to learn how to mouth paint. Sometimes my head jerked unexpectedly, and I'd ruin the painting. I nearly gave up, it was so frustrating and extremely difficult, but while I painted, my mind returned to ballet and eventually I was able to open a dance school. I couldn't dance but I could teach from my wheelchair using my Possum controls and I could design the costumes and sketch the choreographic moves. I love movement and long for movement, but I try not to think about it, I paint it instead. I always say to handicapped people, build on what nature gave you rather than spend your lives complaining about what God took away. I know that sounds harsh, but really it is the only way to get through life.' She stared out at the faces in the room, everybody seemed to be hanging on her every word. 'You may not believe it now, but you will push boundaries, you will achieve the seemingly impossible. But you will find your way to fulfil your dreams.' There was a shuffling, some frowning, and a few were leaning forward, one hundred percent engaged.

One of the mothers made a comment. 'My daughter has taught me so much. All the funny things she did as a baby and toddler. I could have shielded her from the rough and tumble of life, but I didn't, she had to learn, I had to learn too. There have been moments of such happiness for us as parents, just seeing what they are capable of. When she was born, I was sick with worry and didn't think I'd bond with her. But one day as I bent over her cot to change her, the end of the scarf I was wearing fluttered down. She smiled up at me and tugged the scarf with her little feet. It was such a magical moment I'll never forget. We never mollycoddled her, and she was brought up believing she could do anything.'

'That's wonderful,' Elizabeth said smiling. 'Thank you for sharing that with me.'

'Try everything, you don't know what you're missing until you've tried it,' one of the children piped up, 'That's my motto. And please, miss, when are we going to do some painting?'

While Elizabeth had been talking, Joy and another member of staff were setting up easels, arranging paint palettes and blank canvases in preparation for the art workshop. Soft natural light streamed through the windows, the faint scent of oil and acrylics lingered in the air. Tables were lined with brushes of varying sizes, tubes of paint and jars of water.

Elizabeth joined Joy in offering guidance and encouragement and soon the room buzzed with creative energy and a sense of empowerment as people took brushes in their mouths or between their toes planting the first daub of paint on their canvases.

A few people took their time before diving in, while a couple of people immediately threw in the towel claiming they had no creative bone in their bodies, couldn't paint and didn't want to learn. Jasper was pleased to see Toby having a go. He was taking his inspiration from the view to paint a small fishing boat. It wasn't bad.

Before Elizabeth left, she said she wanted to leave them with a final thought.

'Life will seem hard for you all right now, leaving institutional life. It's often not until we leave that cocooned world that we become aware that we have a disability, because in your world it was a level playing field. But remember that regardless of your handicap, each one of us is different, unique and you will find your own skills and never give up on your dreams.'

Jasper escorted Elizabeth to the front door after everybody had thanked her for coming and then he strolled round the room, admiring the artwork. One girl, Lisa hadn't even picked up her brush. She was staring at the canvas, almost mesmerised by its whiteness. Jasper looked at her and she had tears in her eyes.

He stood behind her and gently asked, 'What are you thinking, Lisa?'

'I don't know where to start.' She looked so glum.

'The canvas represents your life, it's for you to set your mark and paint your dreams. Never be afraid to have a go even if it goes wrong. If you never try, you'll never know. There's nothing to lose and everything to gain.'

CHAPTER 15: TOBY

After they'd returned home from Jersey and as the summer drew to a close, Toby grew nervous about starting college, but despite his apprehension he was also excited at the prospect of the unknown; meeting new friends, learning new subjects. At his interview, the head of the Academic Studies Department had convinced him to study two A levels rather than three due to the challenges he faced in writing with shortened arms and mouth. This decision ensured he had the best possible chance of success. He chose English literature and geography. Reading was one of his passions and maps had always fascinated him.

He was prepared for lots of writing, and it would be a strain on his body, but he was desperate to learn and make something of his life.

'How do you write?' the head of department had asked him at interview back in the spring. 'Are you able to write fast and take notes?'

Toby couldn't resist a playful quip. 'You, sir,' he teased with a grin, 'can only write one way. I, on the other hand, have three ways of wielding a pen.'

Toby explained how he'd gripped a pen in the hook of his artificial arms from a young age. A pencil was fastened on with an elastic band to stop it slipping. He'd found it tedious having to concentrate on the action of writing rather than on what he wanted to write. Thankfully, his mum had hated the artificial arms as much as he had, and they were abandoned.

He boldly lifted his foot and plonked it on the head's desk sending a few pieces of paper fluttering to the floor. The man looked shocked but sat back and watched wide-eyed as Toby skilfully grasped a pen between his toes and effortlessly began to write his name.

'See, sir, versatility at its finest,' he declared, suppressing a mischievous grin.

From a tiny age he'd learned to hold a pen or pencil between his toes and by the time he was seven this was the main way he wrote, but he was slow back then and got painful cramps on the arch of his foot. Over the years though, writing with his toes became easier and quicker and his writing had become neater. He'd also learned to write with a pen between his teeth, but not a pencil because of the risk of lead poisoning.

'I also have a Possum typewriter.' It wasn't his machine, he'd used one at St. Bede's. The Possum was an adapted electric typewriter made by IBM and allowed the keys to be automatically depressed when he made a choice from a light board on which a keyboard layout was displayed. He remembered how tedious it had been when he'd joined St Bede's, having to learn fifty or so number codes, because each letter was represented by a two-number combination. He selected keystrokes with his toes by pressing a switch using a knob attached to a footplate when the desired character was illuminated. The only problem with it was that it didn't allow him to read what he'd typed and there was no facility to edit and correct mistakes. It wasn't easily portable, and he didn't want to risk damaging it. The other problem was that the machines at St.

Bede's were now a few years old and always breaking down. When they broke down, they had to be sent away to be fixed and this meant they were out of action for too long. It was frustrating.

'You have your own?' The head looked impressed, but Toby explained that it belonged to the school and was a heavy machine fixed to a trolley.

Toby couldn't imagine having a Possum at home, where on earth would he keep it? There wasn't enough room. And the terrible racket it made, it would drive Bill mad and not to mention the heat it generated, it would be unbearable especially in the summer. He imagined Bill mopping his face with a face-cloth or buying an electric fan to stay cool and complaining the whole time.

'I'm afraid we don't have anything like that here, we're not really set up for people with individual requirements.'

Bill leaned forward in his chair and scratched his chin. 'Maybe you need to become more inclusive.'

'Yeah, but we don't have a lot of handicapped students here, and the funding situation is pretty dire, especially with this government.'

'I'm the caretaker at St. Bede's,' Bill had interjected, 'and I'm sure they won't mind Toby using the Possum in the evening or weekend.'

'Let me think about that one. There might be funding for a typist to assist you. But what I will do is arrange for one of the students in your class to work with you and you can share their lesson notes. Where there's a will, there's always a way. We can overcome this.'

On the first day, Toby didn't want the distraction of babbling parents and so he declined the offer of a lift to college. He wanted to walk, get used to the route he would be taking each day and he wanted to be alone with his own thoughts.

He found himself in the bustling street outside his college,

FEAR TO FEARLESS

blending into the flow of students eagerly funnelling towards the grey concrete tower block.

There was something invigorating though about the buzz, the feeling that he was part of a bigger picture. He listened to the chatter around him. Friends who hadn't seen each other all summer were sharing holiday stories, while others anticipated their first day at college. As he reached the glass double doors leading to the academic studies department, the crowd were thrusting forward, pushing, shoving their way through and up the metal stairs. With the lack of manners unsettling him, his heart began to pound in his chest as panic shot through him.

It was way too crowded and he felt very uncomfortable.

I might get knocked down.

A stampede of feet like a herd of elephants, a sea of faces shot past him, bumping into him, racing to their classes. What was the rush?

Thinking quickly, he decided it was best to pin himself against the wall. With no arms to hold onto the rail, the fear of losing his balance loomed large. Each step felt like a precarious dance, amplifying his sense of vulnerability.

Reaching the top of the stairs having walked up with his shoulder grazing the wall for support, he headed along the corridor until he reached his classroom, room 15.

At the door he was greeted by a tubby man with fat spilling out of his collar. On the shoulders of his tatty blazer was what looked like the aftermath of a flour fight, thanks to his dandruff. 'You must be Toby,' he said in a lilting Welsh accent. Toby caught a whiff of his rancid garlic breath and recoiled. 'I thought you'd like to sit at the front,' he said smiling and pointing to a label on the front table with his name on it.

He wanted to choose where he sat but this didn't seem to be an option. He wondered why he'd been put at the front because there was nothing wrong with his eyesight or hearing. But then he realised it was probably to allow him more space to move around and to use his feet when he needed to. Then he saw the small foot desk on the floor to hold his paperwork. Wow, this made him smile, they had considered his needs and there was even a mug with his name on it complete with a straw. This put him at ease on the one hand, but also made him feel like a goldfish in a bowl. The last thing he wanted was to be watched by the whole class and viewed as a freak.

In front of him was the teacher's desk. It was massive, big enough to get about six people around it and there was a blackboard behind the desk and a pull-down overhead projector screen. A funny looking contraption sat in the middle of the desk. He wandered over to take a look while the teacher greeted each student. The contraption was a chunky box with a sheet of glass on the top. An arm extended vertically from one side like a *War of The Worlds* alien and there seemed to be a magnifying glass. He read the label, Premier Overhead Projector. He was intrigued, he'd never seen one before.

He was about to take a closer look when two lads came rushing in and bounded over to him. They looked him up and down. 'You must be the Toby everyone's been talking about. Nice to meet you. I'm Tom and this is Dave,' the taller one piped up.

'Yup, I'm Toby and as you can see, I'm pretty 'armless.'

Tom and Dave chuckled. 'Glad to see you have a sense of humour, mate. Don't worry, we won't ask you to do a high-five.'

'I dunno, I might be able to, I could be a magician.'

'Come and join us at break, mate, we're going for a fag.'

'I don't smoke, I've got enough fire in my spirit, don't need it in my lungs too, but I'll gladly join you for some fresh air.'

Dave looked at Tom and smiled. 'He's funny, I like him.' Then he turned to Toby and slapped him on the back. 'See ya later, mate.' They sloped off to the back of the room and Toby wished he could join them.

He stared at the notice on the table next to him which read,

'Toby's scribe' and wondered who this would be. As he stared, a flash of colour by the door made him glance up, stopping his thoughts in his tracks. There in the doorway was a tall stunning redhead brimming with confidence, her hands in the pockets of her denim jacket. The most striking girl he'd ever seen. She was wearing hotpants, and her slender long legs seem to go on forever. He was mesmerised and felt the momentary stopping of his heart. She had such a presence, he couldn't take his eyes off her. She scanned the room as if looking for her best friend, then when she saw Toby, her eyebrows shot up and she flashed him a smile. His chest tightened, he was transfixed, couldn't move as if his bum was glued to the seat. As she flitted over to him, a trail of heavy perfume wafted in her wake. Up close, he noticed her eyes and his breath caught in his throat. They were the most stunning green orbs he'd ever seen.

'You must be Toby. Hi. I'm Mandy, your scribe. I'm going to be your ears and hands.' She was panting as if she'd run up the stairs.

Her shiny mop of red hair cascaded in tight curls down to her shoulders and as she plonked herself down next to him, she flicked her hair out of her eyes with that self-assured confidence of hers.

'Hi.' He felt himself go red. He hadn't expected his scribe to be a girl and felt a mix of flustered surprise and self-consciousness.

Bloody hell, I can hardly believe it. Looks like I'll be spending a lot of time with this stunning girl.

He mumbled a response which made her laugh, and this put him at ease.

'It's the first time I've ever left somebody speechless.' She grinned. 'We'll get on fine.'

Every seat in the room was now occupied. 'Class settle down.' The teacher, now at the front of the classroom, clapped his hands. 'Settle down, you'll have plenty to catch up on in the break.'

As the teacher spoke, Toby glanced round at his new classmates. They were an eclectic

bunch. Not one of them was dressed in similar clothing to another. A chubby lad had a mop of hair like Gilbert O'Sullivan, all curly and Toby wondered if it was permed. A fabric parrot perched upon the shoulder of another lad clad in a black suit and rainbow tie, while a girl's eyelids were coated in sky-blue eyeshadow, reminding him of Elizabeth Taylor playing Cleopatra or Liza Minelli's cabaret make-up. Each student was the architect of their own style, fashion the fearless way, experimenting, wearing what they loved, not worrying if something didn't match, pushing their own boundaries. They were comfortable in their skin, and it translated in the way they dressed. But above all, Toby thought, the most beautiful thing they wore was their confidence. They weren't worried about fitting in, they craved the unique, distinct and that made him feel comfortable.

I think I'll fit in just nicely.

'First things first,' the teacher said. 'I'm George Gush and I shall be your tutor for the year. Firstly, let me welcome you to our college and I wish you all a successful year.'

Even the tutor was strange. His beige trousers were too short revealing odd socks, one bright green, one red, and his shabby leather shoes were the size of boats. There was something a bit mad science professor about him, but without the wild hair and white overall. As he spoke, he foamed at the mouth, making Toby think of a mutt with rabies.

'So that we can get to know each other, let us go round the room and introduce ourselves, then we'll crack on with the detail of how things work at the college.'

There were a few groans and when it came to Toby's turn, he found he couldn't speak. He hadn't a clue what to say, he hadn't been listening to what others had said and nothing had sunk in. His voice went all squeaky, his brain was like scrambled egg and his heart was still racing.

'It's okay,' Mandy said in a kind voice. 'I can see you're a bit lost for words, I always seem to have that effect on people, I'll tell the class the little I know if that's okay?' He nodded eagerly. She turned round in her seat and said, 'This is Toby and as you'll find out, he's a terrific character, full of fun and a cheeky chap.'

Toby went red. What did she mean, a cheeky chap, a terrific character? She'd only just met him. Maybe she'd been briefed.

'And he's the only one of us that's presented a bouquet to the Queen.'

A few students gasped.

'Will you be helping him?' one lad called out. 'You lucky bugger, Toby.'

Somebody whistled and the teacher said, 'That's enough.'

'Yes, I'm going to be his scribe although Toby is very capable but may need some help to keep up. As you can see, he has no arms and was born like this due to his mother having taken the drug thalidomide during pregnancy.' A deadly hush descended; all eyes were on Toby. He just wanted the teacher to move on to the next student but realised he was the last.

The idea of the entire class watching him write with his mouth or foot filled him with dread. The prospect of everyone gawking, sniggering, and mocking him was daunting beyond his worst nightmares. What would he do if that happened, how would he react? And then he felt frustrated with himself, he had to toughen up to survive this jungle. It was going to be hard surviving college, he'd always known that. It was a completely new environment. He'd been cocooned at St Bede's where everybody was handicapped and they'd accepted him. Here though, he stood out like a Belisha beacon.

'Anyway,' Mandy continued, 'I hope you'll all look after him.'

It was as if she could see into his soul. She knew exactly what to say and how to put him at ease. 'I know you're worried about people staring and maybe yes, they will be curious when they see you using your feet to write and eat, but they'll also think you're pretty cool. I know I do.' She gave him a warm smile. 'Everybody's on their own journey, they have their own worries and insecurities they feel self-conscious about, and they worry that others will notice. Just because we can't see their insecurities doesn't mean they don't exist. Stay strong, be proud of who you are.'

He felt so happy to have someone like Mandy by his side and her words left him astounded. She seemed to have the insight of someone far beyond her years.

The following morning when Toby bounded into class, a girl rushed over to him all excited and gushed, 'Hey, I was talking to my mum last night about you and it turns out I could have ended up like you.'

A lad sitting further back overheard and piped up, 'oh no, not you as well, that's spooky. My mum said she had morning sickness with me, but her doctor couldn't prescribe it because she was taking thyroxine, so she had to grin and bear it.'

'Well,' Toby said, deflecting and trying his best to sound witty and hard, 'lucky you both dodged that bullet.'

Luckily for Toby, Mandy came into the room and had overheard the conversation. 'We've all got a lot to be thankful for, all the more reason why we need to look after Toby. He's our mate, he's one of us. He might be different but he's still one of us.' She thumped her bag on the table and sat down.

Toby cringed. He didn't want the spotlight to be on him. All he wanted was to blend into the crowd, to be treated the same as everybody else. He had no desire for special treatment.

A few days into the first week, Mandy collared him at breaktime. The third period had just ended. 'Hey, Toby, let's grab a coffee and you can tell me how you're finding things.'

Toby leaned down, and picked his satchel strap up from the

table with his teeth and hauled it over his neck. They headed for the door.

'I can't grab a quick anything.' He laughed. 'You don't realise what a challenge everything is for me. Rush, rush, rush, that's all we ever do in this place.' Exasperated with it all, he didn't remember St. Bede's being like this, not when every student faced different complications.

Someone bumped into Toby on their way out of class and it was almost the final straw for him. Heat pricked around his neck, and he threw Mandy a withering look.

'Hey, careful,' Mandy said to the student as they flew out the door.

'See, that's exactly what I mean, rush, rush, rush.'

She gave him a sympathetic smile and as he brushed past the door, the strap of his satchel became entangled with the handle, and he lurched backward. He tried to untangle it, but Mandy did it. Her laughter made him more irritable.

'Bloody thing. I hate being rushed.'

'I gather that, but calm down, I'm here to help, I know this place can seem overwhelming, it's not what you're used to.'

He turned bolshie. 'I'm not a cripple, I have to sort some of these things out for myself.'

'Sorry, I didn't mean to laugh at you, but seeing your arse sticking out as you tried to pick up your satchel with your tongue was kind of hilarious.' As she sniggered, she gave him an affectionate wink and hug.

'Yeah, I suppose it did look funny. Student hangs himself with satchel, first week of college.'

In the canteen, Mandy fed coins into the coffee machine and when the drinks were ready, she carried them to a table. He couldn't have managed this on his own and wouldn't have bothered getting a drink. He took a sip, and the kick was almost immediate as the caffeine hit his bloodstream.

'How's it going then, apart from all the rushing around? You enjoying the lessons?'

'Yes, but I wish I hadn't chosen geography. I'd rather do history.'

'You could swap, it's not too late. Just speak to the tutor.' She leaned over and threw her empty cup in the bin.

The first Geography lesson had sent him into a spin, he was hating everything about the subject. After visiting Jersey, Toby had found himself captivated by the Second World War, devouring every book in the library on the German occupation of the islands, and had asked Jasper and Bill a ton of questions about the war. The geography lesson had left him uninspired and disengaged and he'd found himself daydreaming about the cellar at Bonaparte House and pondering the part played by the Trimbles during those years.

This afternoon he had another hour of geography to look forward to and already he was dreading it. He thought he was going to enjoy the subject but didn't feel at all motivated, and the teacher's delivery and approach didn't help to inspire.

Draining his coffee, he said, 'I don't want it to prey on my mind for another day, I'll speak to the tutor later and ask to switch.'

Changing subjects proved effortless. Walking home, he felt happier. Not only had he managed to switch courses, but he'd also set up plans to hang out with Tom and Dave at the weekend.

As he entered the cottage, he spotted a white envelope propped up against a jam pot addressed to him.

'Hi Toby, there's a letter for you.'

They both stared at the envelope.

'St Neots,' Toby said, referring to the postmark. 'Where the hell is that?'

'Haven't a clue, son, but it looks official.' Bill slit open the envelope and eased out the letter. The page was typed and read, 'Dear Toby…'

CHAPTER 16: TOBY

'It's my letter, let me read it.'

Toby was furious. He was capable of reading his own mail, but Bill was hogging the letter. He wished he could snatch it and read it upstairs in privacy.

Bill put his glasses on and in a posh voice said, 'Oww, it's from the Thalidomide Trust.'

Intrigued, Toby rose from his chair and stepped round to peer over Bill's shoulder.

"Having trouble getting around? You may be entitled to vehicle assistance." Sounds intriguing,' Bill said, glancing up at Toby. 'You'll have to give them a ring, find out more.'

'Maybe,' Toby said with a shrug.

Bill read on. 'Your entitlement might depend on your classification.'

'I'm not a library book,' he joked.

He had a feeling he knew what they were referring to: the 'X' and 'Y' list which had been created to differentiate between those with definitive proof of their mothers having taken Distaval and those without proof. The 'X' list were all the children accepted by Distillers as officially thalidomide. Toby knew there were around three hundred and forty on that list. But he was on the 'Y' list which consisted of around a hundred and sixteen children not yet accepted as genuine thalidomide victims because the High Court wasn't satisfied their mothers had taken the drug and had no formal proof. But Toby had recently been assessed at Roehampton and it was possible he was now being treated as if he was on the 'X' list and therefore eligible for support.

He headed upstairs to get on with his homework and didn't give the letter further thought until a couple of days later when he arrived at college completely soaked, like a drowned rat. It hadn't been raining when he'd left home, otherwise he might have worn his mac. The sky had clouded over to a heavy and oppressive gunmetal grey, fists of wind and rain punched his face, the water slicing into puddles on the road. He cut through the college car park and seeing a few of his fellow classmates arriving by car, felt envious. Most of the time he didn't feel disadvantaged. Right then in that moment as cars passed him, he hated being different. If only he could drive a car, be independent like them, but that was never going to be possible. He'd always be reliant on either walking or public transport. It would take a genius to invent a car that someone without arms could drive. The Thalidomide Trust letter sprang back into his mind.

The rain was pounding down on the car roofs like marbles pinging on metal and he increased his pace, desperate to reach the double doors of the building. Just then he heard his name and twirled round, the rain dripping from his fringe into his eyes as he saw Mandy emerge from a red Mini. She locked the door and dashed over, splashing in the water, hastily putting an umbrella up for them both to shelter under.

'Bloody hell, have you just walked through this? You must be soaked to the bone.'

'I don't have much choice. My dad can't always give me a lift and the bus service is rubbish.'

They reached the building, and she nudged the door open with her shoulder and shook the umbrella out. 'I guess it would be challenging for you to drive a car, but I have seen handicapped people drive around in those funny little pale blue three-wheelers. Perhaps you could get one.'

'They're hideous things. Imagine turning up to college in one of those.' Toby chuckled. 'I'd be a laughing stock. Wouldn't do my reputation much good. Anyway, driving's out of the question because of the steering wheel.'

'I guess so,' she said as they joined the thong of students heading up the stairs. 'Those cars look flimsy. Bit of wind and they'd probably tumble over. Aren't they made of fibreglass?'

'No idea.'

Sitting in wet clothes all day was awful. Wet fabric clinging to his skin was so uncomfortable and reminded him of a camping trip years ago with his dad and it pouring, the whole weekend. He was chilled to the bone and couldn't concentrate on his lessons, the sensation of being wet was too distracting. He never wanted to repeat the experience of walking into college in heavy rain. He now knew what the term drowned rat meant.

All day his thoughts kept circling back to the letter. Perhaps he should investigate it.

It was still pouring when the final bell signalled the end of the day, and since Bill was working late, he couldn't give Toby a lift. Luckily Mandy offered to drop him home. When they reached her car, she opened the passenger door, and he got in. Before she turned the ignition, she offered him an Opal Fruit, unwrapped one and popped it into his mouth. He smiled; she was clearly addicted to them, and lime flavour was her favourite. Problem was that lime was his favourite too.

As they drove he felt increasingly awkward, he didn't want to be one of those people who always cadged a lift off mates, and didn't want her to feel obliged to help every time it rained. And besides, she lived in the opposite direction to him.

Toby had only been home for half an hour when Jasper called round. He often popped over to catch up with Toby when Bill was working late.

'How's college?' he asked as he wandered into the kitchen to put the kettle on. He took his coat off and gave it a shake before grabbing a tea towel that lay on the worktop to dab his wet hair. 'Horrible weather today, surely you didn't walk back?'

Toby smiled. He was used to Jasper coming in and making himself at home. He couldn't imagine him using a tea towel on his hair in his own home, Sandy would go mad. 'No I didn't because my new scribe, Mandy, gave me a lift, but I don't want to rely on her, she lives the other side of town. Wish I could drive, but that isn't going to happen, is it?'

Toby plonked himself down on the settee. 'That reminds me, I had a letter from the Trust, something about being entitled to vehicle assistance. Can you read it, see what it's about?' He nodded towards the letter in the pile of papers on the kitchen worktop.

Jasper went over and found the letter. As he read it, he exclaimed, 'That's intriguing. Where's the phone? I'll give them a call.' He checked his watch. 'It's not yet five, they'll still be in the office. I'll find out more.'

Toby watched as Jasper spoke with the Trust, amused by his notebook at the ready like a true journalist.

'You're going to love this, lad,' Jasper said after the call. 'How do you fancy learning to drive?' He was grinning from ear to ear and for a moment Toby wasn't sure if he was joking. 'You're entitled to lessons and a car.' He then went on to explain the new Motability Scheme, offering handicapped drivers a conventional car modified to cater to their specific impairments.

'No way, you serious?' His voice was wobbly, and his heart skipped a beat. It felt almost unreal, like the best of every Christmas and birthday combined. The excitement surging through him, it was almost overwhelming. 'So, I wouldn't have to drive one of horrible blue spaz chariots?'

'Blimey, now you're triggering memories, lad. When I lived in Manchester there was a firm that used to repair them down by the Bridgewater Canal. I went out on a friend's narrow boat one day and we had a collision with one.'

Toby gasped.

'I kid you not. The local yobs had nicked it and sent it off to a watery grave, fifty-foot narrow boat versus fibreglass tripod, no contest.'

'Wow.'

'They're going to be phasing them out, they're dangerous. There have been reports of cars overturning in strong wind and even setting on fire.' Jasper went to fill the kettle. 'My car mechanic down in town might know more. We should nip round there sometime.'

The following day after college, Jasper took Toby down to his garage to speak with Jim, the mechanic.

Jim's eyes lit up. 'You've come to the right person. I know all about those Ministry approved vehicles. I've worked on Model 70s. Top speed 60 miles an hour.' He laughed. 'Trouble is, we can't match the vehicle to the individual's needs. I took a Hillman Imp steering rack and fitted a shoe plate, all connected to the front wheel to allow the client to steer the car with his one good foot. Those cars are unstable and unreliable. I'm glad they're phasing them out and introducing this new scheme.'

Toby applied to the Trust to ensure he didn't miss out on the opportunity for a modified car. No more traipsing into college in the rain, soaked to the bone.

Months stood between him and the delivery of his Motability car, a wait that would test his patience. He just wanted to get out there and now that he knew he was eligible and on the list, his eagerness was fuelled. To experience that independence and freedom he so craved, to arrive to college in his own transport, truly a dream come true.

CHAPTER 17: TOBY

Toby was in the refectory eating lunch, scanning around looking at different people. His fellow students were curious, staring at him eating with his feet, but he was used to people's reactions after a lifetime of eating this way. Some were polite, quickly averting their gaze in embarrassment when he caught them watching, while others saw him as an entertainer and came over to marvel at his party or circus tricks.

He just grinned and chuckled to himself. This was all new to them. Playing to the audience he picked up a chip between his toes and offered it round, raving about how tasty they were. They looked on in horror.

'It's okay,' he said, grinning, 'you'll get used to me.'

An older student was pinning a poster to the noticeboard at the entrance to the refectory. Finishing his lunch, he wandered over and read the bold red title.

'The Debating Incubator.'

He frowned. What a weird title. It made him think of babies in hospital or chickens under a lamp. Intrigued, he read on.

Is there something that irks you? Are you finding life a challenge?

We are a weekly discussion group. We discuss and debate any topic from politics to religion. No topic too small, irrelevant, or off limits. Pop along next Wednesday, 5pm, to find out more.

Over the next few days, he mused about speaking in public. He'd never stood up and spoken to a group of people, but he asked around to see if anyone fancied going along with him. A couple of lads in his history class liked the idea and so did Mandy.

Toby had always admired politicians and some of the foreign correspondents on TV and wondered how they managed to speak without prompts. He struggled to remember what the teacher had said two hours ago. He particularly enjoyed listening to the fiery Reverend Ian Paisley who regularly popped up on the news spouting nonsense and always pointing his finger in a way that reminded him of a Nazi salute. His voice was unique and instantly recognisable and sent a tingle down his spine. He was outrageous, his fire and brimstone ways, even to the point of inciting violence, but he was such a great raging agitator. Toby wondered how these great orators got to be like that.

He'd always been a bit reserved but comfortable around his friends. He'd become more forthright since the great revelation about his parentage and was not afraid to voice an opinion even if it got him into hot water or a heated argument with either his dad, Jasper, or at times both together.

He spoke to Jasper about the club the next time he saw him. 'I'm not sure whether I should join this debating club? I've been thinking about great speakers, I mean how did people like Hitler and Churchill hold the attention of such huge audiences? Was it more about what they said or how they said it? What made them so inspirational?'

'I guess it takes great skill and practice. Hitler and Churchill were able to really engage with their audience and connect with their emotions and sway them with powerful words. Maybe it's about really understanding the power of rhetoric and being able to tap into the emotions of the crowd. Go along. What have you got to lose? It's another skill to learn and could stand you in good stead.'

'So, have you ever given a talk, an interview on the news? I can just see you on the ITN News, with a crooked tie.'

Jasper scratched his chin and laughed. Honestly, I've never taken the stage, but I've read that they say to imagine the audience is naked. Maybe that's a trick to put you at your ease. I guess it's all about finding your own way to connect with the crowd.

And then, Jasper took him by surprise by getting up and with a mischievous twinkle in his eye leaping onto the table. Toby gasped; Bill wouldn't be too happy, the table was wobbly, and he was always having to take a screwdriver to the fixings. But Jasper didn't seem to care and despite the wobbles he was standing on the table posing in a dramatic way.

'Steady on, what are you doing? Dad will go mad.'

'Friends, Romans, countrymen, lend me your ears,' he bellowed, exaggeratedly gesticulating as if he were in a Shakespearean play. Toby stood back and erupted into laughter as he continued to recite lines from *Julius Caesar* in an over-the-top theatrical manner as he embraced the moment. With a playful grin he concluded with a bow and clambered off the table.

His conversation with Jasper and all the antics started to stimulate his thought process over the next few days. He found himself thinking about all the people he'd seen talking without notes. The fiery figure of Enoch Powell came into view, the moving speech of Martin Luther King he'd heard so many times.

I have a dream.

I have a dream too.

The way they inspired, captured the world's attention, he found them so compelling, the power of their words, the choice of their words, their ability to move and motivate their audience and with courage and fearlessness. Something was sparking inside him. In his daydreams he found himself standing on his bed practising public speaking, and the most incredible thing for him was how a speech could change the world.

Toby was still pondering the evening before the meeting, but Bill encouraged him by saying, 'Only way you're going to find out if it's for you, son, is by going along. If you don't like it, don't go again, that's the way I look at it.'

The following day, Toby remembered the meeting when it was already halfway through. He dashed up from the library where he'd been researching the Nazi occupation of Jersey. Ever since returning from holiday he'd been fixated, devouring every book on the subject. The thought of Bonaparte House being a Nazi base had seized his imagination after venturing into the cellar. It was all so intriguing, and he'd loved his visit to the War Tunnels. Arriving at the room, he apologised for his lateness before grabbing a seat near the back. They were in the middle of a lively discussion and hands were darting up. Students were interrupting each other until someone at the front desk banged what looked like a wooden hammer on the table. He looked older than the others but too young to be a teacher. Toby guessed that he was Lawrence, the president of the club.

'Come on, guys, I don't want to have to repeat what I said at the start of the session. I am sure we all have something we want to speak about, and we all deserve to be heard no matter how diverse our ideas are, but let's remember our manners, we're not farmyard animals.'

Animal noises filled the air. Lawrence smiled, regretting his analogy. He strutted across the room trying to calm everyone, his hands in his pockets jangling coins, but he wasn't floundering, and his voice stayed calm, and rather than raising its volume he lowered it and after a couple of minutes everyone fell silent. He went to the blackboard and picking up a lump of chalk scribbled some bullet points.

'Common themes that concern you.' Then he scribbled in capital letters: nuclear disarmament, apartheid, future job prospects, equal pay for women, pollution, educational funding, better college facilities, i.e. bar and pool room. He stood back and rubbed his chin. Quite a wide list, plenty for us to discuss.'

'Are there any other themes?' Casting his eye around the room, he noticed Toby and said, 'What about you? Did you go to St Bede's? What are your fellow students doing now? I expect some have been sent off to another institution and it's a sad fact that most disabled kids end up unemployed.'

Toby hated the word institution, it really irritated him and conjured up pictures of prison, inmates in navy uniforms, mad people locked in padded cells for their own protection. And it was obvious how naive people were about thalidomide babies and people with disabilities in general.

Maybe I can tell my story.

'A couple of my friends have gone on to Herewood College in Coventry. It's a college for young handicapped people and they'll be going on work placements.'

A couple of students started laughing. 'You mean they were sent to Coventry.'

'Very funny, not,' Mandy chipped in.

Lawrence scowled at them, then looking at Toby, said, 'I can see you have some challenges; how would you fancy a discussion on what it's like to be handicapped? I don't want to single you out and make you feel uncomfortable, but I think you might be the only handicapped student this year.' His voice was suddenly filled with passion. 'And that's wrong.' He paused, glanced round the room. 'College should be open to all, there shouldn't be any barriers to further and higher education.'

A few heads nodded and all eyes turned to stare at Toby. How he hated the stares. His cheeks burned; he didn't want to be singled out, if only he could melt into the magnolia walls, observe but not be a part of the group, but at the same time something was stirring inside him, making his heart race and a surge of energy course through him. This was his moment to shine or make a fool of himself, but he wanted to make his voice heard, be somebody, make a difference.

Toby felt slightly unhinged as he mumbled an answer. Mandy, who had been at the meeting from the start interrupted. 'Disability isn't always visible. There could be others in the room with impairments, with their own challenges. Sorry, Lawrence, you think you know what a disability looks like. There are non-visible disabilities too.'

As Mandy spoke, a germ was growing inside him. All those years when he and other thalidomiders were tucked away in institutions, out of sight, out of mind, removed from society, viewed as a burden, the world not knowing or caring about them or how they were coping. He felt a sense of frustration, he was dying inside. It was sink or swim for him.

'Surely there are more interesting things to talk about than one individual. There are all kinds of disability. Mental conditions like depression, the inability to concentrate in class and some women have problems when it's the time of the month. When you look at someone, you don't have a clue what's going on with them. When we see someone who isn't on crutches or isn't in a wheelchair park on a disabled spot or using a disabled toilet, think how quick we are to judge. There could be all sorts of reasons why someone is disabled, or the person could be picking up their elderly mum, but I appreciate it is frustrating when some people do abuse the system.' She sat back and folded her arms.

Toby's heart was quietly melting; she was defending his corner, was fiercely protective of him.

What a sweetie.

By the time Mandy had finished speaking, he felt a surge of

passion. There was so much to fight for in terms of disabled rights and access and a ton of other issues that would make life easier.

'Yeah, you lot have no idea the prejudice we face. There's discrimination everywhere.'

He knew he wanted to do the impossible, say something, do a talk. Words were rattling around his head, taking him by surprise in their intensity, raw emotion pushing through, thoughts that had always been private waiting for a confessional. He straightened his back and glancing round the room, realised that he didn't really want to blend into the walls, he'd rather have a voice. He could be a champion for people like himself, raising awareness and challenging stigma and it could start here in this very room.

At the end of the meeting, the president of the group said, 'hopefully you've found the session useful. Give us a shout, we're always interested in new topics, sometimes we can make a change and occasionally we get local dignitaries along. Last year the local MP came, and we had a lively discussion about nuclear disarmament. Feel free to suggest a visitor.'

Toby, despite being shy and painfully self-conscious plucked up the courage to chat to Lawrence after the meeting. His heart was thumping so hard under his rib cage with the anxiety, but he knew this was something he had to do. He strolled to the front and waited until everybody had left the room before telling him that he wanted to give a talk about thalidomide and the difficulties and he and his friends faced.

'That's amazing, Toby, I'm so pleased.' Lawrence patted him on the shoulder. 'That's very brave of you.'

He could feel his cheeks burn, there was no turning back now, he'd committed himself, and as he left the room a strange feeling overtook him, a sense of achievement. It was birdlike fluttery in his stomach--nerves, but that was natural, of course he was going to be nervous. He'd go away and think about what he could say, write it down and when he delivered the talk, he'd refer to his notes.

The next morning, he saw the president pin something alongside the notice that he had seen the previous day. He cast his eye over it and noticed it was a list of topics for discussion and he saw his name and topic on the list. He felt a surge of pride and then the panic.

Christ, I had better get on with it.

The speaker for the debate coming up next had already been decided, but after that, nothing was pencilled in. There were also voting forms for students to choose the next speaker only two weeks away. It could be him in the firing line, so he had better be ready.

He spent the next couple of evenings jotting down thoughts and notes, he even spoke to Jasper to sound him out. He was curious to know more about his job.

'Do you ever stand up and talk in your job?'

'I just prefer writing, it's easier. Public speaking isn't my cup of tea.'

'Ah, is this going to be something I can do that you can't?' he teased.

This was getting exciting but what should he include in his talk and what should he leave out? What if they asked him questions? Would he be able to speak or would he dry up in front of all those people? How should he structure the talk? He hadn't a clue where to start. What if nobody came? He did not want to look stupid. Or, much worse, the whole college might turn up.

What have I let myself in for?

CHAPTER 18: TOBY

In the days leading up to Toby's speech, students approached him in the corridors, slapped his back and wished him luck. 'I'll be there for your talk,' they all said. The event was starting to attract attention and more students were signing up. Soon there were too many for the usual meeting room, so it was changed to the college hall. This only added to his frayed nerves. He'd barely slept in days, tossing and turning, consumed with anxiety, his stomach knotted, his head pounding. His mood was up and down, like Tower Bridge. Would he forget his lines? Would he stumble over his words? Giving a speech––what was he thinking, offering himself up to the lion's den? Drawing attention to himself was the last thing he wanted. Yet a part of him craved the spotlight, to shine, for people to like him and like what he had to say.

By the day of the event, the seed of fear that had been growing inside him was now a tangled vine of despair.

As he entered the hall, all eyes were on him. He gasped; he hadn't expected every single row to be filled. His heart pounded, and in that moment, he knew this was the scariest moment of his life.

Did they notice what a quivering wreck he was?

A few people had come along out of interest, but word had travelled, and he wasn't stupid, he knew that most were here just to see the college freak. All he wanted was to turn and run. But that would be the end of everything. He'd be finished.

I must see this through.

He sat down at the back where Mandy had reserved a seat. She'd helped him write prompt cards. While everyone was getting settled, she held them up for him to go over even though he'd learned them by heart.

He gazed round the room and estimated there were around two hundred and fifty people.

A sickening shiver swept over him as Lawrence clapped his hands to start the meeting. 'Thank you all for coming along. Today we're kicking off with a talk on what it means to be handicapped. Please give a warm welcome to Toby.'

Clapping erupted and Toby nervously rose from his chair, his legs turning to jelly as he walked to the front of the hall. His heart was banging so hard he thought it might explode out of his chest. He was going to do this.

At the lectern, he cleared his throat and glanced around the hall, his stomach churning.

'Many of you will look at me and wonder how I find the strength to face each day with a smile on my face.' He paused. 'You'll probably notice I use my feet for most things and I'm sure I look funny, but I do things in a different way to you lot.' He stuttered and suddenly he'd forgotten his words. It took him a few moments to gather his thoughts.

'Life without arms has presented challenges that are often overwhelming. Simple tasks that you take for granted, from getting dressed in the morning to eating a meal, requires effort and thought. My mum was brilliant, she let me struggle because she knew it was the only way. After all, she wasn't going to be there holding my hand for the rest of my life. The times I watched as tears flowed down her face. It was breaking her heart, she desperately wanted to step in to help, take away my frustration, but she knew, and I've grown to learn that she wouldn't have done me any favours. Sometimes you have to be cruel to be kind.

I refuse to be defined by my disability. I am more than my limitations, I know I can achieve great things. Each day I face new obstacles, but I find a way to overcome them. Tasks such as brushing my teeth, combing my hair, shaving, tying shoelaces, buttoning a shirt, cooking, preparing a meal, opening a door, reaching for items on a high shelf. You take all of these tasks for granted but for me, each is a challenge. I have to think through everything I do before I do it, I can't just jump on a bus or get dressed in a hurry. I've been very fortunate to have an amazing dad. He's good with his hands and has made me lots of aids. Some of the things he made include a comb attached to a wall mount but these days it's easier to keep my hair short. As I get older, I'll probably have to go to the barber to have a shave or grow a beard like John Lennon. I have long handles attached to some kitchen utensils, and my dishes and plates have suction bases to prevent spillage. I carry books in my backpack which I carry around my neck otherwise it would probably fall off. When I'm older, I'll probably get neck problems with all the contorting and straining, but hey, I'll worry about that then.

Now that I'm nearly eighteen I'll be able to dive into the pub and I'll buy a round.' He winked at the students in the front row to let them know he was teasing. 'But you'll have to carry the glass to the table and ask for a straw for me.'

Toby spoke for about thirty minutes covering subjects like accessibility and public perception to give the audience a flavour of some of the issues they faced, and then said, 'I can't just blend into the background, I will always stand out like a sore thumb. I hope you found that interesting and if you have any questions, I'm happy to answer them.'

Lawrence interjected as hands flew up. 'Thank you, Toby, that was great.' Then he turned to the audience. 'We only have time for a few questions, but please respect Toby's privacy, don't ask anything too personal.'

Some hands lowered, and disappointed faces followed. Toby knew instinctively what they were planning to ask, and it saddened him to see they hadn't matured since school.

At first, they asked questions which he was able to respond to easily. Although the adrenaline was still rushing through him and his face was burning, he was more relaxed and enjoyed explaining how life was for him.

A new hand shot up with a bold, cheeky expression on the student's face. 'Excuse me, but how d'you wipe your bum and what do you do if you get a streaming cold and how do you pick bogies and what if you get an itch, how do you scratch it?'

'Sorry,' Lawrence said. 'That's not the sort of question we should be asking.'

Toby piped up, 'No, hang on, actually I will answer that.'

A few stunned and shocked faces greeted Toby's readiness to answer the deeply personal questions and the hall fell silent.

'I've been asked that before, a few years ago, how I wipe my bum. I was cornered by a group of bullies, humiliated, and forced to answer under duress, and it wasn't easy to run away.'

The hall was so quiet you could have heard a pin drop. Toby ploughed on. 'They trapped me in an alleyway, I was scared for my life, they were threatening me if I didn't answer. That's the kind of thing I have to live with, the world is full of pricks. But yeah, as you can imagine, it's difficult to wipe my arse.' He gave a nervous chuckle and wondered how to get around the awkward question. If he answered it truthfully, they'd laugh and tease him for the rest of his college life. They'd give him a horrible nickname, like arse wiper. Far better to make a joke, brush it off, show he wasn't bothered and hopefully tomorrow they would move on.

'If there's someone else in the toilets, I'll call them in to help.' He felt his face burn and he was cringing inside.

The students roared with laughter and a few girls pulled faces and said, 'Ow yuk.'

'Okay, guys, only kidding, but if any of you girls fancy helping me in the toilet…' He winked but his embarrassment was so intense he was crumbling inside. It was the sense that everyone could read his feelings as if he'd written them in little notes and handed them around. And then he realised there was nothing for it, he'd show them his vulnerability and just maybe they'd understand. 'There will always be those who want to embarrass others just to amuse.' He looked directly at the person who'd asked the question. 'But they're living with a broken soul, and I'd rather be me living with a strong soul, because who I am isn't who you see on the outside, it's who I am on the inside that counts.'

When the meeting was over, some of the students came over and said, 'well done, good on you, mate.' And as he turned, Mandy was there beaming at him.

'That was great, how did you feel?' Lawrence asked.

Relief was washing over him, he was just glad it was over. 'I was so nervous. I felt sick, my mind was racing, I was so worried about stuttering. Did I stutter? Did I repeat myself? People were gawping and it was putting me off, then I relaxed. God, I don't know how politicians do it, day in, day out.'

'They usually have training.'

'Training?'

'My dad is a trainer, it's his job. I'll have a word with him. I'm sure he wouldn't mind giving you a few tips.'

'I haven't got the money.'

Lawrence laughed. 'No, silly, he wouldn't charge you. He loves helping people if he can. I think he could really boost your confidence. I could really feel the passion in your voice and you're funny with it. You could hone your skills. You're not used to standing up in front of an audience, who is? But you did bloody well and especially for your first time. You have a powerful voice, and you could be very good. The ability to speak is an important skill, the ability to get your message across. Just think what TV reporters have to go through, but all sorts of industries as well as government and other organisations need speakers. You never know, you could make a career as a town crier.'

Toby laughed.

'You may not have all your faculties, but you have your voice. All those thoughts we never get to hear. All the untold secrets. I'll speak to the old man and get back to you.' Lawrence patted Toby on the shoulder. 'Be proud of yourself, you did well.'

Toby was just glad it was over, but he was excited too. Lawrence's encouragement had given him a massive boost, and he was intrigued to find out how Lawrence's dad could help.

The following morning on his way to tutor group, he wondered if he'd get any comments from his classmates. Everyone had come to support him. He walked into class to a chorus of whoops and cheers.

I've nailed it.

His heart swelled, it was such a boost to his morale, knowing they accepted him, were proud of him. Buoyed by their praise he headed for his chair with a spring in his step.

Over the next few weeks, he focussed on honing his skills. His mind went into overdrive, crashing through other subjects he could talk about. Lawrence's dad was generous with his numerous tips and insights into public speaking, imparting valuable wisdom and guidance. Toby started to recognise the power of the spoken word, witnessing first hand its ability to captivate, inspire and compel. He loved the tremendous opportunity it gave to put his voice across. Apart from the occasional heckles, he realised it was his chance to speak uninterrupted, something he didn't get the chance to do in normal, regular conversations. His voice got lost, people spoke over him. With no interruptions he could make a difference, educate, inform, inspire. Lawrence even gave him the tools on how to handle hecklers. This was his twenty minutes to put his thoughts across. And then he realised something profound. It was an epiphany moment.

I can speak for those who can't.

The moment he realised this, his mind raced, exploring every possible topic he could address. He wondered what might interest him and what might interest the group. The list on the suggestions board seemed dull, but he appreciated that other students had their own gripes--views they wanted to express. His driver was the way society neglected people with disabilities, leaving them out in the cold, almost an afterthought, overlooked and unimportant-- and hadn't it been like this throughout history?

Accessibility had always been a problem for his friends in wheelchairs, society was just not geared up for people with physical challenges.

Now that he was wondering what to talk about, he started to look at things through fresh eyes and everywhere he went, whether it was to the local leisure centre for a swim, the train station, or the shopping centre, he started to consider how people with different needs went about their lives. One Saturday he watched a mum struggle up a set of steps with her pram, watching from a distance with no passer-by offering to help.

He also spoke to Sue over the phone about her experiences in town.

'It's impossible, that's why I don't go shopping very often.' She laughed.

Sue described the numerous physical barriers she encountered in her town. Inaccessible entrances, narrow aisles, steps everywhere and the absence of ramps. 'The staff in these shops and banks, they aren't helpful or friendly. Sometimes they can be so hostile, it's like they can't be bothered with us. And then there's the problem of toilets, it's a nightmare. And not to mention the public's reaction to us. There's a certain intolerance.'

Toby decided his next talk would be about the difficulties the disabled faced in more detail, highlighting the most important ones. In the middle of the night, he was struck by an idea. He decided to approach Lawrence and ask if he could write a letter to the local MP to invite him to come along to hear his talk.

Lawrence was all for the idea. 'That sounds great, Toby, he's been along before and he's friends with the principal of the college, which all helps. Don't be surprised though if he can't come, he's a very busy man.'

Toby only half expected the MP to accept the invitation, but after sending his letter, he allowed himself to indulge in daydreams of standing before the MP, the rapturous applause, his face in the local paper. It was like a role reversal. He returned from college one day and saw the yellow envelope with a green portcullis on it with the embossed words, House of Commons in large letters. He was ready to pop. He couldn't wait for Bill to return from work before opening it, so he grabbed a knife and tore it open, pulling the letter out with his mouth. His excitement soared when he found out the MP would come.

In the coming weeks as Toby prepared for his speech, he realised it was almost impossible to cover everything he wanted to say in the twenty-minute time slot, so he homed in on the issues he felt the MP could influence: the narrow entrance to the Halifax Building Society, the steps leading to the local leisure centre, the lack of a public disabled toilet in the town centre, the narrow aisles in the Co-op, were just a few examples among many. The list seemed endless.

With so much to do and limited time, he found himself spending a significant portion of it on research for his talks causing his studies to suffer. Even Mandy was starting to moan at him.

'Toby, I can't do everything for you,' she said on their way out of college one afternoon. He hadn't finished an essay, and it was due in a week ago. 'You're spending too long on these talks, you'll slip behind if you're not careful.'

He knew she was right, but he couldn't help it, speech writing was firing him and taking up all his time. Instantly he went on the defensive. 'I'm not asking you to, but it's a struggle for me. I've had a nasty ulcer, it's sore using my mouth to write.' It was true, he did suffer from frequent ulcers, and this made it hard, but the last ulcer had healed a few weeks ago.

She gave him one of her withering looks, she knew it was a white lie. 'I don't want to see you fall behind.' She looked hurt and he felt guilty about all the time and effort she put into helping. She didn't have to do any of it. His whole life he'd struggled, from simple tasks like turning the tap on to opening a can of beans, and it was frustrating as hell always relying on others. She was right, he was falling behind. He hadn't told her, or his family but yesterday he'd been called in to see the principal who was concerned with his progress. The principal asked him what his plans were, because if he was aiming to go to a polytechnic or university, he'd need to put in a lot more effort to achieve good grades. Toby didn't want to admit his failings, but the truth was he was slipping behind for a variety of reasons, and they weren't just due to the debating society. The Possum was always breaking down and because it was a specialist piece of equipment, the engineers came from long distances to fix it and he often had to wait weeks for it to be repaired. Also, despite his supple body, occasionally he experienced foot cramp or hip twists, which hindered his studies.

The frustrating thing was his head was so much faster than

his body. He knew what he wanted to write, he formed paragraphs and arguments in his head and organised his ideas, but the physical process of writing the essay was a struggle.

They reached her car; she'd offered him a lift.

'Honestly, Toby, I don't mind helping, I'm a fast writer, always have been.'

Sometimes he found it intimidating when others were so capable because it highlighted his inadequacies. 'You're lucky, how did you get to be so perfect?' His tone was sarcastic, but he didn't apologise for it because in that moment, he didn't care. He'd sunk into a downer; he was never going to be as good as her or the others in his class.

I might as well give up, go and join my cripple friends at Herewood.

He didn't want to be like this, he felt pathetic. She'd become a good friend, much more than just his scribe and she'd inspired his speeches too. They'd had discussions about disability and how society could be better, how attitudes had a long way to go to improve.

She stopped and looked at him and he could see hurt in her eyes. 'I've told you before, Toby, don't be so stupid, I'm not perfect either, I've got flaws like anyone else. Stop running yourself down, you're clever. I'm good at some things, crap at others. I can't throw a ball to save my life.' She laughed. They reached her car and got in. 'Now,' she said, turning to him before putting the key in the ignition, 'I'm up to date with my homework, let's go back to yours and we'll crack on with your essay. You can tell me what to write and I'll get it on paper.'

It worried him that he was becoming too reliant on her, she wouldn't be around forever.

Later that evening, after Mandy had left, Sue rang for a catch-up. Bill was out at a meeting and Toby struggled to pick up the receiver.

'Hello, who is it?' he said grumpily.

'That's a nice welcome, sounds like you've had a bad day.'
'Sorry, Sue, you've caught me at a bad time, how are you?'
They chatted for a while.
'You seem to be getting on very well with this Mandy, you going out with her?'
He laughed. 'God, no, she's way out of my league.'
'So, am I in your league?'
He'd noticed how flirty she was, ever since Jersey but it was that jealous streak of hers, it didn't do her any favours and was off-putting. As far as he was concerned, they were just friends. He thought now about a relationship with another sufferer, then quickly imagined the challenges.
'If we're talking leagues, you would be my Manchester United rather than my Bromsgrove.'
She laughed. 'Toby Murphy, trust you, football's permanently on your brain.'
'So how's it going at Herewood?' he asked.
'Great, you should come here, they do all sorts of courses, you'd love it and we'd get to spend more time together.'
'I'm hoping to get into university.' But Toby didn't feel hopeful.
If he didn't knuckle down and catch up with his studies, his dream of going to university would slip through his fingers. The pressure was on, and he couldn't bear to admit to Sue, or his family, that he was lagging behind. He wasn't even sure he'd be able to catch up now, there was so much going on and not enough time to do it all.

CHAPTER 19: TOBY

The hall was filled with a palpable sense of anticipation as Toby stood on the stage to deliver his talk, the MP to his right, Lawrence to his left. He felt a mixture of excitement and nerves. Butterflies danced in his stomach and before he'd even uttered the first words, his mouth was as dry as a desert and made his voice squeaky.

As he progressed through his talk, he was aware of the change in his body language. He was more relaxed because he was fired up, passionate, an inner voice driving him forward.

After Toby finished his speech, the MP gave feedback and a few brief comments before having to leave.

People started calling out. 'Typical politician, did you hear him? "It's not my position," and, "we have a government minister dealing with these areas."

'Toby, you shouldn't put up with this.'

'Yeah, what can we all do? Must be something.'

'You could be a disability champion. You and others like you need to be heard, deserve to be heard, not fobbed off by twats like him and he's supposed to be our MP.'

'Disgusting.'

'What a tosser.'

A cheer went up. 'Toby for MP.'

'Whatever happened to human rights?'

'It was interesting listening to his responses to all your questions. The man's quite clearly a fob-off.'

'That lot are so privileged, they only think of their own interests, the needs of white privileged toffs. He probably sends his kids to a private school like Eton.'

'Okay,' Lawrence concluded. 'It's no good complaining, the only people who can change things is us, the people. The key is awareness and the more awareness we create, people will sit up and notice.'

Toby felt a sense of pride. He'd managed to create a stir and liked the noises coming back from the audience.

But will it lead to anything?

CHAPTER 20: TOBY

It was February and Toby was now seventeen. Returning from college one day, he found Bill cutting the branch of an oak with his chainsaw. Over the deafening noise he shouted, 'What are you up to?'

Bill stopped the engine and, resting the saw on his wheelbarrow, replied, 'You'll see, lad,' with a wink.

Toby guessed his dad was making something special for him, a gadget to make an everyday task easier, but he couldn't think what he needed right now. His whole childhood Bill had made various devices to enable him to be independent. He could turn his hand to anything, had real imagination and Toby admired him for that. As he watched him hump logs in the winter chill, a pang of guilt gnawed at him, recollecting all the times he had been difficult and spiteful. The magnitude of his dad's love and dedication reminded Toby to be more appreciative. He wished he could help by carrying the logs, but that was out of the question.

A few days later, soon after he arrived home, Bill rang from the school's workshop. 'Get over here, lad, come and see what I've made for you.' There was an unmistakeable tone of excitement in his voice. Toby's curiosity was piqued and he rushed over to see what his dad had crafted for him this time. He ran down the darkening lane. The trees stood bare, having long cast off their leaves, and the branches were swaying as if they were conducting an orchestra. A wintry chill cut through him, making him long for the spring. He rounded the corner and headed for the large wooden shed to the side of the main building. The workshop was a haven of creativity and craftsmanship and he always enjoyed visiting to see what was going on. As he opened the door, the air was filled with the scent of sawdust and the clank of tools. The shelves were laden with various materials and instruments while a large workbench served as the centrepiece of the shed scattered with an array of tools and half-finished projects. This was a place where Bill's passion and expertise came to life through his big gnarled hands.

As if presenting him with a trophy, Bill handed him a simple wooden disk and Toby was puzzled. There had to be some logic to this strange contraption. Embedded in the centre of the disk was a secure fastening with a small strap. The smooth surface of the disk was polished to a shine.

Bill laughed. 'I can see you have no idea what it's for.' With his finger in the loop, he coaxed Toby's thoughts. 'Still not guessed?'

'Sorry, Dad, you've lost me.'

Bill tutted. 'Slip your big toe into this loop.' He put the disk on the floor. 'Shoes off, come on.'

'If you say so.' He was still mystified.

'Fits perfectly.' Bill clapped. 'It's a steering disk. Okay I know it's wood, the real one will be made of metal, but you can use it to practise driving your car. You'll be steering with your foot. In fact, you'll be handling all the controls with your feet.'

'But what about the gears?'

'It will have automatic gears.'

'Wow, like Jasper's old XJS.'

Bill laughed.

'You'll do the steering and braking with your left foot. And your right foot will be kept busy with the brake pad, the lights, wipers, washers, horn, indicator and of course, the accelerator.'

'All at the same time?' He laughed. 'How do you know all this?'

'Because they phoned the other week to say your adapted Mini will be leaving the workshop next week.'

'Wow. Where's it coming from?'

'Not far at all. Somewhere near Heathrow. It will be delivered to you and the mechanic will give you a guided tour of all its features. You excited?'

He couldn't hide his excitement.

'Wow, I won't have to rely on you.'

This was life-changing, the freedom and independence a car would bring. He was an adult. Suddenly he felt older than his years. Adrenaline surged through his body whipping his heart rate to a frenzy as he turned and ran from the shed. He couldn't wait to share his excitement with Mandy. He could pick her up for a change. He imagined driving down the bumpy lane to college and singing along to some catchy tune on the radio, showing off to his mates in the carpark with a *Starsky and Hutch* three-point turn.

CHAPTER 21: TOBY

Toby was now in his second year of college and the pressures were mounting as he continued to juggle studying and public speaking with the additional stress of researching and applying for university. There were deadlines to meet for the submission of assignments as well as deadlines for UCCA. There was also the expectation of a minimum grade level and the additional problem that he'd dropped his third A level. This was exacerbated by the fact that his toes were sore from all the writing and Mandy had become grumpy with him because he wasn't taking his studies seriously. 'I'm making myself available to you,' she said. She'd become a broken record, 'studies come first, public speaking second unless you want to be a dropout.' The tutor had also warned him that he needed to stay focussed and put more effort in.

In desperation, Toby applied to obscure universities that most people had never heard of, and Mandy would exclaim, 'where the hell is that?' Some of the Welsh universities were known to offer lower grades, little known places like Aberystwyth and Lampeter. Toby received rejection letters from his top two choices, Bath and Exeter. He felt foolish applying for those two, but he'd always wanted to aim high. He felt disheartened until he received a letter inviting him to attend an interview and two-day campus familiarisation at Lampeter. Bill said, 'where the bloody hell is that?'

'It's in Wales.'

'Jesus, lad, that's another country and they speak a funny language there and it's full of sheep, leeks and rain.'

Toby suddenly realised he didn't actually know where in Wales Lampeter was. He unfolded a map on the floor to discover it was in the back of beyond.

'If you think I'm going to drive you all that way, you've got another thing coming, my old boneshaker won't even get to the next village let alone the mountains of Wales. You need a whole pint of phlegm in your throat to pronounce the place names and forget asking for directions, you'll be washing spit out of your hair for a week.'

'Dad, you're disgusting. How will I get there then?'

'My God, it's miles away,' Bill said peering at the map. 'Remember where we came from, Blackpool? It's even further than that. At least there is a motorway to Blackpool.'

'What happens if the course is in Welsh?'

'Surely you've checked.' He started laughing. 'You're a daft ha'porth.'

'There is another option. I haven't heard from Aberystwyth yet.'

'Jesus, boy, what is it with you and Wales?'

Toby tutted. He was annoyed that Bill had taken very little notice of his UCCA application and now he was fussing about the journey to the interview. It seemed very short-sighted. Perhaps he doubted his chances of getting into higher education and that was why he was cracking silly jokes.

After his annoying comments, Toby became quite insistent in not wanting Jasper and Bill to take him to Wales. He was keen to show them he could be independent now that he was a grown man. The other students would be going alone. They wouldn't have parents trailing after them, carrying their bags, and holding their hands. And after all, if he was going to be living away from home, he had to start somewhere.

From Guildford, he took the train to Victoria and had to circumnavigate the grubby underground system across to Paddington.

He scrambled to get onto the packed tube and barged his way through to the other side of the train where he could pin himself against the side so not to fall over. He couldn't just grab a rail to hold on to and right in that moment wished he'd taken someone with him.

As the train jolted away from the station, he glanced round to observe the other passengers hoping they weren't staring at him with that look of concern he'd seen so many times before, but as he turned, he found himself staring into a pair of dark eyes, as black as ravens and as cold as a February morning. His eyelids were heavily made up, a peacock display of green and blue eye shadow and with thick black liner. If it hadn't had been for his bristly stubble, Toby might have wondered if the person was a woman. Black lines rimmed his lips. Blusher sat in magenta streaks across his cheekbones. He was dressed head to toe in black leather, metal studs liberally decorating his nose and ears as well as his chin.

Toby's eyes wandered up to the garish Mohican that extended from his head like porcupine's quills. He knew he was staring but he couldn't pull his gaze away and he was rooted to the spot. Rationally, he knew this guy was about his age and just expressing his individuality and was probably a very nice person, but he felt a churn of discomfort and it annoyed him that he felt so intimidated. He'd been at college for the past two years and had rubbed shoulders with all sorts and thought nothing of it. He wasn't normally fazed. But there was something about punks that rattled him, disturbed him. He wasn't scared of them, as such, he'd seen clusters of them before along Carnaby Street and the King's Road, but there was something about their clothing and heavily made-up faces that unnerved him. The rings through the nose and lips, their bovver boots, he didn't understand the culture at all. He didn't like the music, The Sex Pistols, or the other bands. Rock music was more his style. It wasn't that he was against their ideology, in fact he admired their spirit, their anti-establishment ethos, and the lyrics were the kind of words he aspired to in his speech writing. Words that moved, rocked the world, shook people. Perhaps he wasn't suited to university, there were bound to be all types there, a microcosm of society. It was depressing how narrow-minded he was at times. The punk stepped away and registering Toby's obvious discomfort, smirked. Toby stepped back and hit the glass of the door and the train jolted to a halt. The punk got off and he breathed a sigh of relief. Toby watched him walk off without a backwards glance. A kid without arms was of no interest to him. Suddenly he was seized by the desire to cry.

'All right, dear?' an old woman opposite him asked with a look of pity.

'I'm fine, thank you,' he sniffed.

At Paddington mainline station he was sucked into the crowd on the busy concourse as commuters and day-trippers dashed in every direction. He stared up at the board scanning for the correct train to take him west to Swansea where a minibus would be waiting for him and other students. On the platform, passengers jockeyed for position as they attempted to get as close to the edge of the track as possible in anticipation of the train soon to arrive. He glanced around; three trains were now trundling along different tracks into different platforms and one was his. There was a squeal of brakes, metal scraping against metal, the growl of the engine as it came to a halt. A woman carrying a child barged into him, and noticing his handicap, apologised profusely, and asked if she could help.

'If you could open the door for me that would be great,' he said brightly. It was always nice when people offered to help. He followed her up the steps and through the narrow door, sitting down on one of the grey upholstered benches opposite a man with a briefcase on his lap who was puffing away on a cigar. The woman slammed the door behind them and plonked her child on the seat next to the man while she lifted a heavy bag onto the rack. Toby could see that she looked flustered, her cheeks were pink and her face damp around her hairline and she was irritable with her child. It annoyed Toby that the man wasn't offering to help with her bag. He only had himself to worry about. People like that, Toby thought, took their independence and faculties for granted and hadn't a clue what it was like to have the challenge of travelling with a child or a disability. To rely on the goodwill of other passengers, the honesty of the staff when he asked them to open his bag and get money out of his wallet to pay for the train ticket. He was travelling light, there was no other way, but he'd only be in Lampeter for one night and didn't need to bring much. He had a small bag like a satchel with a long strap and carried this around his neck. He kept his train ticket in his shirt pocket and could just about grab it with his teeth to show the ticket collector when he came to check.

The train trundled along through dingy and grimy trackside corridors slowly picking up speed as if it was trying to pull along a herd of elephants. They passed office blocks and other buildings, parks and endless Victorian semis with long narrow gardens until the city trickled into an uninviting suburbia and then they dived into a long tunnel and darkness descended. Daylight reappeared and there was open countryside where sheep and cows grazed in lush green fields and the landscape looked fresh and bright.

They stopped at Didcot, Swindon, Bath, and Bristol and

shortly after this passed through another tunnel. The child bounced on the seat. 'Mummy, Mummy another tunnel.'

The man grunted in disapproval and rustled his newspaper in an agitated fashion.

'Yes, sweetie, we'll be in Wales in a minute.'

They hadn't spoken during the whole journey and Toby was glad to be locked in his own thoughts but now that they were getting closer to Swansea, his stomach knotted with anxiety.

Out of the tunnel everything changed. It was raining, pelting down from a leaden sky, like an army of fingernails rapping at the window. His face was pressed against the glass as he watched a huge digger at work on a barren wasteland, saw boarded up buildings, fly-tipping in an abandoned car park, stacks of rubble and broken concrete. The landscape slowly became ever bleaker as heavy industry crept into his line of vision and eventually swamped the view. It was dark and foreboding, ghastly and scary, like nowhere else he'd ever seen, but he recognised it from the pictures in geography textbooks. Giant chimneys puffed smoke into the grey sky, gas pipelines, blast furnaces, giant vats and flare stacks all competed for the eye's attention. The scene could have been taken straight from a post-apocalyptic blockbuster. This was hell on earth. It was as if a giant jellyfish had oozed its way across the neat patchwork quilt of fields sucking the life out of everything bright and beautiful.

'Tata Steel.'

It was the first time the man had spoken, and now he was staring at Toby as if he'd just given him the last clue in a crossword.

At Swansea station he got off the train and emerging into the concourse saw a placard with his and a few other names scribbled in big bold letters. Trying to quell his nerves and appear relaxed, he belted over and introduced himself.

Five other students joined them. They all piled into the

minibus and soon they were on their way. Toby was relieved to find the scenery was much prettier as they wound their way past green forests, wild rivers and through quaint villages. On arrival they had a tour of the campus before being led into a large sports hall for coffee and a short talk by a third-year student who was also secretary of the university's student union.

'We're the smallest university but we have the largest bar bill, so if large campuses leave you feeling daunted, this is the place for you, oh and you've got to like sheep too, that's pretty much mandatory.'

Everybody chuckled. This was to be the first of several jokes about sheep and by the last one, Toby was inwardly groaning.

The student wore a huge cream Aran sweater with diamond patterns running down it and Toby imagined that he'd knitted it himself.

His mind drifted. Was this really the place for him? It was miles from home and although Wales wasn't really a foreign country, it felt like it.

Jeez and Aberystwyth is even further away. The back of beyond.

Toby hadn't been concentrating on every word of the talk, but he caught the tail end. 'This is a great place to study. We're surrounded by historical sites, hill forts and castles and we're a stone's throw from Cardigan Bay and there's a quilt centre nearby with its world-famous collection of quilts.'

Quilt making, can't wait.

'And if you're interested in medieval society, you can join the 12th century re-enactment group and learn archery and other skills.

Archery, me hold a bow and arrow?

Suddenly he felt disheartened, as if he was a round peg being forced into a square hole. Nothing about this place resonated with him and he struggled to see himself thriving here. But it seemed friendly enough. It would be easy to get to know people, especially as there was only one bar. He'd heard that some universities were spread over large campuses and had more than eight bars. As a community, Lampeter would be cosy, close-knit, with a real sense of belonging and possibly more understanding and supportive of his needs and smaller class sizes could allow for greater individual attention.

The talk came to an end and the sound of chairs being pushed back filled the hall as people rose, collected their bags, and prepared to head to the canteen for dinner. As they strolled down the corridor, Toby was suddenly aware of being alone. The other students were chatting and laughing to each other and seemed to have paired off. They were talking so naturally, firing questions, sharing anecdotes. Were they avoiding him because he was different, too embarrassed to approach him? He hoped not, but if it was like this now, what would it be like in the autumn term? He felt something open up inside him, a hollow gaping hole. Maybe it was the absence of Mandy always at his side, she'd become such a presence in his life, or maybe it was the thought of change, a new place, new people, the anxiety of having to make new friends yet again. He'd hadn't even been at college for two years and it was time to move on. The thought of more change scared him.

Over the course of the evening which was spent in the bar, Toby struck up a conversation with a boy from North Wales, but it was hard to make out some of the things he was saying because he had such a strong accent, and the bar was noisy.

He strained to listen as the boy told him about his disabled friend who had applied to study psychology at the University of Wales. 'He was so excited as he'd been turned down by two universities and he was getting desperate. I mean, we only have four choices, can't afford to mess up. He thought he'd been called in to discuss his A level results and academic performance, but it was to tell him that because the university building was on two storeys, there was no way they could accommodate someone who drove around in a wheelchair. And not just that, they said they couldn't make any simple changes, their routine was too precious.'

Toby could understand his friend's frustration.

'It was the bland dismissal that infuriated him.'

'Did he find a place somewhere else?'

Toby strained to hear, leaning in to hear every word. It was an interesting conversation, and he didn't want to miss anything. 'He's got another interview next week.'

'Hope he has better luck.'

The evening wrapped up, and the students scattered towards the dormitory block. He collared the lad who was in the next room to him and asked him to open his door. The lock was too high and tricky for him to manage.

The following day, they each faced interviews for their chosen courses. After each student had their interview, they shared their experience.

'Piece of piss,' one of them laughed. 'It was just the head of the department, he didn't ask much and offered me a C and a D. I'm sure I can manage that.' This seemed to be the pattern, a short interview, more like a conversation, with the head of department.

When it was Toby's turn, he entered the interview room and was greeted by a formidable sight, one he wasn't expecting. He stopped dead in his tracks.

A panel of five were seated authoritatively behind a vast desk.

Each interviewer introduced themselves. It would have been easy for Toby to shrink back and be nervous, but instead he made a conscious decision to listen to each of their names. Before him sat the dean, the head of history, a representative of the student union and the university nurse. He knew that his dad and Jasper would ask how the interview went and if he had a query later on, he needed to remember who he'd met.

The dean outlined the purpose and the format for the interview and the head of history fired the first question.

'Tell us why you're interested in studying history and how is it relevant to your career goals?'

Toby delivered his well-rehearsed answer, he was expecting this question. He felt as if he was reading from a script and wanted to come across as natural. He talked about his passion for reading about the past, researching, his trip to Jersey, and told them that he believed it would be a good degree for entry into various careers such as law, education, and government. He was deliberately vague because he had no idea what he wanted to do. He hadn't found the careers adviser at college very useful. When he thought about his future, it left him muddled. In his dreams he imagined being an ambassador for the disabled, maybe working in an office and going out to deliver speeches in front of big groups of people but again that was so vague. He hesitated; he wasn't sure whether to speak his mind and tell the panel about this dream. And then he thought, *hell, why not, what have I got to lose?*

He framed his words but when he spoke, they came out muddled. He was going to flunk the interview, he just knew it.

Toby saw the dean's eyes grow brighter as he smiled and asked the next question.

'I was very intrigued to hear about your public speaking. Tell us about that and any other interests you have.'

Again, he rattled off an answer. This was his passion, and he found his words flowed. He started to relax and enjoyed telling them about the speeches he'd delivered. He glanced at each person around the table hoping not to see bored, impatient faces but each looked genuinely interested in what he had to say.

Next up was the university nurse and he was glad she was last because it showed that his physical needs were being treated as a side issue and not the central focus. How differently he was being treated to the young man in a wheelchair at his University of Wales interview. This panel were concentrating on what mattered most––why he wanted to study history and what his future plans were.

The nurse was a kindly woman in her fifties, and she was wearing a white uniform. He didn't want to be treated as if he were a patient, he wasn't ill, and never had been and he wouldn't be needing a nurse any time soon. He wondered if they thought his internal organs had been damaged by thalidomide because there were survivors with damaged organs and others who had spent their lives in and out of hospital undergoing various operations, for example the removal of fingers and toes was common, operations to the hips, shoulders, and spine.

'Can you explain what special needs you have and how we might be able to help you, both in class and in your living quarters? You had a tour of the student block, kitchen and washing facilities. Did you identify any issues?'

He felt his jaw tightening at the question and was conscious about not appearing too needy, but at the same time he had to be honest and give sufficient detail about his routines. 'At college I have a helper, a scribe, and we sit at the front because I need more space because I write with my foot. I'd need a seat at the front of your lecture hall. I wouldn't be able to move my legs if I had to sit in those narrow rows.' He described the help Mandy gave him. Sometimes she typed his essays and always gave him a copy of her lesson notes because he couldn't always keep up and there were times when he got sore between his toes. Toby paused as he gathered his thoughts and went on to praise the student washing facilities at Lampeter. He liked the fact that the showers had curtains rather than heavy doors and the shower taps were low down and easy to turn with his foot. He told them the locks to the bedroom doors were tricky and that he hadn't been able to master opening his door. He wondered if they had a maintenance guy who could make a few adjustments.

'That's very helpful, Toby,' the nurse said when he'd finished his answer. 'And in terms of the kitchen, there are eight students living on each floor and using the kitchen, so there should always be someone around to open a tin of beans for you, that sort of thing but we'd be happy to assign another student specifically to help you if you would like us to.

CHAPTER 22: TOBY

Toby adored his orange Mini Clubman. It took on a personality of its own with its roof-mounted number plate and "disabled driver, no hand signals" sign. He decked it out with a black fluffy dashboard cover and there were furry red dice hanging from the rear-view mirror, for they were all the rage. His friends had a competition to see who could hang the largest dice in their car.

The car's ignition and switches were on the left of the steering wheel where he controlled the indicators, lights, horn, and other devices. His key was on a lanyard hanging from his neck so that it was easy for him to hook the key between two toes to open the door, then when he was comfortably in the car, he could turn the ignition. He could just about manage to turn the ignition with his hand if he leant right forward but it was a strain on his neck. He pulled the seatbelt across with his teeth, then gripped the belt between his toes and clipped it in. Wearing a seatbelt wasn't compulsory but he wanted to get used to wearing one for motorway driving. It felt strange to pull the seatbelt from the right rather than the left and it took time to learn this new skill.

Learning to drive seemed to take forever and was frustrating as hell especially when Bill was in the car distracting him when he was supposed to be teaching him and laughing at his mistakes. His gross behaviour didn't help, chomping on cheese and onion crisps, lifting the packet, and pouring them into his mouth. On one occasion he was so busy glancing over and telling Bill not to stink the car out that he nearly ploughed into a wall. Being confined in a small metal box with his dad who stank of either crisps or sweat was not the most pleasant of experiences. The early days of learning were the worst when he was still mastering the basics and using the school grounds for practice. On several occasions he tried to start the car when it was already on, repeatedly jarring the ignition mechanism causing horrendous grinding noises.

'But I stalled, why won't it start?' he asked Bill.

'The engine's already running, silly,' came Bill's reply.

'How do you know?' he asked. 'I can't hear the engine.'

'Well press the pedal and see what happens.'

The car revved and jerked forward, and Toby gasped.

He hated the aggressive beeping at traffic lights when he took longer than a split second to pull away after the lights had turned green. The multi-blast was uncalled for, but he'd come to realise that some drivers were impatient around learner drivers and beeping was a knee-jerk reaction.

The first year of learning to drive disappeared in a whirl and then he was in his second year of college. One season followed another, trudging back and forth to college in rain and shine, or cadging a lift from Mandy or Bill whenever they offered. There were times he arrived in class a drowned rat, the bottoms of his trousers caked in mud and in summer his face and neck burned to a crisp. Like so many milestones in his life, whether it was learning to ride a bike, write, type, or vacuum the carpet, he needed help, and it took him longer than most to master these skills. The humiliation of months spent learning how to perform a three-point turn and reverse around a corner, failing miserably, constantly bumping the curb due to poor judgement, never quite managing to do that perfect sweep. Learning to drive had seemed so simple for his college friends, but they weren't disabled. The frustration of being the last one in his class to pass, it had really got to him.

Eventually though he was ready to take his test which took place in July, the day after he finished college.

When the examiner handed him a pass certificate, it was the best feeling ever. Nothing had ever topped that wonderful euphoria, not even winning the trophy in the annual speech competition. There was also a huge sense of relief. He knew he would have been gutted to fail. It was such a surprise to pass, he'd been convinced he wouldn't but during the test everything seemed to go perfectly. The stern examiner, dressed in a grey suit and with a clipboard on his lap made him feel nervous. Then he distracted him by pointing out a beady-eyed robin sitting on a bush watching them as he was about to start his three-point turn. But at the end of the test, the examiner announced that he'd passed, and Toby wept with joy. But then the man added the words of caution, 'just don't drive in London yet,' which dampened his spirits and made him think he wasn't quite up to par yet.

On the way back from the test centre, he glanced at his instructor, a mischievous smile on his face. 'Let's pretend I failed,' he said as he indicated and drove into the bumpy lane leading down to the cottage.

He couldn't wait to tell Bill and Jasper that he'd passed, to see the surprise and delight on their faces, but first he wanted to tease them. They didn't believe he could do it and in truth neither had he--not until he'd seen the certificate.

'Every learner wants to tease their parents. Put on a sad face and don't laugh.'

It was hard to look sad when he felt this excited, but he pursed his lips and looked glum.

He would remember this day forever.

The day he gained his independence. Woo hoo.

Going out on my own will be like stepping onto the moon. A whole new world is about to open up.

Suddenly it seemed as if everything in his life was within reach. He could go anywhere, do anything, not have to rely on others for lifts.

He couldn't believe how lucky he'd been. The weather conditions were perfect, it was almost as if the day had been sculpted specially for him. No bright sun to blind his vision, no thick fog, no heavy rain hammering the metal roof, sluicing the windscreen. Just an ordinary, bland cloudy day, ideal driving conditions.

The car bounced over the ruts in the lane. It was an unsophisticated car with a soggy suspension which meant that he could feel every stone in the road, but Toby loved this dear little orange car.

The lane was flanked with overgrown gorse bushes covered in yellow flowers at this time of year. He glimpsed the cottage. His heart swelled with pride. His three parents, Bill, Jasper, and Sandy were waiting for him. Sandy waved frantically when she saw the car, Jasper was expressionless, and Bill glanced up before fixing his gaze on the ground. He knew exactly what each was thinking. Sandy was optimistic, she believed he'd passed, but Jasper, nervous, wasn't so sure. Bill though, ever the pessimist, was certain he'd failed. He'd even told him that morning, 'I'm hoping, son, that you don't pass first time, because you're crap at parking and need more practice.' But that was how his dad had become. Maybe he was just afraid for Toby, and it came out all wrong. But he was his dad––and even though this was in name only,––for really, he was just the man who'd raised him--and Bill was supposed to support his dreams, encourage him, be happy for him.

Sandy rushed over, clutching his little sister Angela by the hand. Toby sat, stony faced while the instructor got out. Being so lanky he looked ridiculous in Toby's Mini with his bald head tight against the metal roof. When he emerged from the car it always made Toby think of a party popper detonating, minus the popping noise.

'Who, I tell you, who goes through a red light?' The instructor was a great actor and warmed to the drama.

Sandy's hand flew to her mouth.

Jasper rushed over and opened Toby's door. 'Poor chap, better luck next time. I can take you out, practice makes perfect.' Jasper had never taken him driving, he knew this was Bill's role, so why suggest it and risk upsetting him? In any case, since the spring with the new female prime minister in power, Jasper's time was limited. He was far too busy writing articles about the new 'political landscape' as he liked to call it.

Bill shook his head in disbelief and turned away. Sometimes he felt as if he was constantly having to prove himself to avoid disappointing his da and he wondered if this was something that most handicapped people felt.

Toby sprang out of the car with a beam on his face.

'Surprise.' He waved the certificate, the edges of it now soggy.

Sandy reached to take the certificate, a puzzled look on her face before she broke into a smile. 'You've done it. I knew you'd pass even though those rotters didn't.' She turned to Jasper and held the certificate up with a beaming smile.

'I've passed.'

Bill and Jasper beamed and slapped him on the back.

'Thank you,' Jasper said, shaking the instructor's hand.

'It's been my pleasure. He's a great chap, you should be very proud. I feel quite emotional, he's the first disabled person I've taught. There are certain pupils you never forget, but the longer I work for BSM the more difficult it is to remember my ex-pupils which is awkward in the supermarket when I bump into them, and they tell me stories about their adventures behind the wheel. But I won't be forgetting Toby.'

After the instructor had left, Toby followed Jasper and Bill into the cottage. The three of them were a chattering knot: Bill, portly, red-faced from drink, Jasper, film star handsome and his elegant mother, Sandy. Sandy glided past them with Angela at her heel who was dancing like a butterfly and singing to herself. Such a pretty girl, she was angelic, pale-skinned with gleaming blue eyes and a mop of silky blonde curls, always neatly brushed and tied with red ribbons. She reminded him of one of those iced cakes with piped flowers, crafted to perfection, the type of cake that won WI competitions. She'd been sent from heaven–– or chosen from the Littlewoods catalogue. A designer kid plucked from the shelf, made to order, boxed and ready to go.

As he glanced down at her now, her little hand in Sandy's, linked like an unsevered umbilical cord, a dragging sensation moved across his chest, that dull ache he always experienced when his sister was around.

He wasn't a part of their family––and yet he was their first-born.

Discarded trash, that's how he sometimes felt. The mistake. The ruined cake baked at the wrong temperature. An outsider, he was an imposter who orbited a kind of parallel world, like a bird watching from a branch. They were complete, a proper family unit, but where did he fit in? The trappings of family were there in everything they all did together, but it felt plastic, false, and it was as if he were merely acting the part from a stage. For God's sake, he wasn't even allowed to call Angela his sister. Sometimes he wished he'd never been told the truth about how he'd come into the world. Knowing the truth just threw up a raft of problems and emotions that weren't there before. The truth might have set the three of them free, but it had shackled him. Were they really going to let Angela grow up not knowing that Toby was her brother? The damage that could do if she ever found out.

In the cottage, as soon as Sandy let go of the little girl's hand she made a beeline for the stairs, bounding up and giggling. Nobody stopped her and yet they would have known where she was heading.

'Tea and scones, Toby, to celebrate,' Sandy gushed, waving her hand at a plate of scones that looked freshly baked.

'Or commiserate,' Bill muttered. 'Thought a nice spread of food would cheer you up, eh, lad?' He plonked his bulky frame down at the table.

Toby barely registered the cream tea spread across a crisp white linen cloth in his honour. He knew exactly where Angela was going––straight to his bedroom. He had to stop her. He just wanted to phone his friends and give them his news. Most of all he wanted to call Mandy, Sue, and Lucy. His heart swelled with pride imagining how they would react.

Brat. Why was Angela doing this now? She loved to hide in his big wardrobe, but always trampled on his books and clothes and he hated the chaos it caused. Without arms he couldn't grab her and bring her back down. At times like this, the butter-wouldn't-melt-in-her mouth toddler, who Sandy treated like a doll, became an annoying silly little girl he wished had never been born.

At the top of the stairs, he caught up with her.

'Play hide and seek, Tubby.' He raised his eyebrows and smiled at her. The mispronunciation of his name was cute and endearing but one day she'd realise her faux pas and see Toby for who he was––lanky and wiry and just like Lucy, by comparing him to an exclamation mark.

While Angela kept her hands covered over her face and counted, Toby slipped into his dad's huge wardrobe. Bill's clothes smelled of sandalwood and musk and transported him back to a time when he was tiny, and Rona was still alive. His memory of her was fast fading, the one photo he had was dog-eared and creased. Toby pushed through the sweaters and shirts hanging on the rail, all relics of a golden age when Rona cared for her husband's every need and chose his clothes for him. Bill loathed shopping. Frayed cuffs, the odd hole, faded colours–he failed to notice their demise and it wasn't as if he had a lady friend to keep him in check. Bill seemed to have given up on women after a failed relationship with a teacher at the school. Sandy though noticed Bill's shoddy outfits, which of course she would. Sandy and Jasper were so stylish, impeccably dressed and a hard act for anyone to follow. Bill was different, his appearance didn't bother him, but it bothered Sandy. On one occasion she asked Toby to smuggle what she called 'a particularly offensive pair of trousers' to her for mending. They had a ripped hole in the crotch area. 'If I could get away with it, I'd bin them and buy him a new pair,' she'd said with a look of distaste, holding them with two manicured fingers like a pair of pincers.

'The world's your oyster now, lad,' Jasper said from the lounge as he beamed up at Toby now trotting down the stairs, Angela at his feet. 'Not long now and you'll be away at university, first in the family to get a degree.' Jasper was jangling coins in his pockets and for a moment Toby thought that he was going to pull out a fiver. Afterall, his friends had been rewarded with money when they'd passed their tests.

'Stop jumping the gun, I might not get in.'

'Hey, of course you will, don't be defeatist.'

It wasn't defeatist, he was just being realistic, preparing himself for rejection. He had to achieve a C and a D to get into Lampeter and he hadn't the foggiest idea what he would do if he didn't get the grades.

'I can't believe we got you through,' Bill said chuckling as he poured the tea.

'Huh, the royal 'we' is it? I got myself through.'

'And we're all really proud of you.' Sandy smiled and reached out to ruffle Toby's mop of hair before lifting Angela onto a chair and tucking a napkin into her collar.

In a funny sort of way, he was going to miss the kid. All the silly games he played with her. Tickling her with his feet until she wet herself with laughter, watching *Andy Pandy* together, his foot in her hand as they cuddled up on the settee, teaching her how to do tasks with her feet which always amused him.

'You proud of your big brother?' Sandy asked Angela. 'He can drive a car now.'

Her brother.

In that moment, a surge of delight rushed through him. He'd always imagined them sitting her down one day to tell her, but this here now being so natural, so unexpected and coming just before he was about to leave for his next college, was sort of comforting, reassuring, a validation that he was important in their lives.

Ever since her birth three years ago, he'd lived with the jealousy, and it had become an undercurrent swirling around him. He didn't like to admit it, even to himself, but it was the truth.

Bill was chattering away, recalling all the mishaps and blunders. 'I could write a kid's book, Toby's adventures, along the lines of Toad of Toad Hall in *The Wind in The Willows*.'

'Ha ha, very funny.' He knew the story well and as a kid he'd loved it and could recite some of the words. He mimicked Toad's accent. 'Maybe one day I'll arrive home in a shiny new bright red motorcar of great size dressed in goggles, cap, gaiters and an enormous overcoat and drawing on my gauntleted gloves.'

The next morning Toby awoke wrapped in a sense of euphoria, still basking in the thrill of having passed his driving test. Deciding to get some fresh air, he walked into town and wandering past the library he noticed a poster advertising a summer writing competition that called for story submissions. The prize was a residential writing course.

    Intrigued, he stood staring at the poster for several moments as he mulled over a few ideas before heading through the door to pick up a form. As he meandered his way back home, he dreamt of winning the competition.

CHAPTER 23: JASPER

'Hey, Toby,' Jasper said one Saturday morning when he dropped over for coffee. 'You never guess, I had a call from Trimble.'

'Really? What did he want?' Toby's eyes lit up.

Jasper perched his bottom on the edge of the settee. The settee was so grimy, he felt uneasy about leaning back, and it was cluttered with junk. How they could live like this, he'd never know.

'Push the crap aside if it's in your way,' Bill said as he waved at it dismissively.

'His sister sadly passed away a few months ago and he's not well himself, and says he's been diagnosed with cancer and doesn't have long.' Jasper sighed. He wasn't good around sickness and wasn't sure how he would handle the situation. 'There are things he wants to tell me.'

'The confessions of a dying man?' Bill asked.

'He wants to see me.'

'I wonder what about. Can I come too?'

'No Toby, it wouldn't be appropriate,' Bill said.

'No, I'm afraid not,' Jasper added. 'This is something I've got to do on my own, it could be a bit delicate.' He didn't want the aggro of worrying about Toby.

A week later, arriving in Jersey, Jasper collected his hire car and drove over to the Portelet Inn. The inn was a far distance from La Roque, yet he had fond memories of the place from a previous visit with Toby and yearned to return. He wrestled with a sense of guilt about indulging in a getaway, yet he justified the treat, believing his tireless work entitled him to a short break away from Sandy and Angela. This charming, rugged granite inn was located at the end of a remote road. He gazed fondly at the Virginia creeper. It looked as resplendent as he'd remembered. Sliding off to the side was the pathway leading down to the hidden gem, a wonderful cove, the sand tinged with red, the Napoleonic watchtower perched on the rocks. He ducked his head as he walked through to the bar, taking care not to bang it on the low beams which festooned the ceiling. The interior, with its nooks and crannies and mezzanine area was a welcome maze. A few locals were propping up the bar and a family were lounging on the old worn leather settees. The bar man looked crusty and tired as if he was a sailor of former times and he was sharing banter with one of his older customers. Jasper ordered a whisky and went to sit in a comfy chair to relax and gather his thoughts. Looking round, he saw nothing had changed.

The following morning, he took a stroll down to the cove and stood taking in the scene. A gentle breeze blew off the turquoise sea and the waves were lashing at the rocks. He smiled to himself as he recalled the conversation with Toby about the construction of the tower. 'Anything's possible if you put your mind to it,' he'd said. 'Look at man's greatest achievements: the Pyramids, Stonehenge.'

He traipsed back up the steps and as he headed over to La Roque, he wondered how he'd find Trimble. On arrival, he was greeted by the carer who led him up the stairs to Trimble's room.

He was shocked by the vision before him. He'd aged considerably and had obviously deteriorated since the holiday. His rheumy eyes were sunken into his skull as if haunted by his past and he was skeletal, a mere shadow of his former self.

He tried to lift his head, but it just flopped back on to the pillow, and semi-raised his hand by way of gesture as Jasper went over and touched his hand in acknowledgement.

'Hello, Trimble,' he said in a soft voice.

His eyes flashed open wide, jaundiced yellow and bloodshot. He waved his hand towards a chair for Jasper to sit.

'How are you?'

Jasper expected a weak voice to reply but instead he spoke in a strong voice.

'Thank you for coming, Jasper, there are things I need to share with you before I depart from this world and I'm afraid some of it won't be pleasant for you to hear. I need to tell someone, and I think you're the right person. I feel I can trust you. And you won't betray me.'

'Okay,' he said tentatively, settling into the armchair perched by the window.

'Jasper, I've had plenty of time lately to reflect on my life. It's easy to look back and regret some of the decisions we made, especially during the occupation. We hadn't a clue what to expect had no support from England, we were totally abandoned, scared and there were horror stories coming through the BBC about what was happening in the occupied territories.'

His gaze was drawn to the vast expanse of the sea, flat and twinkling under a bright sun. The sky was a sweep of sapphire and he tried to imagine the day that the Nazis invaded. The tiny black dots, like insects arcing over the bay, the black crosses on the underside of their wings, the noise of the deafening engines, the violent rat-a-tat machine gunfire, bullets hitting the sea wall, zinging off in random directions, sending debris and black smoke into the air.

'At first we thought it was a false alarm, these warnings had become a daily event, reconnaissance planes circling then disappearing back to sea. But this time, something was different. The growl of the engine had a note of brutish intent. There was nothing here to deter our aggressors, Churchill had decided not to defend the islands. The whine of the engines became a hum and the hum a strident drone, and then I knew this was no reconnaissance mission, this was for real.'

Jasper listened intently, every so often taking a sip of his coffee.

'We could smell burning aviation fuel in our nostrils, corkscrews of charcoal smoke were drifting across the bay. We had no idea what they were planning to do. Would they round people up, stand them in front of walls and shoot them?' Trimble's breath was raspy. 'Thank God my mum hadn't lived long enough to witness the nightmare. She passed away in '38.'

'Sounds like a blessing.' He felt a sudden wave of sadness; this man was about to bare his soul and he felt privileged he was sharing it with him.

Jasper looked up to see tears trickling down Trimble's face. His face was sunken, and he looked devastated. 'I didn't believe they would invade, I honestly didn't.' His voice was tinny, more a whine as if he was pleading with Jasper to believe him. 'We're a tiny island, what did the Jerries want with us? That's what I believed, but what a fool I was. There was a Jewish family who were close friends to us. I sent those kiddies and their mother to their grave. Me, I was responsible. They were the most beautiful little girls, just sweet, innocent children, but it was a snap decision we took that day down by the docks when everyone rushed to send their children to England. I wish I'd made them go. They were screaming and crying and clutching at their mother's skirt. I wish she'd been stronger, but she couldn't bear to be apart from them. A few months later, the whole family were deported. It came to light after the war that they'd perished in Auschwitz. I should have done more.'

'But what could you have done?'

'There are enough hiding places on this island to disappear, but sometimes the enemy within your own family is the greatest danger.'

Between his words, Jasper heard deep sorrow. He was intrigued.

Trimble was now staring out of the opposite window. He looked as frail and white as an eggshell. 'I looked out one morning not long after they'd arrived and saw an officer on the driveway looking up at the building deep in thought. I opened the front door to see what he wanted. He was walking up and down kicking gravel. I greeted him and asked if I could help, but he was too rude to turn round and say good morning. Instead, with his back still to me he said, "you the owner of this house?" in an officious manner.

I wasn't going to be intimidated by him, so I said, yes, I was and proudly told him the house had been in my family for over two hundred years. It was my way of saying leave well alone.'

Jasper looked closely at him; his face was gaunt, his eyes were glassy, as if he was staring into a void and his lip was quivering. He wondered what was going through the man's mind and how he was going to tease out the information, and if he could. Trimble had always come across as very secretive.

'Our family have been in the market gardening business for decades. When the Jerries arrived, I thought we might as well stay on their good side, I didn't want to ruffle any feathers, so I had Katie send over a big bouquet of flowers to the commandant's wife and a basket of Jersey Royals.

'He demanded to see inside. There was nothing I could do, he just swept in and went from room to room nodding approvingly and when we reached the bedrooms he didn't bother to knock or ask if it was okay to go in. One of my sisters got the fright of her life. She was in the middle of getting dressed and wasn't wearing a bra. I quickly looked away embarrassed, but he hovered there for a few seconds, and didn't take his eyes off her as she grabbed a towel to cover herself. Back down in the hall after his tour of the house, he asked me if anyone else lived here with us. "Yes, one of my farm workers," I told him. "He's staying because you lot bombed them out of their house when your planes attacked the harbour."

"He'll have to vacate his room. You better get ready. My officers will need it," the bastard called from over his shoulder. "I'll be back." And with that, he turned, his heels clicking across the wooden floor and then he was gone.'

Trimble coughed, every word proving to be an effort. It pained Jasper to watch him struggle and he wondered if he should leave him to rest and return later. He gazed out of the window remembering the holiday with fondness, the walks along the beach with Toby and just when he thought he'd dropped off to sleep, Trimble started talking again.

'I want our story to be told, I can't think of anyone better than you to tell it. The older you get, Jasper, life takes away rather than gives. The war took everything.'

He'd thrown off his duvet, exposing his bare chest which looked like a sparse parkland after a forest fire. His skin was mottled and translucent, like onion skin and there were several cloud-shaped bruises on his thin arms. There was barely anything of him. How he'd aged and deteriorated since the last summer, ravaged by cancer, a thought which saddened Jasper for Trimble was only in his sixties.

'I hardly slept that night, worrying what was going to happen. I didn't want to be in the same position as Mr Harris.'

'Mr Harris?'

'A man in another village, he dismantled the chapel to stop the Jerries from requisitioning it. He took the iron roof panels off, took the whole bloody church down in one day. By the time they returned, it was just a pile of timber. Apparently, the officer turned a bright shade of purple and shouted a few swear words in German but Mr Harris just stood there as cool as a cucumber, shrugged his shoulders and when they'd gone, he laughed his head off.' His voice sounded gravelly, as if he'd swallowed sand.

'You'd have had a job dismantling this house.' Jasper chuckled.

'I was terrified they'd get their grubby hands on all the silver ornaments and the oil paintings. They've been in our family for decades. Greedy bastards. So, I shifted them all to a barn on our farm and covered them in hay. Of course, when they did arrive, they noticed they'd gone and immediately challenged me. The terror those men instilled in us. I remember my heart banging away. I thought they'd pull out a gun and shoot me, right there in my own home in front of my sisters. That feeling of terror, and that was well before we even knew about the ghettos, the burning synagogues with Jews locked inside, the round-ups, the cattle trucks, the purpose-built camps.

'A few days later, we heard vehicles. The first car appeared on the drive, a smart open-topped Bentley filled with senior officers in full uniform. The second was a gleaming Daimler, then a few less impressive cars containing lower ranks and a couple of motorcycles––all stolen I imagine from local residents as the arriving military could hardly have had time to ship such vehicles from Europe. The soldiers trooped into the house with delight on their faces. I presumed they'd spent months in the cold muddy fields of Europe. This island, with its pretty little villages, green rolling fields and lush beaches must have come as a happy surprise to them. They'd come to commandeer the house as the Nazi headquarters of Jersey.

'I didn't know how to behave in my own house. Were we supposed to salute them and what would happen if we didn't?

But they didn't make us salute, to begin with they tried to make us believe they were civilised. But I wasn't going to let my guard down. They were the enemy, the invader, and it was hard to sleep at night with them under our roof. And my sisters kept their bedroom doors locked at night. Well, one of them did.' He sighed.

The weight of his words settled into the air. Jasper's brain was briefly paralysed as he tried to process the enormity of it all. The room was silent, and all he heard was the rasp of Trimble's intake of breath. He was staring out of the window, his eyes a glassy sheen, the struggle of those years combined with his illness visible on his face.

Jasper followed his gaze. The tide was on the turn and a few large rocks were now exposed. He peered out across the lunar wilderness of rocks and shingle. There were a few people down there, coloured dots on the beach. He remembered crunching across the dry seaweed, the conversation with Bridie most vivid in his mind.

Trimble shifted his position and coughed. 'Over the next few days, the house was turned upside down as they moved boxes and filing cabinets into the front room, taking over most rooms apart from our bedrooms. They expected us to be their lackeys and waite on them hand and foot and jump to their every command. Then they took my Vauxhall 10 and requisitioned it, and we were forced to cycle everywhere.'

Jasper shuddered as he remembered the loss of his beloved Jag after Steadman's bribery.

'Did they notice the missing paintings and silver?'

'Yes, they were furious and demanded to know where they'd been hidden. Of course I wasn't going to admit it. I was shaking inside but kept my nerve when I casually told them that one of their lot had been up in a truck to pick them up.'

Jasper shifted in his chair. 'What is the secret of this house, are you happy to share it with me?'

'If you promise not to publish the story until after my death.'
'Of course.'

They were silent for a few moments and Jasper wondered if he should return the following day. Trimble looked tired.

He braced himself before asking the burning question, 'What happened in the cellar?'

Trimble closed his eyes and Jasper waited, but a few moments later he heard him lightly snoring. He crept out of the room. He'd return in the morning.

CHAPTER 24: JASPER

As soon as Jasper put his head on the pillow his brain fired up, bombarding him with theories about what had happened in the cellar. He could almost hear the machinery of his mind churning inside his skull as he pondered the mystery of Bonaparte House and the missing sister. So far, Trimble had only told him the basics, how the Germans had invaded, how they'd taken over the house as their administrative headquarters and interrogation centre.

He drifted off to sleep and woke when the sun pushed through a crack in the thin curtains filling the bedroom with a soft amber glow. Eagerly he rose and quickly dressed, anticipation fuelling him. Hearing Trimble's story felt like a race against time, a quest to capture the tale before it was too late, the uncertainty of Trimble's remaining days adding an urgency to his movements.

Trimble looked brighter. He was sitting in bed propped up with several pillows sipping tea when Jasper knocked and entered. Without speaking, he motioned Jasper to sit in the armchair by the window.

He glanced out to see the tide was in. Waves slapped rhythmically at the water's edge and there were a few children running in and out of the sea.

Poor chap, Jasper thought. The mechanics of his body were fast failing, and his bed had become a lonely but warm refuge for a man whose time in this world was drawing to a close. How he wished now that he'd got to know him better during that holiday, but it had had been embarrassing, breaking Trimble's trust the day they'd sneaked down into the cellar. He'd behaved like a naughty schoolboy and had certainly felt like it--he was no better than Johnny. How he cringed now with the shame remembering. That desperate thirst of his for a story.

Jasper itched to ask about the cellar, but he had to play it cool. He sensed that something huge had gone on down there, even if he didn't know what. After talking for a while, taking a deep breath, he decided to try an indirect tack. 'Can I ask, the activities in the house,' then he lowered his voice and leaned in conspiratorially, as if expecting the walls to overhear, 'did the Allies discover what had gone on?'

Trimble made a clucking sound and stared ahead. He fell quiet for a few moments. The silence in the room pulsed with tension before finally he spoke.

'Well, Jasper, you have to remember that many crazy things happened in the occupation, some good, some bad and some outright unbelievable but please remember we had no choice. It was either comply or die.' He spoke with the weariness of someone who had anticipated the question or possibly he'd been asked that many times before.

The air seemed to still as Jasper waited for him to continue.

'When the war ended and the news came out that it was over, crowds round the harbour were shouting, singing, cheering. Streams of British soldiers poured off troop carriers in the bay, trudging through the thousands of well-wishers. Women throwing themselves at these newcomers showering them with kisses, begging for sweets and cigarettes. The Pomme D'Or, which had been the German naval headquarter for the duration of the war was now filled with British uniforms and military men. The Union Jack was raised, and people sang 'God Save The King."

He fell silent for a few moments, then continued. 'The officer who'd first come to the house was the last to leave. They came for him. Took him away in an armoured truck. They were lining them all up on the beaches. Before he was carted off, he turned to me, smirked, and made a trite, flippant comment. He brushed my shoulder and said, "No harm done, my friend", as if he'd merely spilt wine on my carpet.'

Jasper gasped. He looked at Trimble and saw a brooding darkness in his eyes, the secrets he hadn't yet revealed.

'Towards the end, when they knew they'd lost and the news of their defeat came out, the area command's priority was an island-wide concealment of what had been going on here for the past five years. Anything at all that could be viewed by the Allies as contrary to the Hague Convention, it needed to be destroyed. At gunpoint, I was ordered to build a bonfire. All the documents, every shred of evidence went up in flames.

'They covered their tracks, but ultimately they paid the price.'

'Did they though? Many served short sentences, some escaped justice.'

Jasper was thoughtful. He was still none the wiser about what happened in the cellar.

'There were photos in the window of the town's post office of the liberation of Bergen-Belsen where a Jersey man had miraculously been found alive. Newsreels of the camps were shown in the cinema.' He paused, looked haunted, grey tinging his skin. 'I'll never know.'

He was talking in riddles now, maybe the effects of morphine were muddling him, or his illness was making him weak.

The next day, Jasper resolved to ask about the cellar and the tower.

He leaned forward in his chair and fiddled with his pen. 'You've lived in the house all your life and throughout the occupation. You're in a good position to know, what is the link between the tower and the house? When we were here, you indicated that the cellar and that part of the house was out of bounds. Are you willing to share this with me?'

Jasper watched him. His face was pallid and drawn tight over his bones. His eyes, once bright, now gazed distantly, their lustre dimmed by the encroaching embrace of death.

'There was a secret passageway built from the tower to the beach. When the house was built––and originally it was the coastguard's house––, rather than fill the foundations, they kept it. When I was a young, I used to pretend to be a pirate. But during the occupation, it was used for far more sinister activities.'

'What sort of activities do you mean?'

His chest heaved with a cough, a stark and jarring sound that seemed to rattle his very being. 'It was an ideal place to keep prisoners and people were brought here and tortured to provide answers, and if they didn't give answers, they moved them to the tower to extract the answers using more extreme methods. Many across the island were brought here. Including my sister.'

Jasper straightened his back. 'I thought your sister was close to a German officer.'

'Yes, she was. Too close. You've heard of pillow talk. All those intimate, private conversations shared in the bedroom away from the public's prying eyes. Profumo paid that heavy price with the lovely Christine Keeler. Because of what my sister knew on both sides she was an asset and a liability to the Nazis, and they believed she had more information than she was revealing. They interrogated her and following that, she disappeared without trace. We never found out what happened to her. I've forever blamed myself for not looking after her, she was my younger sister. We were all foolish back then, we thought we could befriend them, but they just used us all. My other sister was heartbroken and never really recovered. Those rooms hold so many secrets and nobody will ever know the truth, but we do know nothing good came out of them. At the end of the war, we sealed off the passage and never used it again. There are diaries that are locked away here in my bedroom which document a lot of what happened, and you can take them and after my death you can publish them but please don't reveal any of this until after I'm gone.'

'You said the tower is sealed. Is there anything there that reflects what happened in there?'

'Yes, but sadly I can no longer talk about it. It's all in the diaries and the cellar remains as it was when the Nazis left with all the associated equipment inside. I was so heartbroken I decided nobody should go in there.' Jasper asked if his other sister had been into the tower after the war.

'Definitely not, no way. I never wanted her to see in there. I thought I had a strong stomach.'

Trimble's last words to him were, 'The tower and the tunnel are not Thalidomide Trust property, I retained ownership. And after my death, they pass to you.'

Jasper gulped; a lump came to his throat.

Why the hell would he gift it to me?

JASPER TOOK the diaries and left Trimble, returning to London, and was immediately assigned another subject to cover. Since Margaret Thatcher's ascent to power in May, Jasper found himself with an abundance of events and issues to report on.

CHAPTER 25: TOBY

Time was slipping away, and Toby still hadn't thought of an idea for the story competition. It was very disheartening because he'd been so excited about the prize.

A residential writing course.

Coming up with ideas was especially hard because his thoughts were incessantly preoccupied with Jasper's visit to Jersey. Ever since his return, he'd been so cagey. Toby was desperate to hear about his discussions with Trimble, but Jasper had told him very little, and it was hard to get anything out of him. Every time he asked, a haunted look came over Jasper's face, as if the visit had troubled him. He couldn't understand why he was being so secretive especially considering how much they'd talked about the cellar when they were there. All the sneaking around, the late-night chats, the speculation, the musings. They were a team and it had felt exciting when they'd deviously hatched the plan to creep down into the cellar. It was their secret and nobody else knew about it, not even Bill or Sue, and that had felt special somehow. But now Jasper seemed distant, he was hiding something, but what? Toby wondered if it had anything to do with the sister's diary. He wished he could get hold of the diary, he wanted to read it, but Jasper had been dismissive of his requests to borrow it and had it locked away in his house.

It was now late and as he slipped into bed, he hoped an idea would pop into his head. Sometimes the best ideas were hatched in the wee small hours as the brain emptied of all the day's trivia that made it so hard to think. But his mind was so full of Jersey and the conundrum of Jasper's secretiveness, it was hard to think about anything else.

During the early hours, he woke with a jerk, his heart racing and his t-shirt drenched in sweat as he recovered from yet another nightmare involving the Germans on Jersey. He got up and switched on the light.

Jersey. The Nazi occupation.
That's what I'll write about.

It was crazy how this idea hadn't come to him before now. Fired up, he took out a notepad and began to write. He didn't need to know the truth of Bonaparte House, sod Jasper, he wasn't going to reveal what had happened. He'd make up a story. After all, no other ideas were springing to mind. He wouldn't write about the horrors that had disturbed his sleep these past few nights, this was going to be a love story set in 1940 about a romance between a Jersey girl and a German officer.

It took several days to write the story and now that he'd finished and submitted it to the library, winning the competition didn't seem to matter anymore because he'd had so much fun writing it. If only he enjoyed writing essays and taking exams this much. They sapped the joy out of learning and turned it into a test of discipline. Exams were nerve-racking, writing essays was tedious and at times overwhelming. Waiting for exam results was an anxious time. His whole future hung on those wretched A level results.

The day of his results dawned, and Toby was up early to wait for the postman's arrival. Bill dashed outside to grab the mail as the postman emerged from his van and came back up the path waving the envelope at Toby.

'Give it here then.' Toby was standing on the doorstep in bare feet.

'How much you going to pay me?' Bill teased.

After Bill had finished playing silly buggers, Toby flopped onto the settee and using his metal letter opener, slit the envelope and slipped the piece of paper out with his teeth.

He stared at the results, unable to believe what he saw.

Hours later, still dumbfounded, Jasper and Mandy popped round to see how he had done.

'Come on, what did you get?' Jasper asked excitedly.

'C and an E,' he said glumly.

Jasper looked shocked and Toby felt his disappointment like a slap on the cheek. 'What do you mean, you got an E? Which one?'

'English lit.'

'What the hell.' Jasper looked flabbergasted.

'If you got a C in history, you could easily have achieved a C in English lit too,' Mandy said with a groan as Bill handed her a can of coke.

'I revised the wrong stuff.' Toby felt like a prize idiot.

'I'm not happy with you, Toby,' she droned on. 'If you'd spent as much time studying as you do preparing your speeches, you would have walked it. I spent a lot of time helping you, but you were more interested in the debating club. I don't know what you'll do now as I won't be around next year to help you.'

'I don't want to stay on.' He felt completely flat.

'What choice do you have? You can resit the exam in November.'

'Look, Mandy, I'm really grateful, sorry I'm so passionate about my speeches.'

Her eyebrows were arched, and she looked all haughty. 'Perhaps you should make public speaking your career.'

'What did you get, Mandy?' Jasper asked.

Toby felt suddenly bad, he'd been so down all day after receiving his results, he hadn't even thought to ask about hers.

'Thank you, Mr Cooper.' She smiled warmly at Jasper before throwing Toby a frosty look. 'I got 3 A's, I've got a place at Bath, my first choice.'

'That's fantastic,' Jasper gushed.

'I still can't believe you got an E in English lit,' Mandy said. 'You've let everyone down including yourself. We all helped, the whole class will be disappointed because they went out of their way to help too. You've squandered the opportunity.' Her words hit like punches and sank into his body like shards of glass. She looked royally pissed off. He felt a twang of guilt and wondered with a sense of doom what comments he could look forward to from his other classmates.

Bill plonked himself down in his armchair. 'I wouldn't worry too much, it's only a piece of paper. You just need common sense.'

Mandy wheeled round to face him, looking shocked at Bill's dismissiveness, but she said nothing.

'I want to be more than you are,' Toby said to Bill in a cocky tone.

Bill looked affronted. 'What do you mean, more than me?' he snapped.

'A dead-end builder.' Toby let out a mirthless laugh.

Bill got up and hovered beside Toby, his hands on his hips. 'You ungrateful little shit.' His spittle landed on Toby's cheek. 'If I wasn't a builder, I wouldn't have made all those devices for you. What Rona and I went through to give you a good start. All our extra money went on you.'

'Yeah, all that extra money you could have spent on booze.'

'That's enough, you two.' Jasper looked at Toby. 'I'm gutted, you had all the warnings. You were quite capable of achieving two good results. You need to get your head out of the clouds and focus on what you want to do with the rest of your life, boy. At least you've got one good grade, you'll just have to revise hard and take it again.'

'I don't think I really want to go to university,' Toby said downheartedly. 'Certainly not Wales. It's too far away. I want to talk and debate. I know I've cocked up. I want a job helping other disabled people. I want to do some good. Maybe I can get a job related to that.' The idea had never crossed his mind, but this moment of sudden clarity was like a light flicking on.

Bill started laughing and quipped, 'Toby, the MP for disability or with those grades, C and an E you could join the Church of England.'

Toby felt heat rise to his cheeks. He hated it when Bill mocked him.

'That's enough, Bill, we need to help him,' Jasper defended.

'I'm not a baby, I don't need any of your help.'

'You're an idiot,' Bill said.

Toby was really pissed off now. His whole family was against him, and his classmates.

He got up and stormed off out slamming the door.

That evening, on the phone with Sue, she wasn't any better either. He called her hoping for a sympathetic ear but instead she called him a right prat. 'There's you always spouting off about studying hard and getting good marks and you don't perform. You had all that help and assistance, far more than I got.'

'I thought you'd understand.' He felt completely worthless and inadequate.

'It's just that at school you were full of what everyone else should be doing.'

. . .

IN THE WEEKS that followed Toby's disappointing A level result, he contemplated his next steps. Reading the rejection letter from Lampeter was heart-wrenching, much more than he'd imagined. He hadn't been keen on going there, but now that he couldn't go, he wanted to. He reminded himself that anything that was out of reach and unobtainable was more attractive and appealing. That was just the way it was. If only he could wheel back in time, revise more thoroughly. He knew he could do it, despite his physical challenges. The college had been brilliant, he'd been given extra time in the exams in a room all to himself and a scribe from the examining board. His classmates had been fantastic, and he'd made some good friends. Some of them were going on to university and some had job offers. The sensible thing to do would be to retake the exam, he knew that, but the thought of an extra year at the same college left him feeling a mix of emotions. Mandy wouldn't be there. She'd been such a huge part of his whole college experience. He didn't want to walk those corridors without her shadow beside him, imagining her voice, her laugh. And without her, was he even capable of improving his result? Having relied on her for so long, it was hard to believe in his own strengths and abilities. Doubts were setting in and taking hold.

He left it until the final week of August before deciding to retake his exam. He resolved to knuckle under and study hard. The exam was in November and after that he needed to occupy his time until the next university year began. That was another conundrum, how to fill that time. Some of his classmates had decided to take a gap year travelling through Europe, taking advantage of the affordable Interrail ticket that allowed access to thirty-three countries. He thought about joining them for part of the journey, but he didn't have the money and couldn't see Bill helping. And so that left only two options: voluntary or paid work. It would be good to save, Toby mused. He'd get his grant to study at university, but he'd probably need some savings to see him through the three-year course.

It was the last week of the summer holiday, and he received a phone call from the library. All the entrants were being asked to come into the library on Saturday for the announcement of the winner and the mayor would be awarding the prize.

CHAPTER 26: TOBY

Toby rose bright and early on Saturday, eager and prepared to head to the library. It was an important day--the day the winner of the short story competition would be revealed. He was like a shaken can of Pepsi, ready to pop, fuelled by the possibility of his own work being recognised.

As he skipped up the steps to the library, a sudden thought struck him, something he hadn't considered until now. There was no ramp or any access for wheelchair users or mothers with prams. He wondered, what did people who couldn't get up these steps do? Did the library have some kind of book delivery service for people stuck at home? Toby had always cherished his visits to the library. To him, it was more than just a building, it was a sanctuary, a peaceful oasis away from the chaos of home. The very idea of being denied the joy of wandering amongst the treasure trove of shelves laden with countless stories and knowledge, struck him with a sense of horror. The thought of someone being unable to experience the joy simply because of a few steps at the entrance, or because a desired book sat just out of reach on a high shelf, felt deeply unjust to him.

He breathed in the smell and thought how comforting and

reassuring it was. Maybe it was the scent of the books, an odour of knowledge and emotion calmly resting between the covers. Each corner of the library was like a corner of the earth, with its own micro-civilisation, a cathedral to the mind and although Toby was only eighteen, visiting the library felt like a privilege. To have access to the minds and souls of so many writers and not have to pay a penny.

'Morning, Toby,' greeted the friendly library staff, a familiarity that he appreciated. Being a regular, they knew him by name and made him feel a part of the community.

'I'm here for the story competition,' he said before glancing over to the large gathering in the domed section of the library.

The librarian scanned the list in front of her for his name before putting a large red tick against it. With her severe hairstyle that reminded Toby of a pudding basin, and her beige attire, she was the archetypal librarian, perfectly suited for the profession she'd probably been destined for. Why did librarians always dress in beige? Toby wondered. The colour of porridge, camels, and hearing aids, ideal if you didn't want to be noticed. He wondered if librarians dreamt and slept in beige and read beige books, or did they just know the title of books and the table of content?

'Well done, Toby,' she beamed, 'looks like you've been shortlisted. There are six of you. Good luck.'

His heart skipped a beat as disbelief and excitement swirled inside him. He had submitted his story on a whim, never truly believing it would capture anyone's attention, let alone be considered for an award.

'I don't know what to say,' he stammered, a smile forming on his lips.

'You better hurry up and take a seat over there.' She nodded in the direction of the group gathered at the back of the library. 'The panel are about to announce their shortlist.'

Toby nodded, still in a daze as the news sank in. He'd

enjoyed writing the story, it had been a welcome escape after the intensity of studying for his A level exams, and it had made him feel alive.

Just as Toby took a seat at the back of the meeting, the senior librarian, a crusty fella well into middle age with a rim of dandruff around his shoulders, began to speak. His grey suit seemed to blend with the dust motes dancing in the slivers of light pouring in from a small window behind him and illuminating the bald patch on the top of his head. There was a certain sternness to his posture which made Toby nervous.

The librarian announced the shortlist of six names which included Toby's, and the announcement was met with applause. Toby felt the heat rise to his cheeks and wished he'd brought Jasper along for support. This was such a pivotal moment in his life, one he knew Jasper would share with pride. He realised then, with a stab to the heart, how indifferent he felt to Bill's presence.

The librarian introduced the lead author.

'Each of you will meet with an author who will provide feedback on your story, the strengths of your plot and your writing, how you could improve and enhance your story, and then three of you will be chosen to give a short talk in the town hall followed by a question-and-answer session. This will be a ticketed event so if you would like to invite family and friends along, the tickets will be available at the library desk over the next fortnight. Giving an author talk when you'd rather be hiding in the comfort of your own home is one of the toughest challenges you can face. But it's an important part of being a writer because it means you get to meet your readers and they get to meet you.'

Someone raised their hand. 'What will the talk be about?'

The librarian swept his hand through his hair and released a blizzard of dandruff. 'The author will give you more details but essentially the talk will be about your life outside of your story and include humour, just be yourself. As writers, we're not by nature public speakers but it is an important part of being an author, a skill to be honed which is why we are including it in the competition process. Readers want to know more about you and your life.'

There were a few groans from the audience.

'We've made a shortlist of six, but now our job is to select three of you to give this talk and the final winner will be chosen because of his or her talk as well as their story.'

A few people sighed as if they'd been misled, but Toby didn't feel dismayed or frustrated in the slightest. For him, this was an exciting prospect. It was even more thrilling than writing the story itself. He couldn't wait. This was the ultimate challenge, a test of his skills as a speaker, another opportunity to speak in front of an audience.

A few weeks later, he met with the author in a secluded room within the library. Jim Blakey was a local writer but unfamiliar to him until the librarian showed him several of his crime novels and although he wasn't interested in crime stories, he read one of the novels in preparation for the session.

He was an approachable guy and Toby instantly clicked with him. 'I loved your story,' he began in a warm manner, leaning forward in his armchair and filling a pipe with tobacco. He had the kind of diamond-patterned skin that came with heavy smoking and a ruddy complexion. Toby watched him tamp down the tobacco and take out a match to light it. Thin plumes of smoke eddied into the air.

He was curious about Toby's writing process, considering his impairment, and wondered what challenges and obstacles he faced. As he was so easy to talk to Toby found himself opening up. He shared his life story, explaining how his condition was the result of his mother having taken Distaval, shedding light on the reasons behind his current state. When he finished, he realised how cathartic it had been.

'When I was your age,' he said, 'I was always fascinated by war, and I was particularly interested in the Nazi regime. What inspired your story, have you been to Jersey?'

Toby told him about the holiday and visiting the War Tunnels and the strange mystery of Bonaparte House.

'I've always thought the Nazis developed thalidomide as part of their chemical weapons programme and tested it on concentration camp prisoners,' Jim said.

Toby stared at him in sheer horror, the revelation hitting him like a bolt from the blue. Was he hearing correctly, surely this couldn't be true? It wasn't a theory he'd come across, maybe the man was confused. It was just too awful to contemplate the thought that he could be indirectly connected to one of the darkest periods of history. This was so profoundly disturbing that he was lost for words.

Jim frowned and looked almost apologetic as if his information was wrong. 'I don't know where I've heard this, maybe it's just a theory, but I do know the Nazis were testing all sorts of drugs in the camps and experimenting on prisoners. Mengele is the most well-known physician, a ghastly man, he did the most awful things, dreadful atrocities the world will never forget.'

Toby was confident in his knowledge. He understood that thalidomide was developed by a German company in the 1950s before its use by pregnant women from 1957 onwards. Now he was confused. He couldn't help but wonder, if there was a Nazi connection, had it deliberately been kept hidden from the victims of the drug? He puzzled over why he had never heard this theory before. How much of the truth had been concealed?

For the rest of the interview, Toby couldn't focus. He felt unsettled. It was as if a cold shadow had settled over him, making his skin crawl with a strange sensation.

Jim guided him through how to prepare for his presentation and the specific topics he should address.

As he walked home, he realised how little he knew about

thalidomide and wondered how much the Thalidomide Trust knew but were keeping to themselves. And his friends, had they heard this theory before?

When he reached home, he bolted straight to his room. He had a few items of clothing that needed altering. The lady who normally shortened his sleeves was ill. Sandy had a sewing machine and had offered to make the alterations. He'd take them round and ask her about thalidomide.

CHAPTER 27: JASPER

Jasper was working from home, cradling a mug of fresh coffee as if it were a lifeline, pondering his next assignment. A whirlwind of thoughts was rattling through his mind when Toby's car came into view and turned onto the drive.

'Toby's here,' he called through to Sandy.

He waved at Toby as he got out of the car. It was nice to see the lad driving, he was still getting used to the car and didn't take it out very often.

He put his mug on the windowsill and rushed to open the front door. It was always a pleasure to have his son's company and perfect timing; he wasn't ready to crack on with his next assignment, he hadn't a clue where to begin. He sighed. Readers just didn't appreciate the craft that went into a story. News was time dependent and fast out of date, yet it took time to reflect on stories encountered, not just for the factual representation and accuracy, but also for understanding the broader implications, the tone and analytical insight that needed to be conveyed as well as any ethical considerations. Every story presented a challenge, and with the new Thatcher administration and the controversial plans and policies that were being pushed, there was plenty to report on.

Sandy bustled into the hall and gave Toby a hug. Jasper's heart flipped. It was so lovely to see the connection between Sandy and Toby deepening. Over the last few months, he'd really noticed a genuine warmth and affection between them. How different they were from a few years back––no longer awkward, detached, or rigid and strained as their interactions had been. The journey from that point of stiffness to their current state of ease was remarkable. The contrast between their past and present selves was testament to the power of time, effort and love.

'Well, spill the beans,' Sandy gushed. 'How did you get on at the library?'

'I've been shortlisted. There are six of us.' Toby beamed and excitedly explained that they'd thrown in something extra––a chance for the contestants to chat about their story and take questions from the audience.

'What a great idea, it's an important skill that few authors have. Most of them hide away in their ivory towers beavering away, it's a lonely existence. But giving talks, the reader gets a sneak peek into your mind. And you already have those skills, that's a huge win. I'm impressed with the library service, it's a great opportunity.' He slapped Toby on the back before leading the way into the kitchen and flicking on the kettle. 'I'd crack open a bottle of champers if we had one.' He turned and winked at Toby.

'You're acting like I've won. I've got a one in six chance.'

'Don't worry about winning, it's the taking part that matters, it's all good experience and will look great on your CV.'

'I suppose.' Toby flopped onto a chair.

'Is that the clothing you want altering?' Sandy asked, nodding to the bundle on the kitchen table. 'Been buying new clothes again?'

Jasper laughed. 'Hey, you can't speak, Sandy, all your shopping sprees. You're practically keeping the Army & Navy store afloat singlehandedly. I caught you smuggling those bags into the wardrobe the other day, thinking I hadn't noticed. Without you, they'd have gone under by now.'

'Ha ha, very funny.' Sandy tutted at Jasper before turning to Toby. 'I can't do them right away. Okay if I get them back to you in a couple of weeks?'

'Of course.'

'Hey, Toby,' Sandy said. 'We should have a shopping day sometime.'

Jasper put a mug of coffee in front of Toby, then remembered to get a straw for him.

'This private session with an author, how did you get on?' Jasper asked as he sat down at the table and handed Toby a plate of cookies.

'It was good. He liked my story, but there was something he said that I can't stop thinking about.'

'What was that?' Jasper leaned in frowning.

'He said that he'd heard that thalidomide was developed by the Nazis in concentration camps. Do you know about that?' He glanced from Jasper to Sandy.

Sandy's eyes looked like they were on stalks. 'That's quite a claim. Wow. I can't say I do.' She frowned at Toby. 'It was developed by a German firm, but long after the war.'

'Not that long after the war,' Toby corrected. 'But how long does it take to test a drug? Maybe years.'

'That was the whole point,' Jasper said. 'It wasn't properly tested. Did that chap say where he'd read that?'

'No, I've no idea.' Toby shrugged.

'It wouldn't surprise me. There are treatments in use today that were developed and tested in the camps, even the contraceptive pill. Hypothermia treatments for example are heavily based on experiments that took place in the camps. Prisoners were left to freeze while their core temperature was monitored.'

'Oh my God, that's horrible. Why would they do that?'

'They wanted to increase the chances of survival of soldiers in the Russian winter in the battles on the Eastern Front and pilots forced to ditch in the North Sea.'

Toby shuddered. 'I don't want to think about those horrors. Whatever experiments the Germans did to test thalidomide, they failed.'

Just then the trill of the phone could be heard from the hallway and expecting it to be the office, Jasper dashed to answer it.

'Good afternoon, Mr Cooper, I'm Mr Trimble's solicitor.'

Jasper was taken aback. This was probably bad news. 'How is he?' he asked cautiously.

'I'm afraid he passed away yesterday. He left a message for you.'

Jasper went cold. 'Can you read it over the phone please?'

He heard the crumpling of paper, and then the solicitor cleared his throat before speaking.

'Jasper, it reads. The story that shakes the very roots of my soul needs to come to light. I've lived with these shadows, and now, in death's embrace, I find the courage I lacked in life--to share them. As we discussed, I've chosen you, not just for the strength of your pen but for the depth of your understanding. When I'm gone, let these stories breathe, let them live and let them teach. It's a heavy burden but one I believe you're destined to carry. Promise me, my friend, that you'll tell them, not just for me, but for all who suffered in Jersey during those years. Let the world know and maybe we will find peace in the truth unveiled.'

Jasper was silent. The solicitor went on to say, 'Mr Trimble has left some property to you which will be dealt in due course.'

'Property?'

'Yes, the tower and a small piece of land.'

After the conversation, Jasper stood in the hallway processing his thoughts. He felt numb. This was the end of a chapter, but also the start of a new one. He didn't know how he felt, a mixture of emotion and sadness, but he also felt the heavy weight of the task sitting on his shoulders.

The tower.

The thought of going in there after all this time, it sickened him. He couldn't do it alone and wondered who he could take with him.

Since Trimble's illness, the Thalidomide Trust had abandoned the holidays and were now making plans to take the thalidomiders to Tenerife where the weather was guaranteed. In all likelihood, they would sell the property. There could be one problem though. Would it be difficult to sell the property without the tower? He had to see the deeds to the property. A sense of foreboding crept over him.

What the hell am I going to do with a tower?

Turn it into a holiday home, donate it to the war museum?

'Are you okay, my love?' Sandy asked on his return to the kitchen. 'You look ashen.'

'I'm okay, just some sad news, but news I'd been expecting.

Toby looked awkward and getting up he said, 'I guess I better leave you to it. I'll let you know how the contest goes.'

After Toby had left, Jasper said to Sandy, 'I didn't want to say anything while he was here, but Trimble's passed away. When I came back from Jersey, he kept on at me wanting to know what Trimble had told me. He's still young, it would have given him nightmares.'

'You took the same attitude with me, but I'm not young.'

'You'll always be young to me, my sweet.' He kissed her on the cheek.

'Trying to butter me up, what do you want?'

He reached round and squeezed her bottom.

She batted his hand away. 'When you've written up the story and it appears in the paper, Toby will be the first to read it, so either way, he'll find out.'

'I'm not sure what I'm going to do yet.' Jasper was conflicted. 'I'm not going to be rushing to tell the story.'

Jasper went back into his study but couldn't settle for the rest of the afternoon. His mind kept returning to Bonaparte House. By now the Thalidomide Trust would know about Trimble's death and would be considering whether to find a new housekeeper or sell up. Jasper picked up the phone and dialled the number for the Trust.

Gary, who ran the day-to-day affairs of the Trust, answered the phone, and they chatted for a few minutes about Bonaparte House before Jasper said, 'I need to tell you something. Trimble called me over to Jersey, there were things he wanted me to know about the house.'

'What things?' Gary asked, sounding completely surprised.

'The house has a very dark past, there were things that went on there during the Nazi occupation of Jersey. Acts of torture, down in the cellar and in the tower. I've had a call from Trimble's solicitor, and he's left the tower and a piece of land on the property to me.'

Gary went quiet for a few seconds before he spoke. 'That can't be right, we own the whole property. We had a full buyer's report from a local firm of surveyors.'

'What was the name of the surveyors?' A thought was kicking around his head. What if the firm was a long-established Jersey business and knew what had happened up at the house.

'Hang on a tick.' There was a rustle of papers and Jasper heard him huffing. 'Here we are. 'Le Sueur & Coutanche.'

A thought whirled through Jasper's mind. Both were popular Jersey names, Jasper knew that much. He remembered reading about Alexander Coutanche, the Bailiff of Jersey during the war.

Coutanche and other prominent members of the island's government and legal systems actively and willingly enforced the pernicious Nazi legal rules and provisions without question and sometimes with apparent enthusiasm. Everything from carrying out punitive measures against the Jewish citizens to confiscating radios and enforcing curfews, these people were an integral part of a self-policing Nazi terror state. Many people were betrayed by such informers. He'd read about Louisa Gould, for example, dobbed in by a friend they reckoned, then sent to Ravensbruck and murdered in the gas chambers for harbouring a Russian slave.

'Did you meet the surveyor?'

'No, everything was arranged over the phone.'

'Did they sound old, young?'

'What is this, twenty questions? Why do you want to know?'

Jasper could have explained his train of thought, but there wasn't much point, he'd make his own enquiries.

'It's okay, it's just that I don't think they even went in the cellar or the tower, because if they had, they would have discovered the gruesome implements Trimble referred to.'

'Sounds like a tall story to me. Maybe Trimble was having you on. He was probably delirious on morphine or had a vivid imagination. Anyway, I'd always thought Jersey had a not so bad experience compared to countries like France or Poland. The German officers treated the locals well.' He heard the shuffle of papers. 'I'm just skimming through the surveyor's report, there's no mention of damp or structural issues.'

Jasper fell silent, a cold chill sweeping through his body. This was subterfuge, a cunning cover-up which reeked of deceit. The men who ran this firm of surveyors had to be old guys who'd lived through the war. He was certain of that. Witnesses to the dark shadows of the Nazi occupation, maybe even entangled in its sinister web. He needed to go into the tower and cellar, he had to see it all for himself.

'What will you do, sell the place?' he asked Gary.

'Yes.'

'Whatever is down in the cellar and tower could affect the sale. You'll probably want a clear-up.'

He chuckled and Jasper had the sense that he wasn't being taken seriously, that he didn't believe the horrors of Nazi Jersey.

'I won't be able to, I'm in a wheelchair. If you're so interested you're welcome to go and investigate, you can pick the key up from our solicitor and I'll let them know to expect you. The whole place will need clearing anyway. I need to speak to the solicitor, there must be some confusion, I was led to believe we owned the whole property including the tower.'

After the call, he chewed things over before ringing Sam, his boss in London to tell him that he needed some time off to go back to Jersey to dig into the story about the Nazi occupation.

'Bit of a coincidence, I've just come off the phone with a buddy of mine who's eager to meet you. He knows loads about history and is really into the occupation. John Nettles. He's in Jersey and could meet you over there. You might have heard of him, he's an actor.'

'Nope, name doesn't ring any bells.'

'Seriously, mate?' Sam chided. 'You mean you've never watched *The Liver Birds*?'

'That old tripe, Sandy likes it, I hate it.'

Sam made a noise through his teeth. 'How about, *Enemy at The Door*? You watch that?'

Jasper knew the drama; it was set in Guernsey during the German occupation. How exciting, he was about to meet an actor. 'You should have said. The one who plays the police detective?'

'That's the one.'

'If he thinks he might be useful, he can join me for a look round the cellar, otherwise I'm sure the curator of the War Tunnels would accompany me.'

Jasper ended the call and sat at his desk for a few moments wondering what horrors awaited him back in Jersey. The answers lay just beyond that creaking cellar door. But at least now, he had some company.

A while later, Gary called him back. There was a heavy sigh before he spoke and in a weary tone, he said, 'it seems that you were right, there's a clause in the contract, Trimble retained ownership of the tower and a small piece of land connecting the tower to the house. I have absolutely no idea why we agreed such an absurd arrangement, it was when my predecessor was alive, but he's now passed away.'

'I'm not sure what I'm going to do with a tower once I've had a sniff around. I could sell it back to you, that way you can sell it all off together.'

After the call, Jasper picked up the phone and booked his flight to Jersey and accommodation. A sudden chill came over him. Normally he looked forward to returning to old pastures, but this one filled him with trepidation. Jasper was not a wimp, but this was stepping into the unknown and he was unsure what he would find.

CHAPTER 28: TOBY

The day of the speech competition finally arrived, and Toby sauntered into the library, expecting the usual quiet and hushed voices. Instead, this normally serene space had been transformed by a whirlwind of frenzied activity. Camera crews from London Weekend Television buzzed around like bees at a picnic, while the lively banter of local radio DJs filled the air. It was an unexpected fanfare, a far cry from the low-key event he'd envisioned. Suddenly thrust into the limelight, he felt like a star on the rise making an unforeseen Broadway debut and he was thrilled and intimidated in equal measure by the grandeur of the moment.

He was one of three who had been shortlisted after their author interviews to give a talk about their story. There was an opportunity for members of the audience to ask questions. Toby began to fret about what people would ask because this was something that couldn't have been prepared in advance.

He gave his talk, and after the clapping, the room fell silent and then a hand shot into the air. Toby smiled. He hadn't noticed his college mate, Dave, sitting at the back. Thank God. If he had, he might have gone to pieces.

'What inspired each of you to write your story and what message do you hope will come out of it?'

'My trip to Jersey last summer really inspired me. I visited the War Tunnels and read about the romance between a German officer and a Jersey woman. An unlikely love affair and that intrigued me.' And then without thinking, he blurted, 'It made me think of my relationship with my friend Lucy and the impossible dream that we could be a couple, the unobtainability and fantasy of it.' Toby felt his face go red and his heart was thumping. He gave a nervous laugh.

What a twat.

He wanted the floor to open up and swallow him.

One of the female judges said, 'Ah how sweet.'

'It's a romantic notion in my head and I like to see a happy ending, but difficult relationships don't always have a happy ending. I just hope that one day I'll meet someone who loves me, like my mum and dad did and that we'll be able to have a family like other people.'

Feeling emotional, Toby cleared his throat and thanked Dave for the question.

The judge stepped in. 'Okay thank you for that, the next question, please.'

An older woman rose to her feet and stuttered the next question. 'How would you turn your short story into a novel?'

'The competition only allowed me to write a short version of what I wanted to say and could easily have been much longer had I not had to adhere to a maximum word count. I hope you have enjoyed what I have written as that would show I'm working in the right direction. To turn it into a novel, I'd need to revisit the structure and then I could go into a lot more detail. I would add more characters.' He suddenly thought of a good idea. 'Perhaps the judges might have some advice.'

'If you won the competition, what would you hope to get out of the week's writing course?'

He hadn't really considered this, but now he knew the perfect answer. 'Firstly, I would like to learn how to become a better writer and speaker and the course might provide tips on how to turn the short story into a novel. I just find the whole arena of writing and speaking exciting. Being an avid reader, you can learn so much and I'd love to write and inspire others in the same way books inspire me.'

'Thank you. Toby, that's a lovely sentiment to end on.' Then the chief librarian addressed the audience. 'Now that we've heard all the contestants, we'll take a short break while we make our decision. Tea and coffee will be served while you're waiting for us to return.'

During the interval, Toby and Dave browsed round, Toby at the history books, Dave at the noticeboard.

A short while later, Dave went over to Toby. 'Come over here and have a look at this.'

'What have you found, the porn? Didn't think they allowed that in the library. We're not in Mr Singh's corner shop now.'

'Don't be daft,' he said, pointing to a poster on the noticeboard.

He stared at the poster on the board. 'You got to be joking. Jasper would hit the roof and so would my dad. I'd be a laughing stock and they would seriously take the piss out of me. And besides, I'm not sure where I stand at the moment.'

'You don't have to tell anyone. We could go along, suss it out, see if we like it. I've heard the beer's cheap and there's loads of birds. Only one problem, we might have to speak posh. We are talking Guildford after all, they might all be toffs and snobs, we'll have to see.'

'Okay, you're on.' Toby roared with laughter and he felt himself relax after the seriousness of the past hour. Their joviality was cut short as the bell sounded for the return of the judges. Everyone took their seat and waited. It felt like being in court. The judges filed in like soldiers with smiles on their faces, and a babble rose from the audience. A sense of anticipation rose. The lead judge spoke and thanked everyone for their entries and the effort they had put in and said how enjoyable it had been to listen to each story. The winners were announced in reverse order. In third place was a girl with a story about her holiday to Venice, in second place was an older lad with a story about time travel.

Toby was sweating. He'd heard the other stories and thought they were very good. He didn't for one minute think his was good enough to win but had been happy enough to take part and gain the experience. It had helped him to pass time before the next term of college.

The judge rustled his papers. 'Ladies and gentlemen, before we announce the winner, the lead judge would like to say why we have chosen this author as the winner.'

One of the judges stepped forward. 'The reason we have chosen this story is because it satisfies the criteria we set in terms of the essential elements of a short story. It was also important that the story was engaging and entertaining and drew the reader in. It had essential elements of reality linked with information that had been well researched and accurate and we could empathise with the characters. The story has been well written and for a first effort is to be highly commended in every way. The judges hope that following the week's tuition the winner goes on to develop a passion for writing. Thank you to everyone for taking part and we will announce the winner shortly. To award the prize may I please invite local writer to present the prize; ladies and gentlemen, please give a warm welcome to the esteemed novelist, Fay Weldon.'

Fay came to the front and said some pleasant words. 'I'm delighted to announce the winner of this year's short story competition is Toby Murphy.' A huge cheer went up and Toby was astonished and felt a sudden sickness. His mouth went dry. Would he have to make a winner's speech?

A moment later he was standing on the podium receiving the trophy and congratulations from all the judges. It felt surreal, he couldn't take it all in. One of them took his little finger to shake it, the female judges put their arms round him and Toby beamed with so much pride. After the applause had died down, Fay Weldon asked him a few questions which he answered candidly, and she invited him to say a few words. Toby stuttered and spluttered and thanked everybody. He gazed to the back of the audience, suddenly noticing Jasper, Sandy, Angela, and Bill. He said, 'You came, you came,' without thinking the mic was still switched on. Everyone turned to look, then started clapping and laughing. Toby sat down and saw the TV cameras and the local press. He'd completely forgotten they would be interviewing the winner and he'd be appearing in the local news.

'Okay, Toby, TV and local press are ready when you are.'

'Hang on a tick, can I just see my family first?'

The rest of the day disappeared in a haze with interviews and photographs and everyone coming up to congratulate him, and he hadn't a clue what he'd said to anyone.

Over dinner he watched the local news. Bill took the mickey out of him as usual. 'Jesus, boy, your hair was out of place and there's a grease mark on your t-shirt.'

'You can't talk, you scruffy bugger.'

At that moment, the programme flipped to a shot of Toby in action and then the report was over.

Bill beamed at him. 'My God, you were confident, I'm proud of you, lad,' he said with tears in his eyes.

Toby gulped, overcome with emotion. 'Blimey, Dad, you don't say that very often. The last time he'd seen tears in his eyes was when his mum died.

The phone didn't stop ringing for the rest of the evening.

Toby sank into bed shattered, but he couldn't sleep, he was still on a high. The one thing that kept coming back to him was Dave's comment about beer and birds. He finally drifted to sleep.

CHAPTER 29: JASPER

After opening the heavy iron gates, Jasper drove onto the crunchy gravel driveway to Bonaparte House. John Nettles was already there, checking out the place, his hand blocking the morning sun from his eyes. Jasper was immediately struck by how good-looking a fella he was. Striking blue eyes, chiselled features, coffee brown hair. He seemed to glow with the warmth of the Mediterranean, the kind of looks that launched a woman's dreams. He was wearing a short-sleeved shirt, and as he drew closer pulling up aside him, Jasper noticed the fine lines of muscles in his forearms. He had the look of an actor about to become famous, it was the way he carried himself, like someone too clever and talented for an ordinary existence.

Jasper got out of his car and after exchanging a few pleasantries and chit-chat, they wandered around the outside of the property, admiring the garden and sweeping views over the bay. It was a warm day, but the sky wasn't a faultless blue. Clouds hung over the sea like enormous chandeliers in a mansion. 'This place is so special.'

'I've always been intrigued by this little-known chapter of

World War Two. Look at it,' Nettles said. He swept his hand as he glanced round, smiling at the view as if absorbing its beauty for the very first time. His voice was plummy, but he had a slight accent that Jasper couldn't place. 'It was a peaceful summer resort until 1940 when it came under the heavy jackboots of Hitler's regime.'

'Did you grow up here?'

He laughed. 'God, no.'

Jasper was embarrassed. What an idiot he was. He usually prepared so meticulously; he hadn't had a chance to ask Sam about John's background. He didn't even know how the two of them had met. He put it down to nerves, for days his mind had been consumed with the dreadful possibilities of what they might discover in the cellar.

'I just love history, but I grew up in Cornwall. Cornwall's changed a lot since I was a kid though. Lorries used to roar down to Fowey every hour of the day and night and everywhere was dressed in white dust. The clay slurry used to drain into St Austell Bay, and it turned the water a beautiful turquoise blue and visitors would say, "look at that, isn't it the most beautiful blue sea you've ever seen," and of course it was clay slurry mixing with the sea.'

'I love this coastline,' Jasper said. It tells a thousand stories, through its castles and fortifications.'

'Indeed. And the Nazis wanted to get a foothold inside the British Empire. They were obsessed with these tiny islands.' He turned and waved towards the front door. 'Shall we go in? I know something of this building, that it was a Nazi base. Sam was telling me you came over recently to chat with the old fella, Trimble?'

They hovered near the front door. 'That's right. The family were market gardeners, a business that had been around for decades. He had two sisters. One of them worked in the family greengrocers in St Helier. Early in the occupation, an officer visiting the shop was so impressed by her efficiency that he asked her to work here instead. She was living here anyway as the house had been in the Trimble family for years. She had a relationship with an officer, maybe that same chap I'm not sure. Of course that wasn't unusual. Girls who got involved with German officers were called Jerry bags.'

Jasper had picked up the key from the solicitor. He turned it in the lock and the door creaked open. A musty smell hit his nostrils. The familiar smell of cooking, perfume and other human activity was gone. The place needed ventilating.

Nettles chuckled. 'They were hardly uncivilised barbarians, they were ordinary men just like us. Smart, handsome, sexy, you can hardly blame the women.' He put his briefcase on the hall table and glanced round.

'The sister became very important to the Nazi operation, very knowledgeable, indispensable almost, and for that very reason, towards the end of the war when the Nazis started to lose, they knew the Allies would arrive and needed to protect themselves, cover up what they'd done. They burned the paperwork in the garden, destroyed as much evidence as they could. His sister knew too much. She was their biggest liability and would be a key witness at any trial if they didn't get rid of her. She had to be disposed of. Trimble didn't know what happened to her. He wondered if she was taken to the women's camp, Ravensbruck, or Auschwitz, but he also wondered if she died down in the cellar. He said there were things that happened down there, but he couldn't find evidence. He thinks they may have tortured Resistance heroes down there, people who attempted daring escapes in boats. There's an area he couldn't go into, he was too scared about what he'd find. It troubled him for the rest of his life. That's why he called me. He wanted me to investigate and write the story. We need an expert to go down there with us, maybe one of the War Tunnels' curators, but we can certainly have a look today.'

'I'm sceptical, I'm afraid, but we'll see. Contrary to popular belief, there was no Gestapo here. Policing was undertaken by the Jersey police. Except on Alderney and its slave labour camps, the islands were spared the SS and Gestapo. The German army behaved well, they prided themselves on being gentlemen.'

Jasper took out a hammer from his bag and explained that they would have to break the lock to one of the doors. He found the cellar door key in the old mustard tin in the cupboard, and after opening the door, they headed down the damp brick steps into the cellar.

At the bottom of the steps, they stood in a dark abyss that led into the underground passageway. Nettles went into the room to the left at the end of the steps and stared up at the marks on the ceiling and the floor.

'What do you think?'

'I'm not sure.' He rubbed his chin, appearing to be in deep thought.

They closed the door and now a few feet ahead, Jasper stared at the next door, the locked one that led to the once forbidden area of this underground chamber. A cold shiver ran down his spine. The thought of what lay behind it, hidden in the shadows, filled him with dread. Yet there was no turning back now. The secrets entombed in the depths of this forsaken place called to him, a silent whisper urging him forward. It was as if he could hear the ghost of Trimble's sister beckoning him on, urging him to rescue her, but she was long dead. With a deep breath and his heart pounding with fear and trepidation, he raised the hammer and brought it down with a heavy blow, smashing the lock on the door.

They were in.

He lifted his torch, and its light painted the walls with its searching glow, the beam dancing across the damp bricks like a ghost looking for its final resting place.

Moisture clung to the cool, uneven walls leaving them slick to the touch as they felt their way in the gloom. Cobwebs were everywhere. Echoes of dripping water played a constant, eerie symphony and patches of mould dotted the bricks with hues of black and green. The air was heavy, filled with the earthy scent of wet soil and decay. The ground beneath their feet was uneven and littered with debris and leaves, and there were stacks of crates and boxes and rusty implements that looked like farm equipment.

They came to a wider part of the passageway and Nettles stopped, took a few paces back and stamped the ground. Jasper pointed the torch at the ground. Something under the debris rattled. Nettles bent down and brushed the debris aside to reveal a rusted iron grate that looked like a drain cover but larger. The area around the drain cover had been reinforced with concrete.

'What the hell is it?'

'I'm not sure yet.' He grabbed the torch from Jasper's hand and shone the beam into a cave-like area under the ground. The cave was wide enough for a man to stand in and Jasper reckoned it was tall enough for a man, maybe six or seven foot in depth.

The air seemed to go still, and all Jasper heard was the rasp of the intake of Nettles' breath.

'Holy crap.'

'What is it?'

John leaned closer to the grate before giving it a yank. It didn't budge. Jasper noticed four bolts holding it firmly in place at each corner. The right screwdriver would open it, but there didn't seem to be much point, it was just an empty hole that had been reinforced with cement and stone.

He looked up at Jasper and in the torchlight his skin looked like a polished coin. 'I think I know what this is.'

'And?' A prickling sensation spread over his scalp.

'I think we should get out of here, grab a coffee somewhere, but first let's go further along, see if this passageway leads into the tower.'

Ahead, the passageway grew darker now that they were further from the main cellar and relying on the torch as their sole source of light. They felt their way along the rough, cold walls, the air carrying a heavy oppressive silence, punctuated by their cautious footsteps and the distant, muffled echoes of the world outside, another realm away from this hidden artery.

At the end of the passageway, they approached the open, round space of the tower. Slivers of light poured in from the high barred windows, reminding Jasper bizarrely of his primary school, a Victorian building with windows so high to stop the children from gazing out and being distracted.

The air grew colder and there was a draught coming from the cavern. They emerged into the tower's base, a silent sentinel and monument to Napoleonic history. How Jasper wished now that it had been preserved from those days, untainted by the chill of Nazi history.

He felt a dread deep in the pit of his stomach as he looked round for clues about what had happened here. He walked over to a rusty filing cabinet, yanking one of the drawers and when it didn't open, he gave it a hard kick. As it crashed onto its side, the drawers flung open, but they were empty.

'Anything of use has either been destroyed or recovered in an Allied raid.' A chill ran down Jasper's spine when he saw what Nettles was doing.

Examining a Nazi banner.

Jasper had only ever seen the iconic flag with its red background and black swastika in films and books.

The room was cluttered with old dusty boxes, but a pile of clothes in one corner attracted Jasper's attention. He picked up a tatty camel-coloured skirt and a beige handknitted woollen jumper that had deteriorated significantly, torn, and dotted with mould. It had a small logo knitted into it, a blue forget-me-not. There was a tiny ink stain on the opposite breast. He recognised the clothing; he was sure it was the clothing Trimble's sister was wearing in the photo in the War Tunnels. He carefully picked up the items, thinking he'd drop in to the War Tunnels later and check out the photo again.

It was as if Nettles could read his mind. 'Those clothes, all the women wore beige, no way of telling if it belonged to the sister.'

'Yes, but worth taking to the museum.'

Back outside in the sunshine, John offered to drive them into St Helier, and they followed the coastal road until they reached a pub for a pint.

'So, what do you reckon the hole in the ground is?' Jasper asked after they'd ordered and taken their drinks to a table by the window that looked out over the bay.

Jasper took a sip of his beer.

Nettles looked at him. 'How much do you know about the different torture methods used by the Nazis?' He wiped froth from his upper lip.

'Not much, I'm not a sadist.' He let out a mirthless laugh.

'They took inspiration from a time centuries ago. Some were executed at the camps, usually with a large audience to serve as a warning to others. Block 11 at Auschwitz was where some of the most horrific punishments and extreme torture took place. There were many different devices and methods used to extract information. They were incredibly brutal causing immense pain. The guards made their lives a misery. But never in a million years did I imagine that level of cruelty on these islands.'

Nettles stared blankly into his beer.

'How do you mean?' Jasper was puzzled.

'I've always been told it was a benign occupation, but please excuse the expression.' He swept his hand over his face. 'The hole in the ground, it's one of the most horrific torture methods ever to be used.'

Jasper was incredulous. 'But it was just a hole.'

Nettles pursed his lips, a serious expression sweeping across his face. 'I wish it was just a hole.' He made a sharp intake of breath before continuing. 'It's a small cellar, or dungeon called an oubliette. Imagine being stuck in a chimney chute, that's how it was. You could touch the walls on either side with your elbows, it was so small the prisoner couldn't crouch or move, you were just locked in one position and forgotten about. You just waited for the end and hoped it would be sooner rather than later. It was literally like rotting in hell. Just for the fun of it, the officers would urinate on you from above. They might even spear you to attract the rodents. The rats would eventually come for you and without being able to move, how could you bat them away? They'd cut chunks from you. A variation of these chambers was found inside Auschwitz, in block 11. One man was so desperate, he ate his own shoes. If you were lucky, you were taken out, given a meal, then locked up again, or you were just left to starve.'

Jasper's mouth had fallen open. He was horrified. 'But if that's where the sister ended up, surely her bones would be there too.'

'That's the mystery, we'll probably never find out the truth of what happened.'

'And the first room, at the bottom of the steps as we came down into the cellar. What did you make of that?'

Nettles was thoughtful for a few moments as he stared out of the window. He sniffed, turned back to Jasper. 'I looked at the markings on the floor and ceiling. It indicates there might have been a Boger Swing there.'

'What the hell is that?' Nettles really seemed to know his stuff, but Jasper found it all a bit macabre.

'It's an iron bar suspended by chains and hung from the ceiling. The prisoner would be brought in for questioning, stripped naked and beaten. The beating would continue until only a mass of bleeding pulp hung before their eyes.'

'Trimble talked about bloodcurdling screams coming up from the cellar. How terrible it must have been, bad enough the Nazis taking over his home, but turning it into a hammer house of horrors.'

'You can find an example of an oubliette at Warwick Castle if you're interested.'

Jasper laughed and waved him away. 'I don't think I'll be turning this into a hobby, but I will head over to the War Tunnels this afternoon and see what I can find out. Do you fancy coming with me?'

No, I'm sorry, I'm meeting with my agent, there's potentially a new project based here on Jersey, but I can't say any more.' He gave a wink.

'Okay, I'll go over there and let you know how I get on.'

'This morning has been interesting, it's given me one or two thoughts, but I can't say any more than that.' He made a clucking noise.

At the War Tunnels, Jasper went to the ticket office.

'Hello, Mr Cooper, the curator is expecting you, but he's tied up for the next twenty minutes. He'll join you when he can, but please have a look around while you wait.'

Jasper wandered off and headed straight to the photo gallery. After locating the photo he was most interested in, he pulled out his magnifying glass and had a closer look at Trimble's sister. He needed to be sure. He wanted to check his hunch. Nettles had said there were many jumpers like it. He squinted and peered closely, focussing in on the jumper.

'Oh my God, I was right, it's the one.'

Just then a voice came from behind him. 'What have you discovered?' It was the curator. 'That was taken when several notable German officers visited the islands.'

'I was just checking the detail to see if the clothing matched some clothing I've found at the house, and it does.'

'Interesting.' He put his finger on the glass. 'This chap, the embodiment of pure evil. Dr Mengele.'

A chill ran down his spine. The thought of Dr Mengele at Bonaparte House, it was shocking beyond words.

'But this chap, Otto Ambros.' The curator lightly tapped the glass protecting the photo. 'He's less well known. He was a Nazi chemist. He's known for his wartime work on nerve agents like sarin.'

'Not heard of him.' Jasper scratched his head. 'What happened to him?'

'He was put on trial and served time but was released early in 1951 for good behaviour.'

'How shocking. That's no time. And after that, do you know where he ended up?'

'He went on to work for a German company, Chemie Grunenthal. The company was the first to introduce penicillin into the German market.'

A sickening shiver swept over him. Penicillin wasn't the only drug the company were known for.

'What's up?' the curator asked. 'You've turned as white as a sheet.'

He looked at the curator. 'You do realise they also developed thalidomide?'

CHAPTER 30: JASPER

As soon as Jasper returned from Jersey, Toby was on the phone asking about the trip. The lad's curiosity was admirable, but Jasper wasn't sure how much to reveal. He was young and impressionable, and he didn't want to give him nightmares, but at the same time he knew he'd keep the questions coming. And the simple fact was, these horrors were a part of history, a subject that Toby was passionate about. On a whim, he found himself blurting it out, the cellar was in effect a torture chamber.

'Bloody hell, I wasn't expecting that.'

'It was all a bit chilling, but nice to go back to Jersey.' He tried to sound bright, he didn't want to dwell on it. 'It's such a lovely island. Anyway, enough of me, how are you?' he asked. 'Have you decided what you're going to do yet?'

There was a heavy sigh, the sigh of defeat, as if he were battle weary rather than someone raring to take on the world.

'Go back to college and resit the exam, and I thought I'd take an extra A level in politics. I've no idea yet who my scribe will be, I wish Mandy was staying on.' There was hesitation in his voice and Jasper knew he found the uncertainty daunting, which was perfectly understandable.

'You don't sound convinced.'

'It's not that so much. Sometimes I just feel life is hopeless, no matter what effort I put in, I'll face endless knockbacks.'

'Don't get disheartened.'

'With my handicap, it just seems like it's going to be impossible to find a job. There's so much stacked against me.'

Jasper's heart went out to him. He wanted to encourage him to stay positive, but having interviewed several of the older thalidomiders, he knew the challenges they faced. One young chap had been turned away by an employer with the harsh words, "we're running a business here, not a kindergarten and in my opinion your deformed hands will slow you down, I need fast workers." And the endless disappointment they commonly faced, applying for countless jobs, and getting nowhere. And even when they did find work, there was the challenge of transport to and from the workplace. Trains and buses weren't accessible to wheelchairs. To take a train, they had to ring up and book for a guard to be on the platform to put out a ramp and often it didn't happen. Taking a train wasn't a pleasant experience and people in wheelchairs travelled in the guard's compartment, penned in between bicycles and Royal Mail sacks. There weren't always passenger lifts at stations and so wheelchair users had to go in the goods lift that had horrible metal caged doors, and zip along a waterlogged, dirty underpass to the opposite platform. And it was next to near impossible to travel around London with only a few underground stations having lifts and accessibility.

ON THE SUNNY morning of the August bank holiday, Sandy expressed her disappointment that Jasper had to work instead of enjoying the nice weather after days of rain. But he was due in the office, he often had to work unsociable hours, and most of the time she accepted it without fuss.

Jasper loved his work, and it didn't bother him that he was missing a sunny bank holiday. He had a buzz about him as he arrived back in Fleet Street. After grabbing a coffee from the machine, he spent most of the day holed up in his office and then when Sam appeared late morning, he headed briskly into his office for the weekly briefing.

Sam glanced up as he rounded the corner and pushed through the glass door.

'Jasper, good to see you. Nice weekend? What are you looking so chuffed about? You've got a spring in your step today.'

He plonked his briefcase on the floor and sat down. 'It's my lad, Toby, he's won the short story competition. You should have seen him standing there in front of everyone, tall and proud and pleased as punch. I couldn't believe all the publicity, I thought it was going to be a low-key event. They had Fay Weldon presenting the prize, and the local press and regional TV were there.'

'That's wonderful, good for him. What did he write about?'

'It was a story set in Jersey, inspired by our holiday. It's going to be published in a collection of short stories of the winners across the South-East.'

'He's a chip off the old block then. Perhaps he'll become a writer too.' He laughed. 'He could be your PA.'

'He'd have to learn to write faster.'

'Has the boy decided what he's going to do yet?'

'He's got an A level to resit then I guess he'll be looking for work or going on to university, but it won't be easy.'

'Seriously though, has he ever thought about following in your footsteps?'

'I know he loves his public speaking.'

Sam lit a cigarette. 'I've never met the lad, but I'm impressed.

How would you like to bring him in? Maybe I could think about taking him on as an apprentice.'

'That's a bit cheeky.'

'It's not what you know, it's who you know.' He gave a great bellowing laugh. 'Got to pull a few strings to get on in this life.' He paused. 'Leave it with me.'

Jasper wasn't expecting this and was taken aback.

'I'll have a look at his story and let you know what I think, I can't promise anything, mind.'

'You serious, mate?'

'Of course I am, you know I'm always happy to support the underdog, could even be a story in it for us, armless boy does good.'

They both chuckled.

Sam took a deep drag of his fag, and looked thoughtful. 'Maybe he would be interested in looking at stories that we wouldn't normally cover, be interesting to get a young person's perspective rather than old fogies like us. Breathe some new life into these old walls. We've all got to start somewhere. But as you say, the lad's still young and inexperienced.' He swivelled his chair. 'Anyway, food for thought, how's your Jersey story coming on?'

'To be honest, Sam, I'm struggling. I gave old Trimble my word but revisiting the place, seeing what was down in that cellar, it's knocked me for six.'

'How do you mean?'

'It was incredibly upsetting; we discovered a torture chamber.'

Sam's eyes looked like they were on stalks. 'Really? Readers love hearing about gruesome stuff. I'm sure you can whip up something, excuse the pun.' He laughed but Jasper didn't find it funny.

'There are plenty of other stories to cover, if you'd rather leave it for now.'

They went on to discuss the main newsworthy topics that required coverage which included rising unemployment.

Just then, the trill of the phone from Sam's desk rang out like an ambulance siren. Jasper watched as Sam answered it, his podgy fingers wrapping around the handset.

As the caller spoke, Sam stared at Jasper, his expression turning to stone, his eyes wide. 'Holy Jesus.' He swivelled his chair round to face the window and ran his other hand over his head. Several moments later, he came off the phone and turned to face Jasper with a grim look on his face.

'Forget Jersey, you're going to be very busy.' He took a deep breath, wiped his brow, and said, 'That was Jim at Reuters. Lord Mountbatten's been killed by a bomb blast.'

Jasper was speechless. *Monty.*

'Bloody IRA. Apparently, minutes after his boat set sail off from the Irish coast with family and friends, a planted bomb detonated. Fifty pounds of gelignite exploded. Jim said the boat was there one minute, and the next it was like a pile of matchsticks floating on the water.'

Jasper's hands flew to his mouth in horror. 'The Queen will be devastated. Maybe he was an easy target.'

Later that day, he went home in a sombre mood and had only just walked through the door and kissed Sandy, when the phone rang. It was Sam sounding even more downcast. 'More news is just in; eighteen British soldiers have been killed near the Irish border at Warrenpoint. Today will mark the heaviest death toll for the British army in ten years.'

'Bloody hell, I'll be onto it first thing tomorrow.'

'No, Jasper, time's of the essence, I've booked you on the last flight to Shannon this evening. A taxi will pick you up in forty minutes and Liam, our Irish correspondent, will meet you at the airport.'

'Oh, bloody hell, better get my skates on.'

As Jasper packed his bags, he was concerned with all this

news about IRA atrocities. He wouldn't be around much for Toby's start back at college, but the lad seemed very keen to begin politics A level and he'd even mentioned something about joining one of the political parties with his mate Dave. Jasper had taken on the role of union rep a few years back and had served for a year. He'd drummed into Toby the importance of workers' rights and fighting against injustice. He could just see him getting involved with the Young Socialists, protesting against Tory plans and the inevitable cuts that would come with a government more interested in the business classes than the struggling poor. He'd be a proud father. But he couldn't imagine they'd be much of a group though, not here in Tory Guildford among the Surrey elite and city slickers.

When all this IRA stuff was out the way, he'd look forward to hearing Toby's news.

Over the next few days, he was swamped with work, so he floated an idea to Sandy.

'How about you take Toby to Guildford? Treat him to lunch out and some new bits of clothing, college will be starting back soon.'

CHAPTER 31: SANDY

Life with a three-year-old was hectic and relentless. Like all mums of young kiddies, Sandy had grown eyes in the back of her head along with an extra pair of ears. Amidst the chaos of mashing Weetabix, chasing Angela around the park, and making endless Marmite butties, she spent a lot of time thinking back to Toby's birth and the relationship they now had, trying to figure out what she could and should do to make his life and their relationship a better one. So much was outside of her control, she could only guide and suggest. She wanted him to have the opportunities in life that Angela would have or the prospects and options open to any young person, but she knew this wasn't likely and that life would always be a mountain of challenges to climb.

When she reflected, it was always with sadness, a veil of hopelessness hanging heavy. There was one particular day recently that stuck out in her mind. She'd taken Toby on a drive into the countryside for a walk. They were heading for the Surrey heathland, a wide open space that graced the fringes of Guildford. He sat in the passenger seat, his small battered canvas satchel resting on his lap. He wore a black t-shirt that must have been through the washing machine a gazillion times, and his beloved Man UTD track suit bottoms, despite the fact he'd outgrown them. Sandy thought it was quite sweet and endearing the way he kicked about in the same sloppy loafers and t-shirts, but she longed to take him under her wing, update his wardrobe with a few fashionable items even if it meant paying for alterations if she couldn't tackle this herself. They chatted as they always did, covering topics as varied as the merits of the Sherbet Dip Dab versus Parma Violets and which was his favourite *Dr Who* episode and why. She'd asked him quite casually what he wanted to do after college and university. He stared out of the window a little nonplussed, a different reaction to the one she imagined he'd give had Jasper asked. She'd thrown in a few suggestions, building on previous conversations she knew he'd had with Jasper, hoping to encourage a few ideas and pave the way for the life that awaited him, even though her heart was troubled by the difficulties she saw ahead.

'You could be a public speaker, a reporter, a teacher.' These weren't new suggestions.

He'd stayed silent for a while and stared out of the car window as they tootled along, until eventually he'd turned to her and said, 'I think, I'd like to cut people's lawns, but who would employ me as a gardener?'

She'd laughed loudly then turned to frown at him.

'Really, Toby? You're bright and capable, you've got a brilliant future ahead of you if you want it. There are a ton of jobs out there, jobs you've never even heard of yet.' She tried to sound upbeat, but inside she was crumbling. When Angela was at nursery school, she helped at St Bede's reading to the students and helping to interview new members of staff. A few teachers stayed in contact with the thalidomide families, keeping up to date with their news in cards and letters on special occasions like Christmas and birthdays. One young man had applied for over a hundred jobs and hadn't been invited for a single interview. Another young woman worked in a part of a factory in West London, a special section designated for disabled workers on the production line, but the pay for these employees was minimal. A limbless woman with full faculties was living in a small residential unit in Newhaven and she had to share a bedroom with a ninety-year-old lady.

Sandy was a little perplexed and disappointed by Toby's response, but she guessed he didn't want to talk about it with her, which she found hurtful. She was trying to live his future in her head and that wasn't a good thing.

'Because gardeners always look so happy,' he'd replied.

She thought it was a funny answer to begin with, but it was only when she glanced at him as they swung into the gravel car park on the heath and pulled up that he stared back at her with an expression of such sadness that she wanted to weep, realising in that moment that he was striving for something far more elusive than a career in quantum physics.

Happiness.

Like trying to catch a butterfly.

With happiness, everything fell into place and nothing else really mattered. And it was in that moment that Sandy wanted so much for him to just be happy and not to worry too much about the future. She didn't know what motherhood to a disabled boy was supposed to be about, who did? Not to mention all the missing years that lay between them like a vast wilderness. It was the difference between reading about breaking an arm and actually breaking it. You could learn about the experiences of others, the terrible pain, entering another realm entirely, but you had to break your arm to feel that pain. She didn't really know his strengths and weaknesses; she hadn't been around to see him grow up.

Motherhood was like that.

Most mothers developed that bond from the outset, that

need to protect and nurture that child at every cost and that was how it was with Angela. She would have died protecting Angela stopping any harm that came her way and even though babyhood and toddlerhood were hard, there was something natural about the process. Every day flowed into the next. But it wasn't like that with Toby. There was this invisible barrier. The mothering process was stilted as if she were taking a journey over a rocky terrain watching each step to avoid the hot coals, navigating the jagged pieces that might cut her feet. The constant analysis in her head, the turmoil, the confusion, was she saying the right thing, doing the right thing, being who he wanted her to be? She was trying to fill the void but didn't know how to. The missing years could never be recovered no matter how hard she tried. Toby had already had another life of which she knew nothing, and of which she hadn't been a part of. And in the same way, he knew nothing of her life.

Day by day over an unknown period of time, her emotions were chipped away, subtly enough for her not to notice. She didn't know how she felt about Toby, warmth one minute, a rush of love another but mainly the feelings were deadened by a cold blanket of numbness. And so, when Jasper suggested she take him into Guildford to treat him to new clothes for college, the idea excited her, it was an opportunity to play a motherly role and even better that Toby had liked the idea. But it also filled her with dread. How would she cope?

Emotions aside, there were the practicalities. Finding someone to look after Angela, but that hadn't been difficult, the neighbour stepped in and offered.

Just as Toby arrived at the house, the phone rang, the neighbour informing Sandy she felt unwell and couldn't have Angela. After the call, Sandy turned to open the front door. This was a major blow to the afternoon, and she realised then how much she'd been looking forward to Toby's company without Angela there.

'I'm sorry, Toby, the neighbour can no longer have Angela, we can either leave it till another time or if you don't mind her coming too. We'll have to stop off at the park though, she doesn't really like being dragged round the shops.'

'I don't mind,' he said flatly, kicking the gravel. 'She can come too.' Sandy couldn't work out if he was pretending not to mind but when Angela ran out to greet him and he reached down in an awkward posture to tickle her, he looked relaxed and happy enough.

Sandy was disappointed when Toby clambered into the back of the car, she had hoped to chat to him as they drove, but she now realised that Angela was going to be the focus of the day. It would be fun though to watch the pair of them enjoy themselves. Toby was good with Angela, patient, and loved to tease her and she rose to it. Things could get out of control though when she started to wallop him. He'd duck to get out of her firing line, then he'd gently nudge her with his feet but the nudge usually turned into an innocent tickle.

'Now, Toby, today is a treat, I don't want you looking at prices, I know what you're like. You've been after a leather jacket for a while, well that's what you're going to have, and you jolly well deserve it, you've worked very hard these past two years. And I think a pair of flared jeans, that's what everyone wears these days and some new t-shirts.' When he stayed silent, she glanced at him in the mirror, sensing his discomfort as realisation struck that she was treating him like a six-year-old. It was awful to think it, but maybe he had accepted her invitation out of politeness, duty, wanting to keep her sweet. Did he even think about the growing mother-son bond between them, or was she just another adult in his life, an annoyance and inconvenience?

'That's very nice of you, but you don't have to.' When he was polite like this, it made her feel uncomfortable, as if he was treating her like a distant relative or acquaintance. He shouldn't have to thank her.

'I get an allowance from the Thalidomide Trust.'

Toby had been assessed at Roehampton for eligibility for funding. This involved a physical examination and proof, usually from a mother's medical records, that thalidomide had been taken. Toby had told her the examination had been degrading which hadn't surprised her because she'd heard stories of young victims being photographed half-naked and interrogated and tested to assess their physical capacity and perform certain tasks. Following these assessments children were separated into two categories. If you were on the X list you were confirmed to have thalidomide-related impairments, but because Bill couldn't produce evidence that Distaval had been prescribed, Toby's diagnosis was more uncertain and so his compensation was reduced, and he'd been placed on the 'Y' list. But at least this was progress because for years Bill wouldn't take him for assessment because of the circumstances of his birth. Sandy, Jasper, and Bill had agreed it was best that Bill didn't come forward and admit to the authorities that he and his wife Rona had stolen Toby from the hospital. The consequences would be devastating for everyone. They agreed to keep it between themselves rather than upset a large apple cart. Toby was getting some compensation and he had three loving parents. It was easy to count money, but not so easy to count or purchase love.

'I'd love a leather jacket, call it an early Christmas present, but I can't wear jeans, they're too tricky to put on and I can't do zips and buttons very easily.'

Sandy came to a halt as the traffic lights went red and she changed gear, her cheeks flushing with embarrassment. Why hadn't she thought of this? She couldn't recall ever seeing him in trousers with zips. She'd never wanted to pry too much on personal questions just enough to show she cared rather than be nosy.

'Sometimes trousers have a long tag attached to the zip that I can hook my toe around, but the buttons on denims can be stiff. Jogging bottoms are so easy. And some of these flares, they are so wide, they'd get in my way.'

Sandy tried to imagine how it would be for him. When she thought about it, flares would probably be a nuisance every time he picked up a pen. It would be a bit like her wearing floaty sleeves, they weren't practical.

'You've set me a challenge, Toby, to find the ideal trousers.'

Toby laughed. 'Good luck with that one, I've not managed it yet.' He gave a mirthless laugh. 'And then when you've achieved that, find the perfect top.'

'What's wrong with t-shirts?'

'There are all sorts of problems. I look for material that's quick-drying because I'm always getting wet, leaning right into basins and sinks to turn on taps to brush my teeth or do the dishes. Most of the time I take my top off to do the washing up.'

'Your dad should be doing that,' she said, shocked.

'I'm not a complete invalid, he works hard, can't have him doing everything around the house.'

Aside from the sulks she'd heard about, Toby was the model teen. He helped around the house.

Angela joined in the conversation and started chattering about how she could now dress herself, and soon they arrived in Guildford, parked up and headed for Topman and Burton's.

Sandy was about to find out just how difficult things were for Toby.

As they browsed from shop to shop, Angela settled for now in her buggy happily looking around and not making a fuss, Sandy noticed the staff weren't approaching Toby. It was as if he was invisible, but they didn't hesitate to ask if she needed help. She wasn't the one trying on clothes and he wasn't a baby. They ignored him as he rifled through racks of shirts, nudging each coat hanger across the rails with his tongue or his head. The assistants stood on the periphery with taut faces, quietly observing though trying not to make it obvious. She expected them to pounce the minute a garment fell to the floor, but Toby was careful and that never happened.

Bustling over to Sandy, one assistant asked, 'Madam, may I help?' Toby had spent a while searching the racks and had found nothing.

Toby spun round and in a loud voice said, 'I may be armless, but I'm not armed.' He let out a joyless chuckle.

'Of course not, sir, how may I help?' The assistant looked uncomfortable, but Toby stood his ground and Sandy was proud of the way he was asserting himself.

He explained the difficulties he faced. 'Every shop I go in, it's the same problem. I either see a shirt I love, but the sleeves are all wrong or the material isn't quick-drying or there are too many buttons, but the buttons aren't so much a problem because if I buy large shirts, I can get my dad to button up after they're washed ready for me to just slip them over my head. Or I find the perfect sleeves, but I don't like the shirt.'

'I can see why you don't have many clothes, I bet you stick to your favourites,' Sandy said. She thought it was hard enough shopping for herself, finding dresses that swept over her mummy belly and bottom without making them look fat and recently she didn't like her knees, they seemed baggier. She now sought longer dresses and skirts that fell just below the knee. She really couldn't imagine the nightmare that faced Toby.

When Toby turned his back and wandered to a nearby rail, the assistant leaned towards her and in a hushed voice asked, 'Is he one of those cripples affected by thalidomide? I bet you feel really guilty, taking that drug, terrible business.'

Toby turned sharply and looked straight at the assistant with a wry smile. 'Just as well it didn't affect my vocal chords, or my hearing. They're as sharp as a pin.'

The assistant didn't apologise but scuttled away muttering that he would be around if they needed help.

Sandy didn't think Toby would be interested in browsing the department store because it wasn't always the height of fashion for the young, but he keenly suggested it as they passed. Before looking at the clothes, they went up to the toy department and Angela was allowed out of her pushchair to wander around. As she eyed a teddy, then a spinning top, Sandy braced herself for the little girl's demands, but Angela was very good, she didn't whinge for anything. Another little girl came running over to join her and they took the spinning top off the shelf to play with it on the floor. The assistant looked over and smiled and Toby knelt down to watch them play.

'That's fun, Angela.' And in that moment Sandy suddenly felt sad as she thought of his missed childhood and wondered what sort of toys he'd played with.

'Were you able to spin a top, using your feet?' she asked.

Barely having the chance to answer her, the other little girl glanced up and noticed Toby's arms. Now that she'd spotted them, she was no longer interested in the spinning top but stood staring at Toby, her arms folded, her head cocked to one side, and a frown on her face that bordered a scowl.

'It's okay, little girl, I don't bite.'

She got up and turned in a hurry, dashed back to her mother, burying her face in her mother's skirt and let out a howl.

Sandy tutted. 'Take no notice, Toby,' she whispered.

'It's okay,' Toby said wearily, getting to his feet. 'Don't worry, I'm used to it. Shall we have a look at the clothing now?'

All that Toby endured day to day, the struggles he faced, brought a wave of sadness made worse when they headed for the stairs as they passed the little girl who was now peeping out from behind her mother's skirt as if to check the scary spider she'd just seen had scuttled away.

Toby seemed to quickly forget what had just happened; it was a regular event for him, he took it in his stride and his attention was now drawn to a black leather jacket on a plinth. It had a row of metal studs running either side of the zip and the collar had groovy tassels. Sandy clocked the expression on his face; he loved it but didn't dare ask to try it on.

'That's quite something isn't it?' Gazing up, he had a look of wonder on his face as if it was a museum piece.

'I'll call the assistant over, you can try it on.'

'But the sleeves would have to be altered and that would ruin it.'

'Nonsense, Toby,' she said, tutting as she turned to find the assistant who was already heading towards them.

Toby tried the jacket on, flapping the empty arms to amuse Angela who sat in her pushchair giggling. There were tassels running down the sleeves and as they flapped, Toby looked as if he was flagging down an aircraft. He twirled and bowed, and Angela reached out, her chubby hands grabbing the tassels.

'Do you fancy the punk look?' Sandy asked with a smile. 'It suits you.'

'I love it.'

'We can alter it for you,' the assistant said.

They went over to the desk where the assistant took out a table of prices in a folder, peered over his glasses and quoted a ridiculous price for alterations that amounted to half the price of the jacket. Sandy gasped. Toby shook his head and looked disappointed.

'We'll take it, I'm sure we can find someone to alter it,' Sandy said.

'Our seamstresses are very experienced, be careful, leather isn't easy to work with, you don't want to ruin it, it's a lovely jacket.' He hesitated and frowned. 'Shame really to chop off the sleeves, bit of a waste.'

Annoyed, Sandy arranged her face into what she hoped passed for a smile and forced herself to stay quiet as she took out her cheque book. Sometimes staying silent was the right thing to do and when she glanced at Toby, she could see the daily struggle of his life visible on his face.

'What choice do I have?' Toby asked him boldly. He gave a bright smile, but the assistant offered only a curt nod in response as he opened the till with a heavy hand, and Sandy had the sense that they were being scolded. She couldn't wait to leave the store.

On their way to the park, they bought a couple of baggy, loose shirts in another shop, the type that Toby felt most comfortable wearing.

In the park, Sandy took out a bag of crusts for Angela to feed the ducks and they stood at the waterside as a gaggle of mallards swam to the riverbank and waddled towards them, fighting for crumbs. Angela threw chunks and Toby, determined to join in, reached into the bag with his foot clasping a piece between two toes and swinging his foot in the direction of a large swan.

They wandered towards the play park, and Angela ran off to join a few little children as they climbed the ladder to the slide. Toby and Sandy sat on a bench and watched as Angela engaged with the other children, playing happily. A while later she pointed to Toby and shouted, 'that's my mum and big brother.' The children looked over at Toby with lingering gazes–could they have seen his arms at that distance? They all ran over and ignoring Sandy came to a halt in front of Toby, some with frowning, quizzical faces, others just stared.

'Where are your arms?' one of them asked.

Toby sprang up and launched himself at the gaggle of children, wiggling his fingers at them. 'A lion attacked me and gobbled my arms, but he left me with special powers to eat up children and now I'm coming to get you,' he shouted as the kids shrieked and dispersed in all directions. After that, Toby wasn't allowed to return to the bench and soon all the children in the park either followed him around as if he were the Pied Piper or asked him to chase them. Sandy watched in amusement with mixed emotions of happiness and sadness. It had been an interesting afternoon, not quite what she'd expected, but it had opened her eyes to the difficulties he faced. She would look forward to a proper catch-up with him, without Angela around. Lunch sometime after his writing course would be a good suggestion. It would be good to see how the course went.

CHAPTER 32: TOBY

Toby wasn't feeling confident enough to drive up to Welwyn Garden City alone. The journey involved negotiating a couple of motorways and Central London, but Bill came up with a plan. Toby would drive to boost his confidence and Bill would accompany him, leave the car there and return to Haslemere by train. At the end of the course, he'd take the train back up, and they'd drive back together. It was a bit of a faff, Toby thought. He didn't really want Bill to go to all that effort, he felt bad about it, but hoped to soon have sufficient confidence and experience to go to places alone.

Neither had been to a garden city before and arriving in the central area, they gazed in wonder at how unique and idyllic, twee, and perfectly symmetrical it was with its identical streets and architecture, neat walkways with perfectly manicured lawns and bursting flowerbeds. This was a town that had been carefully planned at the drawing board by visionary architects, a picture postcard world where nothing bad happened. It was utopian, flawless, almost like paradise, except for the fact that this was rainy England where the skies were perpetually grey. It made him think of one of his favourite movies, *The Stepford Wives*, where the women were robotic, and everybody lived in perfect harmony. They parked the car and looked up at the building where the course was to be held. His imagination ran wild as he pondered a darker side to this town. Was there more than met the eye beneath the neat paving, stone statues and pride that seemed to ooze from every street corner? Ever since the discovery of the past at Bonaparte House, he eyed every unique building with suspicion.

Bill carried Toby's bags up a set of stone steps, and they headed up more stairs to the first floor of the building.

'The course wouldn't be much good for people in wheelchairs. Steps outsides and no lift.'

'Yeah, but stop your grumbling, you're here, that's all I'm interested in.'

That was hardly the point, Toby thought, and very selfish. He didn't want to be privileged. Courses like this should be open to all.

On the first floor they pushed through a set of double doors and into a long echoey corridor filling with people making polite chit-chat as they queued at different tables. One of the organisers stepped forward and with a bright smile introduced herself.

'Hi, I'm Audrey and I'll be running one of the courses over these three days. You must be Toby, have you had far to come?'

'Surrey.' Bill dropped Toby's bags onto the floor as if they were weighing his shoulders down and Audrey immediately went to pick them up. She hurried off to a private room to lock them away, telling Toby that they would be labelled and taken to his bedroom later.

He had no idea what to expect from the course, there weren't any briefing notes ahead of the day. Toby found this exciting, he liked surprises. After Bill left, he queued at one of the tables and when it was his turn to be served, he was asked to select three workshops from a list: romance, horror, science fiction, memoir writing, scriptwriting and screenplay, as well as newspaper reporting. There would be an introductory morning of icebreakers and exercises, which, in the words of one of the organisers, would "whet the creative juices".

Toby didn't normally read science fiction but because of his earlier thoughts when he'd got out of the car and looked around, he decided to choose that course. The germ of an idea for a story set in Welwyn Garden City was forming in his mind. He pondered the other choices and decided to select newspaper reporting and scriptwriting because they were the most career orientated. These would look good on his CV and interested him the most. He didn't like soap operas, *Crossroads* being the worst, but appreciated the work that went into writing the dialogue and creating characters. He imagined it was a bit like being on stage in a play or theatre production. Those that took part had far more fun than those who were in the audience. He was also curious to find out how these soap operas were made. Even though he loathed them, soaps like *Coronation Street* were hugely popular.

After coffee and biscuits and a chance to mingle with the other attendees aged between sixteen and twenty-four and from across the country, they dispersed in different directions along the corridor. When Toby looked lost, Audrey came rushing over to guide him to where he needed to be. There were six others in the icebreaker session, and they were asked to pair up and introduce each other and include a fun story.

Toby found the stories hilarious, and his story was about his trip to Jersey and the old lady who mistook the prosthetics sticking out of the sand for real limbs. She ran to the lifeguard in a panic fearing there was a person buried in the sand. Toby loved the opportunity to stand up and give a short unplanned talk and already felt he would enjoy the week. He also loved taking questions because it gave him the chance to express himself.

When the introductions were over there were a few short exercises to get everybody chatting, thinking, and sharing thoughts. The first exercise involved thinking about their hands. Everyone's hand was described in detail, callouses were shown to the group, it was observed the ladies had soft skin, some had bitten their nails, another told the group how he'd sucked his thumb in bed until he was ten. And then it came to Toby's turn. He stood up and waggled his hands.

'These are the hands that God gave me, they're like crab's pinchers on my shoulders and not very effective, in fact not much bloody use at all.'

They all peered at his shoulders as he spoke.

He removed his right foot from his slip-on shoe and waggled it at the group. 'My feet are my hands, and my right foot can feed me, allow me to write, paint and open doors. It helps me get dressed and does most things. It's easier not to wear shoes at all, and if I don't need to I don't, after all, you wouldn't want the inconvenience of wearing gloves all the time. That's why the skin on my feet is as tough as rhino skin. They're workhorses. I have a small scar from when I stepped on glass and a bump on the side that I hope isn't a bunion.'

There were a few faces gazing at him in wonder.

Before they moved into their chosen workshops, they were asked to write a couple of paragraphs about one of the objects on the top table. There was a range to choose from including a carriage clock, a peach, a vase, a book, a candlestick. They could write whatever they liked. It was a simple exercise, but Toby found it stretched his imagination and he was amazed at what he found to write about a silver candlestick. He wondered about including the candlestick in the science fiction story set in Welwyn Garden City.

Toby loved all the workshops. He was fascinated to learn

how about scriptwriting for soaps. The fast-paced nature of soaps meant that scripts were produced quickly, the aim to keep viewers hooked with dramatic twists and cliff-hangers. Working in pairs they created their own engaging storyline for one of the characters on *Coronation Street*. Toby was glad his partner was an avid viewer as he hadn't a clue who the characters were, but by the end of the session, he knew all about the shenanigans of Jack and Vera Duckworth's turbulent marriage. He loved the idea of working as a team, it was more fun than being in the classroom at college. He and Mandy had been the only students to collaborate, but that had been out of necessity, to assist him. But he was left wondering how he would be able to cope in a fast-paced environment. Because of his impairment he was slower than others, needed space around him and that space might need to be arranged in a different way.

The news reporting workshop was intriguing too, and he couldn't wait to get back to share his experience with Jasper. The workshop began with a discussion on newspapers. They sat in a circle and the tutor asked questions about the various newspapers seen on display in the average corner shop. They were encouraged to consider the political biases, story preferences and target audiences of these publications. Because of Jasper, Toby knew far more about the newspaper industry than the others and he described *The Guardian* as left-leaning and *The Times* as right-leaning. The second half of the day delved into the heart of the newspaper and they were asked to think of their own scoop, based on either fact or fiction and when they'd written them, they shared with the group.

On the final evening, before they all went out for drinks, Toby rang Bill from the phone in the corridor with Audrey's help, to tell him not to worry about getting the train up, he'd drive himself home.

'No, you're not doing that.' Bill was adamant.

'Dad, I need the experience, I'll be fine.'

'You can't come back on your own this time, I've got a surprise; we're popping in somewhere on our way home. I'll be up around midday.'

Toby was intrigued and couldn't think where they were going, but the pips started, and he wasn't given the chance to protest further.

CHAPTER 33: TOBY

The next morning, the group posed on the steps of the building for a photograph, everyone beaming proudly with their certificates held high. Toby clutched his certificate under his chin, and laughed because it was a struggle to look up. At times, and this was one of them, he relished his uniqueness. In the past he'd been bullied for being different, now he could use it to his advantage. He often brought laughter to those around him. It was a great way to engage in conversation. It crossed his mind how different his life might have been with arms. Would anyone have shown an interest in him or would he have paled into insignificance? He smiled to himself because today he felt energised ready to take on the world and he realised there were benefits to being how he was. People were already interested in him even though it seemed in a negative way. He'd grown used to the stares of incredulity when he used his foot to feed himself. It probably put them off their food and if he had the power to do that, it tickled his sense of devilishness and now he played up to it.

I am as I am. I'm proud of me.

He realised he was developing a thick skin and a dry sense of humour.

He spotted Bill with a big grin on his face. 'Hiya, son, have you had a good time?'

'I've had an amazing time and we've exchanged addresses, but they'll be writing ten letters to my one.' He laughed. 'I'll put it all in a Christmas card.'

Toby and Bill headed over to the car and the group followed to have a look. He suddenly felt a sense of importance and pride, like a celebrity. His car was unique. He took great delight in being the centre of attention.

'Blimey, it's got no steering wheel,' one of them said.

'Love the colour, Toby.'

'What a groovy little car, just look at those controls.'

'And he's got furry dice,' someone else said with a laugh.

Once they'd all had a good look around, Toby started the car, and they headed off.

'Where are we going then?'

'You drive, leave the navigation to me.'

They headed down the Great North Road towards Potters Bar and eventually turned off into a leafy suburb, along a road called Hillside Gardens. Bill told him to take the next left. He saw the road sign half obscured by a hedge and immediately recognised the name.

'Wow, are we going to see Sue?' Toby said excitedly. 'I can finally see where she lives and meet those hideous parents of hers.'

'I don't think I've ever met them at the school.'

'You better mind your p's and q's, Sue said they're very posh. Ah, but will they be expecting us?

'Ah yes, all arranged. I am capable of doing some things, son.'

Toby pulled up at a pair of twin gates. As they drove through, they were amazed at the house, it was nothing like how Sue had described it. There was a Bentley and a Porche on the drive and Sue's Mini.

'There's Sue's car,' Toby said.

'My God, I didn't know Sue could drive a Bentley.'

They both laughed.

'Ask her how she manages a Bentley, son.' Bill winked at him.

Toby parked up and they got out and headed to the door. A metal ramp was propped against the wall for Sue's wheelchair access. Toby glanced at Bill, suddenly embarrassed by his usual scruffy appearance, the thick morning stubble he hadn't bothered to shave, and his hairy paunch spilling over his trousers. His hair looked a mess as if he'd run his hands through it repeatedly which he probably had, a nervous habit. Looking uncomfortable, his hands were now shoved deep into his pockets. The door swung open on the first ring and Sue's dad stood there bathed in sunlight streaming in through a window behind him which illuminated the thinning hair on the top of his head. His eyebrows were like wild blackberry bushes and his nose, an eagle's beak was his most prominent feature. There was something stiff about his manner and Toby knew he wasn't going to like him. He had the kind of face that could darken into anger.

'Jeremy,' he said stiffly. He extended his hand for Bill to shake. 'And you must be Bill and Toby.' He pursed his lips and forced a vague smile that failed to reach his petrol blue eyes. There was nothing welcoming about him, and Toby couldn't decide if this was because he hadn't wanted them to call round or just his normal demeanour. cast a critical eye over them, appraising them warily as if they were door-to-door salesmen. Toby shuddered and in that moment, as they stepped into the house, he was grateful he had Bill and not this odious man for a father. He was relieved when Sue came whizzing into the hallway. At least she was pleased to see them. She was full of laughs and smiles.

'Hiya, Tobes, Mum's made tea and cakes.'

Toby heard the tinkle of crockery and then Sue's mum emerged from the kitchen wiping her hands on her apron before extending her hand to Bill and smiling at Toby.

'Pearl,' she said in a matter-of-fact tone. Toby stared at her, drinking in her features. There was something very manly about her, but he couldn't think what it was specifically. Maybe it was her large, calloused hands and broad shoulders. She stood tall and sturdy, had a commanding presence like timber in a yard. She wasn't at all feminine, had no grace or delicate ways about her as she led them into the lounge. Toby felt sad for Sue, growing up with such stiff and starchy parents, people who she couldn't have a cuddle with or open up to. He remembered all the things she'd told him, the way she'd been frozen out, treated as an irrelevance.

Sue's younger twin brother and sister, Paul and Wendy joined them in the lounge. Paul perched on the arm of the sofa next to his dad, and Wendy perched next to her mum on the other side. What a cosy little unit they were. A wave of sadness as well as irritation flashed over him. Even the twins looked like stuffed shirts sitting like statues guarding their parents. Toby wondered if they'd ever shared a laugh as a family.

They were only a year younger than Sue.

Replacement kids.

Or replacement statues.

Love appeared to have eluded this family, leaving behind a void where warmth and affection should have resided. He suddenly felt very fortunate, but sad for Sue.

Sue had been sent to St Bede's, cast aside while they got on with their lives, rejected as a defective part, she didn't belong here; it was plain as day as he observed the surroundings and the way they behaved towards her as well as the digs planted subtly into every conversation. It was the small things Toby noticed, from the disdainful way her mother eyed the tyre tracks of her wheelchair across the pink fluffy carpet to the praise lavished on the twins.

Pearl poured tea and handed Bill a cup.

'I can't think why I haven't met you before,' Bill said struggling to hold the delicate handle of the fine bone china teacup with his fat fingers. 'As caretaker at St Bede's, I knew most of the parents.' He gave up with the handle and grabbed the dainty cup instead. Toby cringed at his uncouthness and could feel everybody watching.

A silence descended. Jeremy looked at his wife and shrugged. Pearl shuffled awkwardly. 'We didn't visit often. It was too far.'

Toby wondered if Bill would probe further but he changed the subject. They both knew why their visits were sporadic. Their priorities didn't include Sue. Church and cricket matches came first.

'Caretaker,' Pearl said. 'Does that involve unblocking toilets all day?' She gave a derisory smirk.

Toby wanted to tell them what a responsible job his dad had, but what was the point? They were ignorant pigs.

'You lived in Chelmsford at the time. It's nice round here.' Bill's tone was bright as he glanced out of the window. 'What brought you to North London?'

'My office relocated.'

It was like extracting blood from a turnip. They weren't chatty folk.

'What is it you do?' Bill looked at Jeremy.

'Oh, nothing you'd understand.'

Toby was proud of Bill; he didn't seem at all fazed. 'Try me.'

'I'm a financial adviser.'

'I tried that years ago,' Bill said dismissively. 'It was a waste of time. Half the clients didn't have a pot to piss in.'

Toby cringed and stared at the flecks in the carpet.

'I guess I've just been very fortunate.' Toby hated Jeremy's snooty tone. 'You have to work hard to get anywhere in life.'

'And what are your plans?' Bill glanced from one twin to the other.

'We've got another year of A levels,' Paul said, looking bored.

'They're both bright. Must be a trait of being a twin, or all the private tuition I've paid for. I've no complaints. We're very lucky to have two outstanding kids. They're going to sit the Oxbridge entrance test when the time comes.'

'Sue's bright too,' Toby chirped, glancing across at Sue and feeling her dejection. 'She's done well in her business studies course.'

Pearl shrugged and looked at Jeremy.

'It's kept her busy and out of mischief I suppose,' he said without enthusiasm. 'Just as well her brain isn't crippled too.'

Toby caught the mortified look on Sue's face. Instead of retaliating, she spun her wheelchair around and glided through the door. 'Come on, Toby, I'll show you my car and the garden.'

Toby was relieved to be outside. The atmosphere in the lounge had been stifling.

'Have you been here for the whole summer?'

'Joking, aren't you? There's a block at college where we live in the holidays. We get all the support we need and it's as good as being independent. All our needs are taken care of. Besides, it's difficult here. Only reason I'm here now is so that Mum and Dad can put a tick in a box, their annual token gesture. I have to sleep on a camp bed in Dad's study and the bathroom is upstairs. It's a bit awkward but I can get upstairs. I lever myself up and Wendy helps sometimes. I miss her, don't miss Mum though.'

'They should use your Trust money for adaptions. With a big house like this, plenty of space surely to make an accessible shower room or bathroom.'

Sue was thoughtful. 'I'm not sure what they've spent the Trust money on.'

'Still no suggestion of you going on holiday with them?'

'No, I've given up asking, but hey,' she said brightly, 'have you heard, The Thalidomide Society is putting on a trip to Minorca next year?'

'Really?'

'You should get a letter in the post about it.'

'Brilliant, I'm game if you are.' A glorious feeling welled inside him and without thinking, he leant down and gave her a peck on the cheek. In their rush of excitement, the thought of more adventures ahead, she pulled him in, enveloping him in her arms. He pulled away and for a couple of seconds they held each other's gaze and there was a moment, just a heartbeat in time when one errant move could be construed in the wrong way. He had to remind himself, she was a friend, strong and dependable, he needed her lifelong support, like a sister; but a part of his heart was drawn to her, he wasn't sure why, whether it was because he felt sorry for her because she was vulnerable, cut adrift by her family. The one thing he did know, whatever it was, they had a very strong bond between them. There was an unspoken trust.

He turned and looked at her cream-coloured Mini Clubman. It had an extended roof. 'So, this is Sid. Great pet name.'

'It's because of the registration plate, but friends call it the Pope Mobile.' Toby peered inside. Unlike his car, it had a steering wheel and normal gear stick and handbrake, but she controlled the brakes and accelerator with her left foot in an extended stirrup. Sue demonstrated how she got into the car. The back doors had been replaced with a lift which took her and her wheelchair from the ground floor up and she clamped her wheelchair in behind the front seats. On the back of the passenger seat was a platform on to which she waddled before hurling herself into the driver's seat. The most important feature was that it gave her complete independence. Once they'd had a look round, Toby showed her his.

'Shame I can't take you for a spin, but it's not kitted out for a wheelchair. We'd have to go in convoy.'

Afterwards, they went through a side gate and into the back garden.

'Dad's had a lot of work done, you should have seen it when they moved in. It was overgrown with nettles and bramble, and it needed a patio and borders.'

Toby cast his eye around. Her parents had obviously benefited from the trappings of a successful career. A series of steps from a stone patio led down to a lush green expanse, bordered by vibrant flowerbeds bursting with a riot of colour and scents. It was a lovely garden, but Toby couldn't see how Sue could access it, not with all the steps and the pathway running along the side which was too narrow for a wheelchair. It was obvious they had no consideration for her needs. They could easily have built a slope next to the steps but had clearly chosen not to. There was nothing for it, they were just mean people, he decided, doing their very best to exclude their daughter. He remembered reading a quote, something along the lines of, "it's not the disability that makes you disabled, it's the attitudes and barriers that others put up".

He expected Bill to come out of the house at any moment, but when he didn't, he plonked himself on a bench and Sue pulled up aside him.

'This is just like old times,' she said, leaning back and looking relaxed. As he glanced at her and smiled, warmth flooded through him and in that moment, he was overwhelmed with such a powerful emotion. 'I miss our little chats. You're the only person I've ever opened up to, you don't judge me or make me feel inadequate. And you're always so kind. Perhaps now we've got our wheels, we can meet up more often.'

He looked away, a lump in his throat. Nobody had ever said

that before. He knew deep down he felt the same as her. He fixed his gaze on the roses and didn't dare meet her eyes as he tried to understand his feelings. 'Lovely roses. I like the yellow ones.'

It was easier to say how he felt about a flower or an animal but much harder to talk about feelings and emotions. He realised then that regardless of their surroundings and how their lives took shape, taking them in different directions and maybe to opposite ends of the country, they'd always come together, like this, maybe sit in companionable and peaceful silence, share their deepest thoughts, a laugh or two.

'What's the social life like at your college?' he asked breaking the comfortable silence. Her eyes were closed, her head tilted to the sun. She didn't move, but he knew she was considering her answer and, in a beat, before she opened her eyes and spoke, his eyes furtively trailed over her body with curiosity. She'd grown her hair, and it tumbled around her shoulders in pretty waves. Her low-cut t-shirt allowed him an appreciative glimpse. He wondered what it would be like to touch them, like teasing at the gift-wrapping before Christmas Day. As she moved and open her eyes they jiggled, and he quickly peeled his eyes away.

She swung round, laughed, and pointed to her eyes. 'My eyes are here, Toby, not on my chest.'

Now he felt a twinge of guilt and ignored the comment.

'How's that friend of yours, Lucy?' The jealousy tucked behind her words made him prickle.

'And that's all she is, a friend.' He shouldn't be having to justify himself. 'She's very busy, doing gigs, dating different blokes, none of whom treat her very nicely.'

'She'll never be without a boyfriend, she's very pretty, they're probably all queuing round the block.'

He didn't want to linger on Lucy, there were other people to talk about. 'You got lots of friends at college?'

'Yes, it's great. We go to this social club for the disabled, it's called Phab, you've probably heard of it. They're all over the country.'

'No, I can't say I have.'

'Toby,' she chided, 'you, a man of the world.'

He thought about the club he planned to join with Dave, The Young Conservatives, hesitant whether to tell her for fear of being judged or laughed at. He decided to keep it to himself, he hadn't even planned to tell Bill or Jasper, not yet anyway. He wanted to gauge how the initial meetings unfolded. The first was in a couple of days' time, but they weren't going to the Guildford branch, there was a meeting in Tunbridge Wells that everyone had planned to go to instead. Dave was super keen, it was all he'd talked about, and he was prepared to drive all over the place, but at least he'd offered to drive.

Sue described Phab and its events, which ranged from parties to activities like ten pin bowling and canoeing, and while it sounded fun, he hesitated about joining a group solely for the disabled. He wanted to mingle with a diverse and politically engaged crowd. They also discussed the work of The Thalidomide Trust and the Thalidomide Society and the differences between the two organisations.

'We had an interesting talk about the Cheshire Homes. Honestly, Toby, you would have really loved it, it was so inspiring.'

He frowned. It didn't sound interesting.

'It was about this bloke called Paul Hunt, he was a disabled writer and campaigner. He lived in Le Court, it's a Cheshire Home not far from you. He's just passed away, but oh my God Toby, he was so inspiring but such a shame he shunned publicity otherwise he could have inspired while he was alive, but I think people will get to know about him and maybe even become more well known now he's died and hopefully inspire more people to fight the cause otherwise everything he said will have been in vain.'

'I might have heard of him. What was he trying to change?'

'For disabled people not to be banged up in institutions, to live independently, to have more control over decisions that affect them rather than being told what to do.'

Toby was suddenly fascinated. Lately, he'd pondered the presence of disabled activists in Britain. He'd read about the American movement, the San Francisco 504 sit-ins, seen the news of people crawling up the steps of the White House, hunger strikes and various other protests, but nothing like that was happening in Britain. Why not?

'He kept a diary of life at Le Court. Paul hated institutional life, all the things we loathed. Being told when to go to bed, when to fart, when to scratch our arses. The strict meal regimes. I was always hungry and squirrelling food under my bed. Really pissed me off, cleaners used to find it and chuck it out. Every aspect of our lives was regimented,' she said.

'He wasn't far wrong when he described it as a prison existence,' she continued. 'Isolated from society and your family, separated from others but not equal. He wrote about the huge loss of freedom but there was nowhere else for him to live. He hated that whole attitude you see in every member of staff, that we don't know what's best for us, so they'll do what they think is right for us. Two fingers to that. Paul wanted choices, to be able to live independently and he fought against the regime, and he called on all of us to form a consumer group.' She glanced at Toby and the passion he saw in her eyes fired him.

Wow, I've really underestimated Sue.

She leaned towards him, her breasts all wobbly and he caught a whiff of her scent. 'What we need is a Martin Luther King of the disabled world. Someone to fight our cause. Make politicians sit up and pay attention and when they pass all these new laws, there should be nothing about us without us. Oh, that reminds me, Toby, how's your fan club coming on now that you're an esteemed published author? Looks like you're beginning to make your mark.'

'I loved every minute, but I don't want to bore you.'

'No, I'd love to hear all about it, how did it all come about? There's so much we need to catch up on.'

He loved the fact she'd asked and was just about to tell her when Bill appeared from around the corner. Toby didn't want to go, there was so much to talk about, and the conversation had only just got going. As soon as he stood up, he felt utterly bereft, he couldn't understand the conflicting emotions flowing through him. He had no idea when he'd see her next.

'Come on, lad, time to go.'

They said their goodbyes and when they were in the car and heading home, Toby asked, 'What kept you? You were ages, can't think what you'd have to talk about. You've got about as much in common with them as a cactus and a cherry.'

'Talk about stuck-up, but they didn't mind me fixing their dripping tap. Anything for a freebie.'

'The more money someone has, the tighter they are. Always the way.' Toby thought about Sue's Trust money, wondering again how it was being spent.

'You don't need to tell me that, son. Your mother's sisters were the same.' It had been years since they'd seen Rona's sisters. Bill didn't get on with them and they hadn't stayed in touch after her death.

'My God, did you see the size of her aspidistra?' Bill let out a deep belly laugh.

He was in no mood for Bill's crass comments, yes of course he'd noticed, that surreptitious glance had nearly cost their friendship. The brief time with her had been wonderful, a reminder of the afternoons they used to spend together in the garden at St Bede's, but today had felt different. Excitement fizzed through him and as he drove, her words played in his mind. What great lines, turns of phrases, were they hers? The way she'd enthused about Phab, the talk, the passion that came through. Why hadn't he noticed this about her before, or was it that college had matured her?

He felt a sudden sense of excitement that she was finding her own voice, such a far cry from the timidity of school. It made him feel warm and gooey and proud of her.

CHAPTER 34: TOBY

'Remind me again why we've come all the way to friggin' Tunbridge Wells? Cheap booze or nice birds?'

Dave chuckled. 'Actually, mate, the MP, Patrick Mayhew, is giving a talk.' They had just parked the car opposite a posh and imposing hotel called The Royal Wells. The sun was dipping below the horizon, a warm glow spreading across the sky, casting a golden hue over the town. A steep grassy bank fell away from the pavement and a path led down towards London Road where the meeting was being held. Elegant and historic buildings dotted the landscape, which gave a pleasant feel to the place, and beyond the sprawling town, like a patchwork quilt under the fading light.

They headed down the path and across the road and a green area to a white Victorian building, number 84, and down some steps. Once again, Toby felt disheartened by the challenges wheelchair users faced in accessing events.

The cosy bar area was buzzing with chatter and laughter as groups mingled. There was a clink of glasses, an air of anticipation and the occasional burst of raucous laughter, the barman weaving round collecting glasses. A couple of men were engaged in an animated discussion as they sat on bar stools sipping beer and puffing on cigarettes.

'What do you expect when you put a woman in charge?' one of them was saying. 'It's bloody typical, they haven't got a clue what to do and always rely on us guys to get them out of the shit. I give her six months, then she'll be out on her ear.'

'Come on, mate,' the other said, 'give her a chance. She's come up with some cracking ideas, she can't be any worse than Ted Heath.'

'Huh. What good has a woman ever done? She should be back in the kitchen washing the dishes. There are only three things a woman is good for, cooking, cleaning and a good time.'

'Whoa, you sound like my old man.'

'Maybe Dennis will keep her in check.' He winked at the picture of Thatcher above the fireplace.

Toby scanned the scene. 'Blimey, Dave, there's a real mix and match of people here, I thought they'd all be stuck up their own arses.'

'There's some cracking birds here,' Dave replied nodding towards a group of women sitting in one corner under a picture of the Queen. 'Told you it was worth coming.'

A few people glanced round and smiled at Toby and Dave, and a young guy dressed in a suit bounded over to introduce himself.

'David,' he said. 'I'm the chairman, thank you for coming. Always nice to see new faces.'

After buying drinks, they grabbed chairs at a table and jumped right into the lively conversation about recent events, from a raft race on the River Medway to a quirky nightwear party.

Glancing at a couple hand in hand, Toby asked if they'd met at the club. The woman pointed to one of the chaps at the bar. 'Andy over there put on a New Year's Eve party a couple of years ago. His parents were away. Three couples got together that evening.' She flicked her left hand in Toby's direction, a diamond ring twinkled under the candelabra. 'And now we're engaged.'

Somebody chirped up, 'I spilled a pint of cider on the carpet. Andy's never forgiven me.' He gave a chuckle.

Toby glanced at Andy, who was stubbing out a cigarette out. His legs were coiled like a snake, and Toby wondered how that was possible. 'I should set up a marriage bureau and start charging you all.' He had a thick North Kent brogue.

'The raft race sounds fun,' Dave said to the girl opposite.

'Yeah it was, until the locals found out who we were. It got pretty dangerous when people started chucking bricks from the bridge.'

'Bloody hell,' Dave said, wide-eyed.

The sexist guy at the bar piped up. 'Only thing I remember from that day is Sarah falling in the water. She was wearing a white t-shirt with no bra.' He gave a raucous laugh.

Keen to change the subject, Toby asked, 'So what else do you guys get up to?' Mr Sexist Creep was starting to annoy him. 'Are you all being groomed for future stardom?'

'Nah, we're here for a piss-up and a laugh, it's not all about politics and ignore what the press say, we're not all stuck-up snobs, but we're all odd in our own way. You don't have to like politics, as long as you're not a raving leftie, we don't want any reds under the bed. The only real politics here is who's going to buy the next round.' Toby looked at the guy talking and watched as he lifted a packet of cheese and onion crisps, tilted his head back and emptied the crumbs into his mouth.

A mousey-haired girl wearing a pearl necklace and royal blue top and jeans chipped in. 'We have our own branch annual conference, for the Kent YCs, in Margate, if you like debating, it's great fun and there's evening entertainment and the hotel even has a jacuzzi.'

'Or as Mayhew called it, a jacutzi,' somebody quipped with a laugh.

Her friend smiled. 'The secretary and chairman were dating. He got her up the duff then did a runner. I tell you, there's more gossip, intrigue and scandal in the YCs than on *Coronation Street*. You two should come to the summer ball at Leeds Castle this weekend.'

'Sounds like a laugh,' Dave said, eyeing up the women around the table like a kid in a candy store. 'What's the dress code, posh togs?'

'Black tie,' the girl in pearls replied. 'But us ladies will be in our long frocks.'

The women discussed their outfits for Saturday and at that moment Patrick Mayhew entered and Andy rose to greet him. 'Great to see you, Paddy, how are you?'

The meeting started with a talk about the government's plans and then Mayhew invited the audience to ask questions. Toby was enjoying himself and felt a warm sense of acceptance from the group; no one had stared at his arms or questioned him about them. Without hesitation he stood up eagerly and waggled his hand. 'Isn't it a false economy to give people huge discounts to buy their council house, selling the family silver, are you going to replace the properties sold?'

'Social housing is just a safety net, we want people to strive to own their own home, have a stake in a property-owning democracy and share in the prosperity of the country and a future. And besides, it eases the burden on the local council. The population's falling and there's a glut of cheap housing so no, we won't need to replace those properties.'

Toby wasn't convinced. He thought it would just boost the private sector and in the long run lead to the government having to pay tenants to rent expensive private homes. He noticed how Mayhew avoided his cynicism about it being nothing more than a vote winner. The subjects being discussed though fired him, particularly the issue of privatisation and he wanted to discuss and debate more.

Mayhew went on to answer other questions. 'We need to break the power of the unions once and for all.'

A guy in front with wild curly hair, dressed in a lumber shirt and baggy cords stood up. Toby caught a whiff of his body odour as he raised his hand to speak. 'I work for the local electricity company, and I think the biggest mistake with privatisation is that these companies are only interested in profits and putting money in shareholders' pockets. Management just haven't got a clue. They're all kids fresh out of college, don't know what they're doing. Imagine what would happen if they privatised the army?'

'Hear, hear,' someone piped up. 'The government's selling off the crown jewels just to raise money which no doubt will be wasted on spurious things particularly if Labour get back in.'

'I can see what's going to happen. It will all go tits up,' the bloke with the wild hair added. 'Imagine a Scottish company owning electricity. And you mark my word, there will be redundancies, cost cutting, shops will go, everything will be pared down to the bare bones, to cut costs and maximise profits, then property will be sold off, they'll pocket the money and run.'

'Yes, it's asset stripping,' a woman in the front row said. 'Lean, mean and ineffective, just like these glorified bankers and nobody will listen and then it will all be too late, like shutting the door when the horse has already bolted.'

'You're all wets,' Andy interjected. 'Take British Telecom, it's a mammoth organisation, you can't get an efficient service, prices are ridiculous, you wait weeks for a new phone and if you try and complain, nobody's at the end of the phone to help. Time we got rid of these dinosaurs and move with the times.'

Toby and Dave bought tickets for the Leeds Castle ball. Dave said he'd be able to borrow a dinner jacket from his cousin who frequently went to posh dos. As a one off, Toby decided he'd hire one, and wear a waistcoat and short-sleeved shirt.

On the way home, he reflected on the evening. He'd found it enjoyable, sharing views, serious conversation interjected with fun, meeting new people even though there were a few idiots in the group. Although he didn't agree with everything in the Conservative Manifesto and wouldn't have described himself as Conservative, he could see himself becoming more involved, using the organisation as a springboard for discussion and change for the disabled.

He smiled to himself and peered out of the window at the road ahead disappearing into the distance like a spool of grey ribbon. If he could get the disability topic on the agenda, speak with MPs, have an influence, wow, what an opportunity.

CHAPTER 35: TOBY

The sun dipped below the horizon as they turned off the A20 towards Leeds Castle, casting a golden glow over the landscape. In his evening attire, Toby felt trussed up like a turkey. His old school shirt clung to his chest, its buttons stretched taut against newfound muscles that showcased his developing physique. Dave said he felt like a penguin.

'Ticket says carriages arrive at 7pm. People aren't coming by horse and carriage, surely?'

Toby let out a raucous laugh. 'Yeah, what will they think when they see your battered old Ford Cortina?'

Dave swerved as he turned off. 'Be serious mate.'

'You can be a right nincompoop, it's just something they put on the ticket, but don't ask me how I know that. I'm not a massive *Cinderella* fan. It's just the toffs' way of telling you what time to arrive.'

'Funny how we're going to a ball, but it's not the kind we can kick around.'

'Yeah, who knew we'd need dancing shoes instead of footie boots for this one?'

They parked, got out of the car, and gazed at the magnificent castle encircled by a tranquil moat. Its ancient stone walls, turrets and towers stood tall and majestic, lit in a kaleidoscope of blue, green, and red against the blackness of the night sky.

Toby gasped. 'This might literally be the most beautiful place I've ever seen.'

Dave was already sizing up the women heading to the castle barn for the event. 'You old romantic. I feel like we've stepped into a time warp, with all these women floating around in long dresses. I better watch my step if I dance with someone. I can be a bit clumsy. Don't want to trip anyone up. Wonder if I'll get my hands on a nice woman this evening.'

'At least you can.' Toby felt a mix of excitement and apprehension. A moment of doubt crept in; his heart quietly ached for Dave's confidence. At events like this he was reserved, shy and self-conscious, he dreaded people staring, sizing him up, laughing behind his back. He wasn't bothered about having a slow dance, he just wanted to jig around, blend in, but didn't want to be treated like the outcast, the frog that no girl would dance with. Being accepted meant everything.

Inside the barn long tables were elegantly draped in snowy white cloths and topped with gleaming silverware. Flickering candles scattered golden light illuminating the room with an enchanting ambience. The bar area was filling as people queued for drinks and took their seats at the tables. Waiters at the end of each table looked like captains at the helm of ships as they surveyed the sea of faces, napkins draped over their extended arms. It was a warm evening, the open doors at the far end of the hall open to the castle grounds, extending towards the moat and castle in the distance.

In this setting, it didn't feel elegant to eat with his feet, so Toby used his hands, balancing his fork on a wooden stand his dad had made for him. It looked like a mushroom but much larger and had a magnet on the top. He could feel all eyes on him, and a couple of people smiled and said how amazing and effective the gadget was.

'Life must be quite a challenge for you, mate,' someone said.

'I get by, it's all I've known,' he replied.

After a delicious three-course meal, coffee and mints, Toby had a shock of his life when the chairman announced the arrival of the band, *Lucy and the Diamonds*.

What the hell was Lucy doing appearing at this event?

During the interval, he nipped to the loo. As he came out and washed his hands, there was a guy standing at the basins. He guessed by the way he was dressed, in ripped jeans and a black t-shirt, that he was in Lucy's band. He stopped drying his hands and stared at Toby. He felt uncomfortable.

'Excuse me, mate,' he said with a frown on his face. 'I know it's a rude question and I shouldn't really ask, but if you don't have arms long enough to wipe your arse, then what do you do?'

Toby groaned. He was tired of being asked that same question and he knew that his answer would be all round the Young Conservatives in no time at all and so he wanted to give an honest answer to stop the speculation and gossip.

'You're right, it is a rude question.'

Stay calm, don't let him rile you.

'You've got to use your imagination, mate. What would you do if you were me?'

'Dunno, probably want to shoot myself to be honest.' He gave a smug laugh.

Toby ignored the comment. 'I find a way but I'm not going to share that with you. It's private, you wouldn't like it if I asked you which hand do you toss with?'

Toby laughed and the guy stared at him as if he was a museum exhibit with an expression that made Toby feel triumphant and laugh even more. He couldn't let these questions get to him; humour was everything.

He walked back into the hall where the tables were being

cleared. Two men began setting up their equipment in the corner. Toby recognised the tallest, Rick, he was dating Lucy. Toby had seen them out and about, hand in hand. A pang of jealousy shot through him. He watched as the guy sat on a stool and strummed a few notes on his guitar as the other guy tested out the drums. It was a while before Lucy made her grand entrance and when she did, it was to a thunder of clapping and cheers. He loved how natural and relaxed she was, like a true celebrity and she looked incredible. Her legs were to die for. Her hair gleamed under the spotlights and flowed around her shoulders like a pair of silky curtains. She was wearing a slinky glittery red top that dazzled, black leather shorts, fishnets and best of all a pair of long suede black stiletto boots.

'Wow,' Dave drawled. 'She's a bit of all right.'

Pride swelled inside him, but it was going to be so embarrassing, Lucy seeing him at a Young Conservative event. 'She's a friend of mine, lives in Haslemere.'

'Get away with you.' Dave nudged him and laughed.

'Seriously mate, she's a friend of mine.'

'In your dreams.' He picked up his beer glass and tutted.

Just then Lucy spotted him and came over, enveloping him in a warm hug, and planted a kiss on his cheek. 'Tobes, fancy seeing you here and look at you, all dressed up.' She stood back to admire his outfit and he felt his face flush.

Standing beside him and clearly waiting to be introduced to this glamorous woman, Dave was shrinking like a violet in awe. And over her shoulder as they hugged, Toby met Rick's eyes and saw a swirling undercurrent of intense jealousy bordering on hatred. He'd stopped strumming his guitar and was staring at them.

Toby mused, *look at me, I'm hardly a threat.*

He quickly pulled away from Lucy. 'Great to see you, Luce, it's going to be a super evening now you're here.'

As he sat down, he watched Rick step towards Lucy, lean in

and say something into her ear. There was a thunderous look on his face. A strange sickening shiver swept over him. Something didn't feel right. He hoped she was okay. He knew from her pas,; she had a habit of dating bad boys.

Lucy stepped onto a raised platform, her legs slightly apart as she gripped the microphone and sang the first notes of her opening song with fiery passion, 'Devil Gate Drive.' People jumped up to dance, but he and Dave stood watching on the sidelines like a pair of wallflowers. Wistfully Toby gazed on looking at couples, wishing he had the confidence to ask somebody for a dance. At the end of the song, like a herd of antelopes everyone paused, their heads tilted as they waited for the next song to begin, deciding whether to dance and how. Lucy sang Blondie's 'Hanging on The Telephone' and a few songs in; she slowed things down with 'How Deep Is Your Love' by the Bee Gees. As people paired off, and Dave went over to ask a girl to dance, Toby felt conspicuous all on his tod, like a lone candle flickering in a dim corner. Just when he considered drifting into the garden until a faster song, there was a tap on his shoulder, and he spun round to see a pretty girl in an emerald satin dress standing there.

'Hi, I'm Petula, fancy a dance?' She had lovely dark wavy hair and a beautiful wide smile.

Toby glanced round, unable to believe she was speaking to him and thinking that perhaps she was being put up to it for a bet.

Still uncertain, he didn't want to make a fool of himself. 'Why would you want to dance with someone like me?'

'Why not, what's wrong with you?' She had a serious expression on her face.

He shrugged. 'Yeah, I'll give it a go, I'm 'armless enough.' He grinned.

That made her laugh. 'My sister's disabled too.'

Why was she telling him that, was she offering to dance with him out of pity? He wondered how to slow dance, he hadn't a clue, but she seemed to know. She took his shoulders and the gap between them closed in as they moved out onto the dance floor. He could feel his heart pounding, could she feel it against her chest? And his hands, they were shaking as they rested on her shoulders. He wanted so desperately to relax, but it was hard. His body was as stiff as a board, he'd never felt so unsure of himself. He sensed onlookers watching and sniggering and his feet, they were suddenly big as boats and clumsy as they stepped around hers. But there was also something magical and exhilarating about the experience. His first slow dance, he felt so grown up, being close to a woman for longer than a brief hug, wrapped in her warmth, the pleasant scent of her perfume, the silk of her dress, the brush of her soft arms, her hair tickling his neck.

He caught Lucy's gaze and their eyes locked. She was singing with such gusto and for one moment it felt as if she was singing to him, her seal of approval, such warmth in her eyes.

Abruptly the lights went on and the room was flooded with harsh brightness, the music stopped, like a cruel awakening from a blissful dream, or the chiming of midnight in *Cinderella*. Toby and his dance partner sprang apart and looked around quizzically. The chairman's voice cut through the hushed confusion, directing everyone to swiftly evacuate the building and gather on the lawn until further instructions were given.

'We need to fully inspect the building before we're permitted to return. I'm very sorry.' There was a bizarre round of applause when he added there would be a free glass of wine later on.

The hall was a chaotic flurry of activity, shuffling footsteps, a mix of concern, disappointment, and confusion on their faces as they spilled out into the garden. Toby breathed in the sweet smell of honeysuckle and spied a peacock a few metres away. Sadly, Petula had disappeared into the crowd.

There were a few mutterings about this being the work of

hoax IRA callers, which apparently it happened frequently at Conservative events. With the number of IRA bombings and shootings at an all-time high, the organisers had to take every call seriously.

'Not another bomb threat,' somebody said.

'Why would they want to blow us up?' another said.

'Could be a few future MPs among us,' a girl added.

'How will they know if it's genuine?' Toby asked.

'I think the IRA give codes, a sort of password in advance.'

Toby wondered how this all worked and how the police knew the code words.

He glanced round looking for Dave. When he couldn't find him, he went over to Lucy who was chatting to the guys in the band. They were discussing the playlist.

'Hey, Tobe, you enjoying yourself? See you had a slow dance.' Lucy winked at him and leaned in to hug him. 'It's lovely to see you so happy,' she whispered. 'They look like a great bunch of people, I'm pleased for you.'

Toby didn't feel comfortable, he didn't like the way Rick was watching them from a few feet away with a menacing sneer on his face. He felt intimidated.

'What the bloody hell are you doing hugging a spaz?' Rick asked stepping forward and resting one arm casually across Lucy's shoulder as if she was a settee.

'Don't be like that, this is my mate Toby, we go back years.'

'Oh, do you now?' He pulled a face, like a spoilt brat. 'That creep you keep talking about.' He made a noise with his mouth and nose as if expelling air.

Lucy turned to him and lightly nudged his chest. 'You're lucky to have me, sometimes I don't know what I see in you.'

It came from nowhere, happened so fast.

The next minute Lucy was sprawled on the patio, wailing in agony, her arm outstretched. Toby stared down at a lump on her wrist, which looked contorted.

Shit, it was broken. She needed to get to hospital.

Where was Dave?

Rick hovered over her. 'Get up, woman, you're making a scene, just calm down.'

Like moths drawn to a flame, a crowd had gathered, their eyes fixated on the unfolding scene. Nobody was helping Lucy, it was as if they were all afraid of Rick.

Suddenly Dave pushed through the crowd and headed towards Toby. 'Come on, mate, we can take her to hospital.'

Rick backed away, he looked scared, his hand was covering his mouth, perhaps worried that Lucy would report him to the police the minute she arrived at hospital.

Phil, the other band member shoved Rick out of the way. 'What the hell have you done, you prick, clear off, if you can't control your temper we don't want a jerk like you in the band. Lucy's worth a hundred of you.'

Rick skulked off.

With Lucy still screaming like a wild banshee, Dave helped her to her feet and the three of them headed to Dave's car.

When they arrived at the A&E at Maidstone hospital, Lucy hurried in, clutching her arm, still crying, with Toby trailing on after her towards the reception desk while Dave parked the car.

Sitting on plastic seats while they waited to be seen, Toby longed to hold her close, shield her from the pain, make it all disappear. But she couldn't be hugged right then, she was delicate as fine bone china. She seemed so small, vulnerable, lost, her soul broken, her agony etched across her face. He felt something open inside him in the deepest most untouched part of his heart and in that moment, he knew without a shred of doubt that he'd do anything for her, the love he felt was unconditional and yet she'd never be his, she'd always be the girl he admired from afar.

She was seen quickly and moments later someone administered her a shot of morphine until the doctor properly assessed her. Afterwards they waited in a side room before her wrist was X-rayed to confirm it was broken and then the surgeons prepared her for an operation to manipulate her bones before putting her arm in plaster. All this time, Toby sat with her while Dave waited in the corridor. The nurses were just fitting an oxygen mask over her face, when Phil, the other band member, burst into the room looking flustered.

'Lucy, love,' he said, rushing over to her and planting a kiss on her forehead and taking her hand. 'I've brought your handbag.' As she looked up, Toby clocked the look of adoration in Lucy's eyes and his heart plummeted.

Phil glanced at Toby through cold eyes and with a dismissive wave of his hand said, 'thanks for bringing her in, it's okay, I'll take over now and look after her.'

Toby rose from her seat and looked at Lucy who was still gazing at Phil.

'If it hadn't have been for you, this wouldn't have happened in the first place,' Phil said to Toby.

A crushing feeling descended as he stuttered, 'Take care, Lucy, I'll call you tomorrow, check you're okay.'

He sloped out of the room feeling totally deflated, his shoulders slumped as he retraced his steps along the hubbub of the sterile corridor, past trolleys, past the sick and the dying, relatives comforting relatives. Sometimes the love of family wasn't enough; was he going to fall in love, get married, have a family of his own one day or was he destined to be alone, would he always be looked on as a freak of nature? And was this how it was going to be for all his thalidomide friends? Only time would tell.

Never mind all that, he mused. He now needed to make some serious decisions about his future: stay at college or strike out into employment, the safe haven of study or the real world of work? Was he ready, was he capable? He didn't want to let himself down, his family down, look incompetent or stupid.

On the drive home Toby relived every minute of the evening and wondered why Lucy had suddenly changed her attention from him to Phil the minute he walked into the room. Was something going on between them and was that the real reason why Rick had kicked off? Lucy was such a vibrant and warm person. She had time for everybody and wanted everyone to have fun. When he was around her, he felt his spirits lift, he felt alive, he would have given anything for her to be his girlfriend, but he knew she was out of his league.

'Hey, Tobe, you okay, mate, you've hardly said a word since we left the hospital?' Dave asked.

'I'm okay, tired, I just hope Lucy will be okay, that put a dampener on the evening.'

'Yeah, and we never did get our free drink.'

'Is that the extent of your aspirations, chasing free drinks?'

Toby reflected and felt sad the evening hadn't ended in the way they'd hoped. To hell with idiots like Rick and Phil. He'd encountered their types before, and no doubt would face more in the future.

The evening had however left him inspired that he had a bright future ahead of him. There was a whole world out there for him to explore and make his mark, so much more beyond booze and birds. He couldn't wait to dive in and grab every opportunity. However, he'd put romance on the backburner because so far it had only brought him heartache. Maybe one day he'd find the right person and they would love him for plain old Toby. Until then, there were far more important things to focus on, starting with himself.

THE END

To be continued in book 6. PRE-ORDER NOW!
   Every Couple's Fear
   Here is the link: https://amzn.to/3Y6VseW

Thank you for reading *Fear to Fearless*. If you enjoyed the story, I would really appreciate a short review on Amazon.

To find out about Joanna Warrington's other books please visit her Amazon page where you can follow her to stay informed about forthcoming books. Here is the link: https://www.amazon.co.uk/stores/Joanna-Warrington/author/B00RH4XPI6

OTHER BOOKS BY JOANNA WARRINGTON

NEW BOOK!
The Baby Hunters.
My Book

In 1975, the shadows of the Magdalene laundry still haunt Kathleen as she daringly escapes from a life of oppression. Now on the run, the priest is hot on her trail. As the priest's attention shifts to other lost souls, the consequences are nothing short of devastating.

Meanwhile, a famous American actress and her wealthy husband have arrived in Ireland to adopt a baby and discover an unexpected offer they cannot refuse. Will it turn out to be a dream come true or a nightmare waiting to unfold?

Enter the O'Sullivans, a struggling Catholic family in Belfast battling the weight of poverty and the turmoil of the Troubles. With a fifth child adding to their financial strain and ostracised by their Protestant neighbours, their house is about to be petrol-bombed. The couple face a momentous choice––hope the conflict will pass or leave everything they know behind for a

OTHER BOOKS BY JOANNA WARRINGTON

new life. Desperation drives Mrs O'Sullivan to come up with a plan that offers the family a glimmer of hope, but at what price?

Inspired by true events, this is a powerful story of joy and sorrow uncovering the profound and catastrophic effects of the Irish Troubles, the Catholic Church's practices in Ireland and the systemic abuse by those in positions of authority.

Slippers On A First Date

> Inspired by real events! Donna's love life is a mess. Years of online-dating has left her self-esteem in tatters. Now 56, she can boast a list of failed relationships longer than a grocery bill. When her spiteful daughter Olivia makes a scathing remark about her mother's love life, Donna sets out on one last quest to find Mr Right. Is it too late to find lasting love, or will she just repeat the same mistakes?
> It's 2020 and England is in lockdown, presenting a whole range of new challenges for daters.

Donna's forays into the world of dating lead her on a series of calamitous adventures involving an unwanted gift, faking her identity, and getting arrested. And finally, her job as a nurse is on the line. When things go horribly wrong, Olivia decides to take matters into her own hands.

The love that Donna has always searched for isn't the type of love she needs. Her journey reveals a few home-truths and ultimately she discovers that real lasting love has been staring her right in the face all along.

DON'T BLAME ME

It's every parent's worst nightmare
When tragedy struck twenty-five years ago, Dee's world fell apart. With painful reminders all around her she flew to Australia to start a new life. Now, with her dad dying, she's needed back in England. But these are unprecedented times. It's the spring of 2020 and as Dee returns to the beautiful medieval house in rural Kent where she grew up among apple orchards and hop fields, England goes into lockdown, trapping her in the village. The person she least wanted to see has also returned, forcing her to confront the painful past and resolve matters between them.

Weaving between past and present, this emotional and absorbing family saga is about hope, resilience and the healing power of forgiveness.

THE CATHOLIC WOMAN'S DYING WISH

A dying wish. A shocking secret. A dark, destructive and abusive relationship.
Forget hearts & flowers and happy ever afters in this quirky unconventional love story! *Readers say: "A little bit Ben Elton" "a monstrous car crash of a saga."* Middle-aged Darius can't seem to hold on to the good relationships in his life. Now, he discovers a devastating truth about his family that blows away his future and forces him to revisit his painful past. Distracting himself from family problems he goes online and meets Faye, a single mum. Faye and her children are about to find out the horrors and demons lurking behind the man Faye thinks she loves.

EVERY FAMILY HAS ONE

The harrowing story of a 14-year-old facing betrayal by a trusted family priest in a close-knit 1970s Catholic community. Imagine the shame when you can't even tell the truth to those you love and they banish you to Ireland to have your baby in secret. How will poor Kathleen ever recover from her ordeal? This is a dramatic and heart-breaking story about the joys and tests of motherhood and the power of love, friendship and family ties spanning several decades.

HOLIDAY

Lyn wakes on her 50th birthday with no man and middle age staring her in the face.
"For readers who enjoy British humour." Readers Favorite. Determined to change her sad trajectory Lyn books a surprise road trip for herself and her three children through the American Southwest and Yellowstone. Before they even get on the plane, the trip hits a major snag. An uninvited guest joins them at the airport turning their dream trip into a nightmare.

Amid the mountain vistas, secrets will be revealed, and a hurtful betrayal confronted.

This book is more than an amusing family saga. It will also appeal to those interested in American scenery, history and culture.

TIME TO REFLECT

A British aunt and her niece set off to explore Massachusetts and Rhode Island. In this calamity-ridden travel tale their relationship is changed forever.

It's a trip with an eclectic mix of history, culture and scenery. Seafood shacks. Postcard perfect lighthouses. Weather-boarded buildings. Stacks of pancakes dripping in syrup. Quaint boutiques. Walks along the cobblestone streets of Boston, America's oldest city––the city of revolution. Throw in plenty of disagreements and you have all the ingredients for a classic American road trip.

Everything is going well, until a shocking family secret is revealed. In a dramatic turn of events, Ellie's father joins them and is forced to explain why he has been such an inadequate parent.

An entertaining but heartfelt journey through Massachusetts from Cape Cod to Plymouth, Salem, Marblehead, Boston and Rhode Island.

Printed in Great Britain
by Amazon